RECEIVED 9 2009

FIC Maste

Masters, P.
The watchful eye.

PRICE: $25.17 (3797/af)

The Watchful Eye

a&b

The Watchful Eye

Priscilla Masters

First published in Great Britain in 2008 by
Allison & Busby Limited
13 Charlotte Mews
London W1T 4EJ
www.allisonandbusby.com

Copyright © 2008 by PRISCILLA MASTERS

The moral right of the author has been asserted.

*All characters and events in this publication,
other than those clearly in the public domain,
are fictitious and any resemblance to actual persons,
living or dead, is purely coincidental.*

This book is sold subject to the conditions that it shall not,
by way of trade or otherwise, be lent, resold, hired out or
otherwise circulated without the publisher's prior
written consent in any form of binding or cover other than
that in which it is published and without a similar condition
being imposed upon the subsequent
purchaser.

A CIP catalogue record for this book is available from
the British Library.

10 9 8 7 6 5 4 3 2 1

13-ISBN 978-0-7490-7995-6

Typeset in 11/16 pt Adobe Garamond Pro by
Allison & Busby

Printed and bound in Great Britain by
MPG Books Ltd, Bodmin, Cornwall

Born in Yorkshire and brought up in South Wales, PRISCILLA MASTERS is the author of the popular series set in the Staffordshire moorlands featuring Detective Inspector Joanna Piercy. She has also written four medical stand-alone mysteries. Priscilla has two sons and lives in Staffordshire. She works part time as a nurse.

Available from
ALLISON & BUSBY

Medical Mysteries

Disturbing Ground
A Plea of Insanity
The Watchful Eye

In the Detective Inspector Joanna Piercy series

Winding up the Serpent
Scaring Crows
Embroidering Shrouds
Endangering Innocents
Wings over the Watcher

Featuring Martha Gunn

River Deep
Slipknot

Other titles by
Priscilla Masters

Medical Mysteries

Night Visit
A Fatal Cut

In the Detective Inspector Joanna Piercy series

Catch The Fallen Sparrow
A Wreath for my Sister
And None Shall Sleep

And for children

Mr Bateman's Garden

'The Watchfull Eye
The Silent Tongue
And the Secret Heart.'

Taken from a Staffordshire jug, circa 1820.

Prologue

The child lay in her cot, eyes frozen, as the door opened quietly. She watched the shadow darken her view as the door was closed equally quietly. She moved her head to follow the shape as it approached her, hardly breathing as the shadow loomed over her cot, stretching a hand out. She whimpered but was still. Only her tongue flicked around her mouth as the hand descended slowly to cover her face. She was helpless and dumb. Only her eyes could move – that and her tongue, flicking uselessly, doing little more than reddening her mouth. It was an impotent thing.

Chapter One

Monday, 10th April

3 p.m. Monday afternoon surgery.

The toddler was sitting on her mother's lap, watching the proceedings with wary, suspicious eyes. She was, he thought, a very beautiful child, with her fair, curling hair, yet eyes so dark there was almost no discernible difference between iris and pupil. But the feature that made this child stand out from other sweet-looking children was her lips, which were very full and red because she had a habit of continually licking them. Doctor Daniel Gregory was fascinated by the pink tongue flicking in and out of the tiny mouth. She even sucked her bottom lip in so she could wipe her tongue almost all the way down her chin. It disfigured her face, drew the eye towards it so you disregarded an otherwise sweet face and appealing eyes. The little girl should be discouraged from this habit and a barrier cream applied before it led to impetigo, an ugly skin infection.

The child's mother was speaking to him, in a shrill, loud voice which demanded his full and immediate attention. Reluctantly he took his eyes away from the child and transferred his gaze instead to her mother, Vanda Struel. From the day he had first heard it he had considered it a very ugly name. Vanda Struel looked as her name suggested. She was small, skinny and tense, mean-looking, with a thin, hard mouth. She was dressed in ill-fitting jeans which had slipped low down her scrawny haunches as she had sat down on the chair, the smallness of her frame making the two-year-old on her lap look outsized.

Dropping his eyes from Vanda's wan little face with its tired, smudgy eyes, Daniel could see the string of a grubby white thong riding defiantly over the top of her jeans. He adjusted the knot on his tie. He tried to concentrate on the mother's words but his mind was struggling to connect them, his attention divided between the child with the watchful eyes and the careless mother with her anxious face and alarming story.

'She stopped breathing, Doctor. She actually...stopped... breathing.'

The words startled him out of his reflections.

He leant forward to be sure of catching every syllable. 'What did you say?'

'She stopped – breathing.' Vanda's mouth was open, waiting for his reaction. Like her daughter's restless habit, her pink tongue flicked from side to side, rasping across lips as dry as bark.

Daniel focused back on the child, who had stopped looking at him and had transferred her curious gaze to her mother. He frowned. Anna-Louise appeared both normal and healthy. Superficially he could detect no obvious sign of serious disease. Nothing unusual apart from the active, anxious tongue and the shuttered expression on the little girl's face.

A two-year-old is unable to relate a history. It must all come from the mother. 'Tell me exactly what happened.'

Vanda crossed her legs, bumping the child against her in an awkward movement. 'We was watchin' telly last night,' she said. '*Stars in Their Eyes.* Anna-Louise was in 'er cot. My mum says she'll check on 'er. Right?' It was as though she was worried that Daniel might not understand her story.

'Next thing is my mum's shoutin' for me, sayin' Anna-Louise isn't breathin'. I went in and she was sort of flopped in the cot, lyin' on 'er back, pale and awful quiet. I picked 'er up, Doctor. She was still as...' Vanda Struel cast her eyes around the room for something suitably motionless. 'As still as your desk,' she finally came up with.

'And *was* she breathing?'

Vanda shook her head solemnly, scattering her honey-coloured hair. 'She weren't.' Her eyes were wide, round and puzzled. Unlike the child's they were dirty blue and she was looking to him for an answer. 'My mum had to give her the kiss o'life, Doctor. Her lips was navy blue.'

Anna-Louise, star of the drama, sat impassively throughout, her eyes wandering between the two adults in the room, her tongue still exploring as much of her face as it could reach.

'And did she breathe after you'd given her the kiss of life?'

'After a while she did, Doctor, but it took ages.'

'How long?'

'Five–ten minutes.'

Daniel's mind was already rejecting this. Five or ten minutes without breathing starves the brain of oxygen. And a brain starved of oxygen begins to die. Fast. He gave her a chance to retract or modify her statement.

'Are you sure it was *that* long?'

The smudgy eyes looked straight into his, opened very wide to coax him into believing this fantastic story. 'Yeah. My brother kept his eye on the clock. Said he'd give us ten minutes and if she hadn't of started breathing again he was going to ring the ambulance.'

'So what did you do?'

'Kept her warm.' Vanda's eyes flickered away as though she suspected he disbelieved her story.

'*Did* you call an ambulance?'

'My mum said it weren't necessary. Breath-holding, she called it. She said I'd done it a time or two when I was a kid and it never seemed to do me any harm.' She hitched her jeans up self-consciously, tucking her thumb in the hip band to push the string of her thong out of sight. Daniel's eyes flickered away.

'But if you hadn't been there?' He was already fingering his stethoscope.

Vanda shrugged.

'Has she ever done this before?'

Vanda shook her head, moving the thin strands of hair from side to side.

'Did she shake or twitch?'

Another bemused shake of the head.

'Did she wet herself?'

'No, Doctor.'

'Were her eyes open or closed?'

Vanda leant forward. '*That* was the funny thing,' she said dramatically, as though she had waited for this question. 'They were open – all the time. Like she was staring at me but not quite all there.' She tried to make a joke of it. 'You know – the folk was home but the lights was out.'

Daniel didn't smile. 'Has she been ill recently?'

'No more than usual. She's always a bit sickly, if you know what I mean.' She looked at him with a plea in her eyes.

Now both of them were studying him. Mother and daughter. Complicit.

He made his decision. 'I think I'd better examine the little lady,' he said. 'Take her into the examination room, if you like, and undress her. I need to take a quick look at her notes.'

He scrolled quickly down the computer screen, his chin propped on his palm. The consultations were many and various. Stomach pain, constipation, diarrhoea, uncontrollable screaming, listless, off her food, temperature, rash, headache (Vanda had reported she had been clutching her head and crying). Anna-Louise had been subject to investigations but so far all had been normal. The temperatures had always settled, the rashes disappeared, the constipation unsupported by physical examination, the screaming child now recorded as silent. And now Anna-Louise had allegedly stopped breathing for ten minutes.

Daniel glanced at the examination room door. Not a sound was coming from behind it. No child struggling or crying at being undressed in a strange place. It struck him as unusually passive behaviour.

He thought for a moment.

It was possible that Vanda was simply overcaring and lacking in confidence with her first child. This sometimes happened with young, single mums. All their maternal instincts came to the fore while they had little experience. But in one way Vanda was lucky. Her mum lived in the same block of flats as she did and was a frequent visitor to her daughter. He'd often seen them together, shopping, little Anna-Louise wrapped up in a pushchair.

Even better – Roberta Millin, Vanda's mother, having divorced and remarried since Mr Struel, was a health care assistant at a local nursing home. Daniel often saw her when he made his visits. A competent, big-bosomed woman with a deep-throated chuckle and a noisy, friendly personality. Popular and extroverted, Bobby, as she was generally known, was the life and soul of The Elms Nursing Home, contributing much towards its cheery atmosphere.

So Vanda had good maternal support in the upbringing of her daughter. She was not alone.

Which gave rise to the thought that if Bobby Millin had witnessed the apparent breath-holding in her little granddaughter it was surprising that she hadn't insisted they take the child to hospital.

It would have been the natural thing to do.

Daniel abandoned the computer and walked into the examination room. Before making any assumptions he must be sure that no organic illness had been missed.

The first thing that struck him as he entered the room was Anna-Louise, wearing only a disposable nappy, sitting still and erect on the couch, eyeing the door with the same wary expression. She did not move her head as he approached but her eyes never left him. Vanda was sitting in a chair in the corner of the room, a good six feet from the edge of the couch. Instinctively he darted towards the child and put his hand on her shoulder. What if she tumbled off?

He was puzzled. With Vanda's heightened awareness of danger, had she not seen that a normal two-year-old might easily wriggle and fall off the couch? For ease of examination it was more than three feet off the floor. And for hygiene the floor was tiled. Hard, ceramic tiles. It would have been quite a bump had she fallen. At the same time as he grappled with this anomaly he was aware that Anna-Louise had not moved or flinched or screamed when he had grasped her. Her only movement had been a curious swivel of her head so she could continue to regard him with those solemn eyes as though she didn't dare to stop watching him. She didn't try to wriggle away from his grasp like a normal two-year-old but submitted herself to his touch. She didn't cry or object. Perhaps it was then that he began to realise just how very different Anna-Louise was from a normal two-year-old. She was a vigilant toddler who had learnt to sit sphinx-still. Why?

With an odd, cold feeling, he scrutinised her face. What was it she could not tell him? Something in her passive, returned stare chilled him.

An examination room is small, which concentrates atmosphere, sounds and presence and he was aware that there was an abnormal detachment between this mother and child. His presence was doing nothing to help. Rather he was adding to the tension.

But he was a doctor and a scientist with a job to do: exclude organic illness.

It was his habit to dangle toys in front of a child he was about to examine, play a little, make friends with them, gain their confidence. One learnt to do that when still a medical student on the paediatric wards. Mothers appreciated it, pushing themselves to the fore because they wished to reassure their offspring, but Vanda remained in the corner, taking no part in the consultation, as though she wished to detach herself from the events.

Daniel was thorough. He listened carefully to the child's heart and lungs: the heart was beating normally – there were no murmurs; the lungs were clear. He peered into her pupils, tested her reactions and responses, palpated her abdomen, felt for her liver, stomach and spleen, all the time asking Vanda questions.

'Waterworks all right?'

Vanda gave a jerky nod.

'Is she eating normally?'

Silence.

Daniel turned around. Vanda was shaking her head sadly, a mournful expression in her eyes. 'She don't eat nothing,' she said.

He turned his attention back to the couch. The child was not skinny but slim. She lacked the podgy arms and legs of some toddlers but she was not undernourished.

She was eating *something*.

Finally he felt for glands in her neck, under her arms, in her groin. Again nothing.

And yet instinct told him something was wrong with this child. For a start she was too submissive. The tongue licking around her mouth was a sign of nervousness. He could not hold her gaze. Her eyes slid away from his. When he touched her she might not pull away or object but there was the faintest hint of a shudder, a small ripple which moved all the way down the small body.

Putting it all together, this toddler troubled him. He handed Vanda her daughter's clothes so she could dress her.

'I can't find anything obviously wrong,' he said, 'except that Anna-Louise needs some barrier cream for the area around her mouth. She keeps licking it, you see, which I think is probably a nervous habit.'

He stole a look at her. Vanda was fumbling with the clothes, her mouth hanging open. He couldn't be sure whether she had understood what he had said. He let the words hang in the air for a while and when there was no response, he spoke again. 'Vanda,' he said slowly, 'are you sure she didn't breathe for as long as you said? Was it really ten minutes or did it simply seem like ten minutes because you were worried?'

He was giving her a chance to retract her statement with dignity.

'It *was* that time,' she said defiantly. 'I know it.' She hesitated. 'It wasn't just because I was worried. I mean, I was, but Arnie was keeping an eye on his watch for me.'

Arnie was her brother. The town psychopath. A body-building toughie who worked for a local building firm – when he *was* working. More than half the time he was cadging sick notes from Daniel claiming he had a bad back.

'Right then,' he said.

All doctors worry about failing to reach a diagnosis – particularly in a two-year-old. Daniel was no exception to this tendency; neither were any of the paediatricians he would refer Anna-Louise to. In these days of scans and tests, enough to fill a hundred textbooks, she must be subjected to some more of them. Anna-Louise would now run the gauntlet of the entire National Health Service. But he had his suspicions that however many tests were performed on this small child no pathology would be unearthed, and so his letter would begin with the words that conveyed a secret message to his colleagues: 'This child's mother claims…'

When Vanda returned to his consultation room, Daniel told her he would be referring her daughter to the hospital, hiding behind the tired old cliché, 'Best be safe than sorry.'

At the news her face altered. Vanda lost the pinched, worried look. 'All right,' she said, breaking into a smile. 'Thanks, Doctor.'

The atmosphere in the room had melted. Vanda could look quite pretty when she smiled, he thought. She had a sort of cheeky, challenging expression on her face and quite big teeth, but they were surprisingly white and regular. Her eyelashes were long and thick, and her skin was still blooming in its youth. Born to a different mother and father, given a different start in life, had she taken other chances, she could have done something else. Perhaps she could have been a dancer, Daniel thought. She had a certain lithe grace which complemented her size.

But as it was she lived here, in this small market town in Staffordshire, in a poky council flat, living on benefits, helped out by her mum and minded by her brother. The one free excitement in her dreary life was to bring her child to the doctors' with a fable dramatic enough to guarantee both attention and sympathy. Perhaps it compensated in a small way for the difficult life she led with this sickly child. As he dictated a letter to the paediatrician in Stafford, Daniel was aware of the inconsistencies in the story. The child was unusually passive and that could be an indication of disease. It was possible that what Vanda had witnessed had not been a true apnoeic event but a convulsion. He could scarcely believe that a mother whose child had not breathed for that length of time – even turned blue – would not have dialled 999. And Arnie? Calmly timing the entire episode as though he had a sick fascination in the fact that his niece's life was in danger?

What was he to make of this family?

Chapter Two

And the Secret Heart

He was peeping over the fence at a line of washing.

The April breeze was making the lingerie dance for him. He crouched down on his haunches, camouflaged against the line of trees, fascinated at the floor show. The cups on the bra were filling with the wind then twisting and turning, seducing him. His mouth dropped open. The line of tantalising femininity stretched the entire width of the garden, lined up like young girls at a dance. Pinks and whites, Siren Black and Vamp Red. He felt the familiar trickle of pleasure. Just to tease him, she'd pegged her underwear out. He knew what her game was. This was a message. An invitation to him. He risked lifting his head one more inch to stare. Knickers. French knickers, wiggling towards him then away, then back. 'Come hither,' he muttered. 'Come hither.' But they danced away. The line of bras. Breasts, cupped together. He put his hands out. He wanted to *feel* them. Cradle them in his hand. His eyes slid along the line. Right on the end was…he felt a frisson of delight. A black suspender belt. Oh Heaven. It conjured up an image of inches of pale naked flesh between sheer stockings and the lace of her panties, the cool touch of that wonderful, precious skin.

Claudine had gone out five minutes ago. From his hiding place against the rim of trees from which he could spy on the back of her house, he'd seen her reverse down the drive in the yellow Fiat. Every day she left the house at exactly the same time – three-fifteen on the dot, to fetch her little girl from school. Although she tended to shop on foot she always drove to the school, never walked – even when the weather was as good as it was today. Bright, breezy and slowly warming towards the summer. Her regular habits made his observations easier.

He particularly liked fine weather because it was only on fine days that she pegged her washing out. Usually on Tuesdays but sometimes Wednesdays.

His attention strolled back along the washing line.

She'd bought new knickers – palest pink this time. In his mind he called it Shell Pink. Four pairs of French knickers with lace on the legs, and two bras to match. Padded bras, which she probably wore because her size was small. He'd read somewhere that French women always wore their underwear in matching sets and that had been why he had first ventured up here. To check. Purely to check out a fact. Nothing dirty. He looked around him furtively. Someone might see him, might misunderstand his intentions.

His eyes scanned the back of the row of houses, out along the damp fields, still on towards the river. He was all right. The entire landscape around him was empty. No one was there.

He smiled. It was lucky for him that these houses backed onto fields that were sliced in half diagonally by a quiet public footpath, giving him the perfect right to be here. He hooked his thumbs into his waistband. Anyone could walk on a public footpath. He sniggered softly to himself.

He'd known Claudine was French the first time he'd served her at the supermarket. She had quite a strong accent. Her being French had intrigued him. And then she had started giving him little hints that she found him interesting. Every time she came into the supermarket where he worked, she *always* made sure *he* served her. He helped her pack her shopping into the bags and she always gave him a wonderful smile, said, 'thank you,' in a soft, flirtatious voice, enticing him, inviting him to love her.

So he did. He was her devoted lover.

The thought made him brave and the line of washing was a secret message, like waving semaphore. He had a sudden, dangerous thought. No one could challenge him while he was on the footpath. That was why they were called public footpaths. He was doing nothing wrong *until he climbed the fence* into the garden. And at one point the footpath was only two feet from the garden gate. Two feet, he thought, wasn't very far at all.

But it was risky. Some people were nosey – like that horrible old Mrs Rathbone and her stupid little yappy dog. She sometimes stood and watched him.

He looked around again.

She wasn't here today. There really was no one. Absolutely no one.

Even when he looked away he could see the fluttering out of the corner of his eyes.

Oh, he groaned. If he could only *touch* those garments, *stroke* the lace, put his *own skin* against the point where… He groaned again in excitement.

The next thing he knew he was walking across the lawn, ducking under the apple tree, moving towards that line of waving, dancing, teasing washing, stretching his hand out and carefully – almost reverently unpegging four pairs of knickers, one of the bras and, *Oh Heaven,* the suspender belt. It was as though it was a person in a dream who did this. Someone else. Not him.

As he ran he whispered to himself, 'Who in the world wears suspender belts in these days of tights and nasty little pop socks? I'm sure she doesn't wear those nasty little things. Who exposes just an inch or two of thigh-flesh except to tease – you?

'She must know how you feel. She has picked up on your secret message and understood it. And this is her message back to you. She knew the garments would please you and so put them here, on show, for you. It is as simple and obvious as that.'

He liked the thought.

He selected the right pieces, the Shell Pink knickers and bra and the black suspender belt, replacing the pegs neatly on the line, taking care that they were evenly spaced, just as she had put them, except that now they had no exciting scraps of material to anchor to the line because they were in his hands.

The chill spring air hadn't quite dried them; they were still slightly damp. He slipped the knickers, bra and suspender belt into his trouser pocket, taking pleasure in the cool feeling which spread against his leg. Then he stood, only for a moment, his eyes almost closed in sheer, erotic ecstasy.

The next second he bolted back to the safety of the other side of the fence and the public footpath.

He had dreamt of doing this for a long time, ever since

he had been walking – quite innocently – along the public footpath that led from the back of the Holy Trinity Church to the row of cottages and watched her, pegs in her mouth, humming, straining to reach the clothes line, which was a little too high for her.

He'd gone home that evening, lain on his bed, closed his eyes and imagined.

But now he had *actually* done it and it was a hundred, no a thousand times better than anything he could have thought of.

He swaggered up the footpath, back into Eccleston, his secrets in his pocket.

3.25 p.m.

Police Constable Brian Anderton sighed, pulled his shoes off and collapsed onto the sofa. He was knackered. These long shifts were a kill. Six-thirty in the morning until three in the afternoon upset his body clock. It was worse than doing nights. Too tired to lift his head, he raised his arm to glance at his watch. Almost three-thirty. Bethan would be home from school soon. In the meantime he could stretch out and take forty winks. With luck Claudine would stop off at the Co-op and he would have fifty winks. He gave a cavernous, hippopotamus-sized yawn and closed his eyes. Claudine would be picking her up around about now.

He closed his eyes and for a few precious minutes he slept, his fingers curled around the yellow Bic cigarette lighter he always kept in his pocket as a talisman.

He was slow surfacing to consciousness, struggling to swim through the screaming, burning demons of Hell that prevented him from absorbing the familiar sounds of the car door slamming, the high-pitched, excitable voice of his wonderful, adored and noisy seven-year-old daughter, footsteps tripping up the path, the rattle of a key in the door, a cold draught as it was thrown open and…

'Daddy, Daddy.' He sat up to the gleeful hug of Bethan, stroked her bouncing curls and kissed her cheek, smelling plasticine, oil paint and baby soap. Claudine was standing behind her. 'Oh, Brian,' she said disapprovingly. 'I can smell those shoes the minute I walk in through the door.'

'Sorry.' He immediately felt guilty.

'Daddy.' His daughter wound her arms around his neck, 'Mummy says I can make some pancakes for tea. With sugar and lemon. I hope you're hungry,' she said severely. 'How many can you eat?'

'A hundred,' he said, tickling her tummy while she shrieked and wriggled and pulled away.

He breathed in the scent of Johnson & Johnson shampoo on her hair and thought how very much he loved this beautiful child.

He sat up. He loved her more than he could have thought possible. He loved her. He loved his family. His fingers fumbled in his pocket, seeking the reassurance. He frowned at the realisation of just how much he did love these two precious females in his life. He would die for them.

If it was necessary.

He clicked the lighter down without igniting it. Families needed protecting. Women needed protecting. His eyes followed Claudine until she disappeared into the kitchen, muttering something about it starting to rain. Brian was hoping she was going to make a cup of tea but no such luck. The scent of fresh washing wafted in from the adjacent room, Bethan trotted upstairs and Brian lay back for one more minute on the couch, thinking how much he still fancied his wife. Claudine was small and slim with faintly olive skin, dainty manners and the impeccable dress sense associated with Parisian women. Her hair, dark brown, was shaped around her face in a neat bob and her eyes, brown too, were wide and deceptively innocent. He looked up.

She was standing in the doorway, frowning.

'Brian,' she said dubiously. He sat up, alerted. He recognised that look. 'I've got a feeling.' For some reason she was looking down at the sheaf of plastic pegs in her hand with as much revulsion as though they had been a handful of spiders.

He felt the first frisson of apprehension, of discomfort. It was the beginning of something. He didn't know what, but he sensed that his period in Elysium was coming to an end, however powerful he might be.

His fingers clutched the lighter. 'What is it?'

'Brian,' she said again, as though she was not absolutely certain of what she was saying. 'I think someone's stealing my knickers from the washing line.' She gave a light, uncertain laugh.

Six-foot four of him stood right up, crossed the room and put his arm around her. 'Are you sure?'

'I can't be – I can't be absolutely sure.' But her eyes were blinking some other message.

Claudine took great pride in her underwear. In fact she was fastidious about it. Brian had watched her rinse through expensive lingerie and peg it out in matching sets along the line, even standing back to admire the effect. It was simply not something she was likely to be mistaken about. If some was missing he would consider it an assault against his wife.

He pulled her tighter to him, pressed his lips to the top of her hair in a guarding, almost paternalistic gesture. 'Some woman's probably jealous of them. Maybe stole them. They could have been blown off. There's been quite a breeze today.' His wife relaxed in his arms.

He muttered his next thought so softly into her hair she hardly caught it. 'I only hope it's not some perv lurking around the place, because if it is it'll go hard with him.' He moved away from her and cupped her face between his hands. 'It's one of the reasons I was so desperate to come here, to Eccleston, because it seemed so clean – so wholesome. Old-fashioned, just the place to bring up our daughter. It probably was the wind,' he said again. 'It has been a bit breezy today.'

'Not that breezy,' she said, still frowning. 'Besides…'

She held her hand open to expose the plastic clothes pegs. 'The pegs were returned to the line,' she said. 'In exactly the same places where I had put them. Only the garments were missing. *That* couldn't have been the wind. I couldn't help but notice they were missing. As if I was meant to. Brian,' she appealed, 'is it personal when people do that?'

'What do you mean, personal?'

'Is it *anyone's* old washing or is it me? Is it because I am French?' He could hear the heat rising in her voice.

'No,' he said. 'Of course not.' He laughed. 'Don't be paranoid, Claudine. It's nothing to do with you being French. It's just the pretty, tempting underwear. Someone saw it blowing on the line and stole it. You and I might find this bizarre, disgusting even, but it isn't usually…' His voice trailed away and his eyes swivelled downwards to look at her.

French girls have a reputation for being free, flirty, more uninhibited than English girls. He recalled the come-hither flick of her eyelashes she had given him almost ten years ago. 'You haven't been leading anyone on, have you, Claudine?'

The soft steel in his voice warned her. Over the years she had learnt to recognise Brian's moods. She did not understand them and he was not a man to confide in his wife. He was the original strong, silent type. But occasionally that could make him scary – almost frightening. But since they had moved to this pretty market town in mid-Staffordshire he had mellowed – or she had thought he had.

She had taken steps to encourage this. They now barely visited France because his French was poor and he thought that people were talking about him. His understanding of French manners led to even more embarrassment. Even now she flushed at the memory of him pulling her away from the social kiss of her sixteen-year-old cousin, Jacques Cabot.

'No, Brian,' she whispered. 'I have not led anyone on.'

He let her go and sat back on the sofa, staring at the fake flames of the gas fire.

His mind had moved away. Jumping straight into the flames. Like Faust or Bolero or a Christian martyr.

She had appealed for his help and finally he had given it.

His fingers stole around the soft plastic of the cigarette lighter.

She had had her underwear stolen too. That had been the first thing to happen.

But however right his subsequent actions had been, awkward questions had been asked and it had been suggested he transfer to a quieter area of the country.

And so he had come, eight years ago, to the pretty, Georgian coaching town of Eccleston, in Staffordshire.

He had not regretted his decision. Here he felt a Fifties Mr Plod. In a year he had collared a couple of lager louts on a Saturday night, investigated a hit-and-run on the High Street, apprehended a motorist or two who had ignored the speed limit or drink and drive law, and investigated an accumulation of milk bottles on an old lady's doorstep, which had turned out to be geriatric forgetfulness. (She had gone to visit her sister in Wiltshire and forgotten to tell her neighbours or cancel the milkman.) There had been two burglaries in two years and his wife and daughter were safe and content. He glanced across the room. Claudine was still standing where he had left her. She didn't move a muscle. 'Don't put your underwear out again,' he suggested.

Claudine objected. 'But I like the fresh scent of washing when it's been blowing on the line,' she said. 'It seems cleaner, somehow.'

'Just put your outer clothes on the line,' he said quietly.

'But—'

'Don't argue.' The words were rapped out like bullets. 'I don't want some nut getting his hands on your—'

'It's some nut?' She was alarmed now. 'Please, Brian,' she said. 'Don't. I don't want to think of it like that.'

'Use the tumble dryer or put them over the radiators – or something,' he said deliberately, as though teaching a four-year-old.

When he had finished surgery Daniel was tempted by the evening, golden with spring sunshine, and decided he would walk the short distance home. The surgery was halfway along the High Street, a converted pub. His own house was at the top of the road, near the end of the town. He only had to walk a few yards and he was home. That was one of the advantages of living in this compact place. Eccleston was a low crime area. He could leave his car quite safely in the surgery car park, protected by electric gates. He wouldn't need a car tonight anyway. His regular features twisted briefly into a sour expression. He wasn't going anywhere.

'Good night.' The practice nurse was leaving at the same time.

'Good night, Marie.'

She seemed to hesitate and he felt unaccountably awkward. Then she walked to her own car, unlocked it and climbed in.

He stepped out into the High Street.

But even on this brief journey two patients stopped him. This was the other side of living 'over the shop'.

'Hello, Doc.' Elias Broughton coughed and wheezed into his doctor's face. 'Thought I might drop in and see you soon. I seem to be getting worse. Those inhalers you gave me don't seem to be doing much.'

Daniel drew back an inch. The man stank of cigarettes. 'You do that,' he said kindly. 'You don't need an appointment in the morning. Just come along. We'll have a chat.' He patted Elias's back. He had some affection for this retired plumber. When he had first come here, ten years ago, and bought The Yellow House with Elaine, Elias Broughton had been a jobbing plumber, anxious to work for and befriend the new doctor. That had been before Holly had been born. Now Elias was retired and sick, suffering from emphysema because of the cigarettes which had constantly dribbled out of his mouth as he had worked. Daniel gave a wry smile. Elaine had made a great fuss about the cigarette smoke and about the damage to their lungs, the smell around the house and, later, the damage to their unborn infant. She had been a great one for smells. Even now, Daniel could recall the wafts of Chanel or Dior or Estee Lauder that had clung to the air in a two-yard inclusion zone all around his wife.

And in that variety there had been a clue. Most women have a favourite scent which lasts for a number of years – sometimes for their entire lives. We can almost conjure up a physical presence by evoking the perfume they wear. But his wife had been fickle from the first, choosing one to be her new favourite only to discard it a little way through the bottle and replacing it with something new.

Just like her marriage. Elaine had been a woman of numerous relationships, her diary, when he had met her, a collection of discarded boyfriends. He'd often wondered why on earth she had married him, until one day – soon after she had stormed out, throwing back the complaint that he had not lived up to expectations and she was blowed if she was going to sacrifice her life for him – he had worked it out. Now *he* was the one to be discarded. Just like her previous boyfriends and her perfume. Which would have been fine had he not had a small daughter who had made the unstable marriage almost worthwhile.

He'd almost made the safety of the The Yellow House when Mrs Rathbone accosted him, her Pekinese yapping at his heels. 'Doctor,' she said in a theatrical hiss.

'Doctor.' She drew up very close. Close enough to whisper in his ear with peppermint-scented breath. 'I've got the piles again,' she said mournfully.

Daniel smothered a grin and tried to ignore Tricky, the

dog, who was now snapping at his trouser leg. 'I need to take a look,' he said.

The attempt at wit was wasted on his patient. 'Not here,' she said affronted, casting her eyes quickly up and down the street.

He smothered another grin. 'No, Mrs Rathbone. Not here. Down at the surgery.'

Her eyes met his with alarm. 'Do you need to? Is it really necessary, Doctor? Can't you just leave me out a prescription?'

'I could,' he said slowly, 'but if they keep on giving trouble I should…'

Mary Rathbone's bright eyes sparkled. 'Will it be ready tomorrow? The prescription?'

He gave in. 'Yep. All right. But it's the only one. If they carry on giving you trouble, book in to see me.'

And now he'd reached the safety of the brass rail and curving steps which led to his own front door.

He put his key in the lock and looked up at the house.

The trouble with buying a property called The Yellow House, was that there was really only one colour you could paint it. Elaine had favoured a bright canary yellow which Daniel had always hated. But Elaine would have her way. 'What do you know about colour schemes?' she had jeered, and he had given in. But the minute she had really gone he had taken his revenge. It had been the first thing he had done – to appoint a house-painter to wash the entire house in the palest of Jersey Cream that Dulux made. Satisfactorily it had been called Lemon Cream. So he had broken no rules.

It had been one of the few elements of satisfaction in those early days – the sight of the painter working his way around his home and watching him cover up the Canary Yellow.

Eccleston High Street was considered to be public property. All the old buildings had Listed Building Status which meant that everyone felt they had a right to say what precise shade of yellow his home should be. Patients often commented that it should be brighter, paler, more subdued. It felt intrusive, as though both he and his house were very public property.

Oh, he thought, suddenly impatient as he turned the key. What did it matter? What did *any* of it matter?

He closed the door behind him with relief and shut out the sounds of the High Street.

But once inside he felt an acute attack of loneliness. When Elaine and Holly had been at home his arrival had always been greeted by sounds. Sometimes Holly crying, when she had been small, a shrill shriek of pleasure when she had been older, or Classic FM, which had been Elaine's favourite. But now, as every day, inside The Yellow House it was as hushed and quiet as a church on a Monday.

Mrs Hubbard had been in today. He could smell the mingled scent of polish and the washing hanging up in the laundry. He could almost feel the cleanliness around him like an electric charge. Anna Hubbard was that sort of cleaner. He could sense the organisation. She would have left something out for tea and emptied the dishwasher, put away the ironing, changed his bed, polished and scrubbed. But instead of comforting him it made Daniel feel depressed. He was forty years old and alone. He and Elaine had split up two years ago and he needed a woman in his life. Not Mrs Hubbard, but someone pretty and sparkling. A girlfriend. Someone who smelt good, felt good, sounded good and tasted good. He wanted someone to walk with and talk to, to share romance and dinners out,

Valentine's and Christmas, holidays too. Even more than he wanted a girlfriend he wanted his daughter back, living with him. He missed her terribly. Everything about her. From the childhood chatter to the toys cluttering up the place, Barbie with her scrappy clothes that cost so much and My Little Pony. He missed those silly plastic bobbles she wore in her hair, which constantly fell out because her hair was too fine to hold them in, and he missed the funny little hairgrips with rabbits or teddies on, which were was always turning up in odd places like the butter dish. He even missed Barbie's awful boyfriend, whatever his name was.

Daniel moved through the hall, conscious of the clatter of his footsteps over the newly polished wooden floor. He went straight through into the kitchen, glancing at the kitchen table. As he'd anticipated, the house was depressingly tidy. Even his post was laid out in a neat pile. He picked it up. A Mastercard bill, electricity, council tax and a stiff, formal-looking letter from Grays & Sons, Elaine's solicitors. More money, he thought bitterly. And what was he getting for it? Nothing. Sweet nothing. He felt a flash of resentment. For the first year after she had stalked out he had been convinced that Elaine would come to her senses and return home. But she hadn't. And now all he got were letters and threats, each one dealing yet another mortal blow to any chance of reconciliation.

He eyed the answerphone warily. One message flashing. Ever hopeful, he pressed play.

His mother's voice filled the kitchen.

'Danny. Danny, dear. How are you?' she cooed. 'Why don't you ring? What are you doing with yourself? I hope you're eating properly and managing...' a pause, '*everything.*

Don't forget, if you're lonely or need someone to take care of you, I can always come to stay.'

He almost shuddered.

Forty years old and his mother was offering to move in. It wasn't the image he had of himself. Hardly the gay bachelor.

In spite of his low mood he smiled. Now that *would* set the patients talking.

He pressed the delete button on the answering machine then sank down on a kitchen chair, swamped by the loneliness which threatened to engulf him. His future stretched ahead like an empty motorway on a dreary day. Bleak and empty, lonely; watching Holly grow up from afar and his mother fussing over him as though he was a three-year-old.

He leafed through the *Staffordshire Newsletter*, found the Lonely Hearts column and grimaced at an advert for an 'Eccleston man'. How was he to meet anyone else? Everyone he knew round here was one of his patients. And to make any sort of advance was not only taboo but would have him hauled up in front of the General Medical Council. A vision of Vanda Struel's grubby white thong appeared in front of his eyes, as though warning him that there would be no chance for him locally. Speed dating? He didn't think he could go through with that. Maybe the web. There were plenty of websites for men like him, men who were desperate for a bit of female company.

But now he had evoked the vision of Vanda his mind wandered laterally. What was her game? What was she up to with her silent little tot with the ever-licking tongue?

He sighed.

Mrs Hubbard had left out one of her specialities – Ploughman's. Stilton cheese, chopped with apple. He didn't want it. He rang the Indian takeaway, the *Darv Chini*. This was one of the perks of being a local doctor. They'd deliver for free. After all, they'd said, he'd delivered their youngest.

Hah hah hah. The laughter had rung right the way around the restaurant, which was actually more like a small parlour.

He faced another evening at home – alone with a curry.

Maybe he should get a dog or a cat. Elaine had hated the thought, forbidding him even to think about it. He seemed to hear her shrill voice still echoing around the kitchen. 'You're not, Daniel Gregory, so you can just forget about it. I'm not having some mucky animal mess this place up. Anyway, they smell.'

He sighed and blamed his mother. Always fussing over him while Elaine had watched, a sneer curling her mouth into scorn for the mothered boy.

Thank goodness Holly was coming for the weekend.

Chapter Three

Friday, 14th April

They wanted hormones.

It was the magic word, the panacea for all that was wrong with their lives. Lack of hormones.

He looked at the girl in front of him. It was April, for goodness' sake. The weather had not warmed up yet. Even so, she was wearing a skimpy T-shirt with no sleeves. In fact hardly anything over the shoulders except what he knew from the Sunday papers were called 'Spaghetti straps'. No bra. And Chelsea Emmanuel was, to put it mildly, well endowed in spite of her fourteen years – just.

She crossed her legs. She had smothered them badly with fake tan. He could see brown-orange streaks around her knees and ankles, dirty goose bumps and a distinct tidemark on the front of her arms near her wrists.

'I need the pill,' she said defiantly.

Daniel sighed.

In 1983 a lady called Victoria Gillick (mother of ten children) challenged a High Court ruling which allowed doctors to prescribe the contraceptive pill to the under-sixteens without the consent of a parent. Since then, in acknowledgment of the focus and clarification she appealed for on the subject, family doctors abide by something called the Gillick Ruling. This allows them to prescribe the pill for contraceptive reasons *provided* the girl is 'Gillick competent', i.e. that she understands the full significance of the act of sexual intercourse and is not being coerced or manipulated. The doctor should still try to persuade the girl to discuss the wider implications of indulging in sexual intercourse at such a young age, but a teenage pregnancy is the result no one wants. Chelsea Emmanuel appeared inappropriate to Daniel.

'Are you actually *having* intercourse?'

Chelsea took a long, cuddish chew at her gum, dropped her eyelashes and crossed and uncrossed her legs without regard to his view of her knickers. 'Yeah,' she said, challenge in every fibre of her attitude.

'I have to point out,' Daniel said, reason making his voice smooth and unthreatening, 'that it is, strictly speaking, against the law. You're only fourteen.'

She leant forward which gave him a full view of her cleavage. 'So?' She rolled her eyes towards the ceiling and he had a sudden glimpse of what it must be like to be the father of a precocious teenage daughter. He gave an involuntary shudder. *Not Holly. Please never Holly.*

'How old's your boyfriend?'

'Nearly twenty,' she said. 'If I don't get the pill off you I'll get pregnant, won't I?'

Probably.

It was the lesser of two evils.

'I'll just check your blood pressure.'

He felt vaguely uncomfortable as he Velcroed the cuff around her arm. She'd turned her heavily painted face towards him, eyelashes fluttering like a bad actress in a Thirties 'B' movie.

He drew in a deep breath.

'Perfect blood pressure,' he said. 'Do you smoke?'

The government paid him to ask questions like these. Cynically he had decided years ago that they concentrated on targets intended to prove the impossible – that the nation was getting healthier.

He tapped the script into the computer, giving her a two months' supply of oral contraceptive, ripped it off the printer, signed it, instructed her how and when to take it, how long she would need to use 'additional cover' for and told her to return to the practice nurse 'for a check' before they ran out.

She stood up, uncomfortably close to his desk, legs apart. He noticed all her imperfections – the irregular teeth, the chipped nail varnish, the smell of cigarette smoke mingled with that of fried food and a nasty, musky perfume, the dark roots of hair striped and straightened into submission, and the incessant, noisy, open-mouthed gum-chewing.

'I'd much rather come back to see you,' she said.

It made his flesh creep.

'It's unnecessary for you to come back to see me,' he said stiffly. 'The nurses do the pill checks.'

'Don't much like your nurse,' she said. 'She's a bit of an old bag.'

He could feel anger rise up inside him. Marie Westbrook, their full-time practice nurse, was in her thirties and anything but an old bag. In his opinion she was an attractive, intelligent and professional woman.

'Come on a Wednesday and see Stella in that case.'

He just wanted her to go.

Chelsea shrugged.

'If you like.'

Daniel was already looking into the computer screen, typing in the consultation. He was always glad his mother had insisted he have piano lessons though it had seemed 'sissy' at the time. The deft skill in his fingers had easily transferred to mastery of the QWERTY keyboard.

He felt a sense of relief when the door finally closed behind Chelsea Emmanuel.

Seconds later he was pressing the key which would move the Next Patient sign across the VDU in the patients' waiting room.

Gone were the days when a doctor had bobbed in and out of the waiting area to summon his patient, running the gauntlet of people angry at the waiting time extending with every one of them who wanted more than their allocated ten minutes.

Guy Malkin was his next patient. An odd misfit of a boy. Not entirely his own fault. Guy had Marfan's Syndrome, a disease of the connective tissue, which accounted for some of his oddness: long, spidery fingers, hyper-extending joints, arms that dangled at his side as long as an ape's. He sat down awkwardly, untidy, all bony limbs, fidgety hands and knees that constantly bounced up and down nervously. Guy was long and skinny, with hunched shoulders. Today he was wearing ill-fitting jeans, huge and too long for him so the flares formed puddles at his feet. The jeans were grubby and worn with a rip, which afforded Daniel a glimpse of a very narrow knee. Guy's eyes were looking all around the room, everywhere but at him. How old was he, Daniel wondered? Fifteen? The computer screen insisted seventeen.

Daniel smiled encouragingly at the gauche youth but the smile seemed to have the effect of making the youth shrink.

Daniel was aware that the time clock was ticking away.

He needed to hurry him along.

'What can I do for you, Guy?'

He was unprepared for the look of panic which froze the boy's face. Eyes wide, mouth a frightened 'O', sweat glistening his forehead, a blotchy, embarrassing rash spreading across his face and down his neck.

'Guy?' he prompted gently.

'I don't think I'm normal, Doctor.'

The million dollar question. What is normal? Guy had Marfan's.

'We-ell,' he began, but Guy interrupted – almost impatiently.

'I don't mean the Marfan's, Doctor.'

'Then in what way?'

The eyes lifted – just for a second then fell away again.

'Sexually, I mean,' he muttered to the floor.

Daniel smiled at the youth and deliberately veered away from sounding patronising. 'I wish I had a pound for every seventeen-year-old who thinks he's abnormal sexually,' he said casually, trying to convey the message that this was no unusual encounter, that the youth was not that dreadful word – different.

Guy swallowed and seemed unable to continue.

Gently Daniel repeated his question. 'In what way, Guy?'

'I find it…'

'Yes?'

'I can't…I've never been with a girl but I want to. I know the girl I want and she wants me. I can tell.'

For all of us there is a match. However strange, unique or unusual, there is someone. For Guy Malkin, for him.

The eyes crept back up towards him.

'You know?'

It came out all of a rush then. 'Can I have some Viagra?'

Daniel was taken aback. A seventeen-year-old virgin asking for the designer sex drug? To prescribe him this would set him up for life, always dependent on a drug to ensure normal activity.

But how could he explain this in ten minutes?

'You've never been with a girl?'

More dropping of the head together with a firm shake.

Daniel tried to make a joke of it. 'So what are you planning to do when you've swallowed a load of Viagra?'

A shrug.

It was scary.

'Look, Guy,' he said finally. 'I'll tell you what. Just go out with girls normally. Don't think too much about sex. Make friends of them.' He grinned at him. 'Most blokes of your age tell whopping big lies about it anyway. Half of them are in the same boat as you. They haven't done it. What's more – they're scared of it. You don't need a drug. Just let it happen in your own time.'

'You don't understand, Doc.' Guy was desperate. 'I really need to be with a girl *normally*. Otherwise…'

Daniel caught the note of panic in the youth's face. It alarmed him.

'What don't I understand, Guy? Why is this need so…'

Guy pressed his lips together, started to hyperventilate with rapid, deep sucking breaths, shot desperate glances towards the door. 'I got to go, Doc.' He was already out of his seat.

And what was called the 'window of opportunity' had slammed shut in Daniel's face.

Guy's brief flirtation with explanation was over. The shutters were down.

'Come back,' Daniel urged. 'In a month or two. You may feel different by then.'

The minute the boy had left the room he knew he'd failed him.

That failure discomforted him for the rest of the morning. He had tried, too clumsily, to reassure him. Before summoning the next patient, he analysed what had been said and still failed to understand how he could have handled the situation differently.

He drew in a deep, frustrated breath and in the words of the American fast food chain, muttered, 'Thank God it's Friday.'

Two octogenarians followed in fast succession, both with a plethora of complaints. Like old cars, he reflected. One system goes, you never quite fix it, then MOTs and services become ever more complicated and finally the car is no longer viable. It dies. He looked at his second elderly patient of the day, Maud Allen, eighty-six years old and still digging in her garden and growing all her own vegetables. 'Have done since the war,' she would bark.

But she was slowing up, almost the last of her generation.

'No arthritis,' she bellowed, 'thank goodness. Nasty business that – arthritis. Painful, nasty business.'

She still wore a hat to the surgery, he noticed, a sort of pork pie, tweedy thing. And a suit which a charity shop would have refused. She must have noticed him looking at it.

'Bought it in the Sixties,' she said. 'Quality always lasts, you know.'

He felt her disapproval as she took in his casual jeans, shirt open at the neck. No tie, no jacket. He could almost hear her comparing him unfavourably with the senior partner he had replaced, Doctor Anthony Morgan. London-trained. Did all his own nights (fool who had no life). And his wife was – *a lady*.

No use quoting *Little Britain* to her!

'I rather think,' she said, 'that I needed to come to you for my thyroid check, but I can't remember whether I had the necessary blood test.'

'Let's look,' he said, 'shall we?'

She hadn't had her thyroid levels done for almost a year so Daniel took some blood and sent it off. 'We may need to adjust the dose,' he warned. 'So what I want you to do is to ring me in a week's time and I'll let you know.'

She put a liver-spotted, slack-skinned hand over his and he met a pair of blue eyes still bright with humour. 'You are good to me, Doctor,' she said. 'So very good.'

His next patient was Maud Allen's diametric opposite. Darren Clancy swaggered in, asking for anabolic steroids, like, to make him more muscly, like, and have a bit more success with the girls, like. Daniel dealt with him calmly, fighting the rising instinct to tell him to piss off. Instead he explained that anabolic steroids were potentially dangerous, illegal when prescribed for body-building, and watched the youth swagger out, swearing as he left and venting his frustration by kicking the door open.

Daniel reflected that he should have crossed the stroppy guy off his list. Instead he'd listened calmly, been polite. What was his role in today's society? He'd trained to treat sick people, for goodness' sake. And now here he was, fending off patients who were trying to rope him in to provide designer drugs to make them more attractive to the opposite sex.

He allowed himself a quiet expletive.

A woman was still sitting in the waiting room, staring at the floor as he passed through. He didn't recognise her so he asked Vanessa, one of the receptionists, who she was.

She moved away from the hatch, out of view of the woman. 'She hasn't got an appointment,' she said. 'But…'

He glanced again at the woman. She was in her forties, sitting quietly and very still, dressed neatly in a dark, full skirt, flat pumps and a white sweater. She didn't look agitated but perfectly composed.

'She wants to see someone now,' the receptionist said. 'I've offered her no end of appointments. She's fairly new on the list,' she added.

'Did she say it was urgent?'

'She didn't use that word.' Vanessa was unfailingly honest and literal. 'But she implied she wasn't leaving until she'd seen a doctor.'

His first thought was the morning after pill. Levonorgestrel. Not quite as urgent as its name implied. In actual fact you have three days' grace from the act, but it did bring women scuttling down to the surgery.

'I'd better see her,' he said.

He crossed the now empty waiting room and approached her. She looked up and for the second time that morning he read desperation in a patient's eyes.

'Hello,' he said. 'I'm Doctor Gregory. Would you like to come into my surgery?'

She looked uncertain and he felt impatient. For goodness' sake. She'd just turned up here. She didn't look like an emergency. It didn't seem as though there was a crisis. And he was offering to see her.

She had a pale face. No make-up, straight brown hair, shoulder-length, tucked behind her ears. Her ears were pierced, he noted, but she had no earrings in. He glanced down at her hands. No rings either.

'What's your name?'

'Cora Moseby,' she said. 'I'm registered with Doctor Satchel. Is she here?'

'I think she's left to do one or two visits. If it's Doctor Satchel you want to see, maybe the receptionist can make you an appointment.'

'I can't wait,' she said very quietly.

'Then why don't you see me?' He had on his best friendly doctor air. It usually worked.

She stood up slowly, picked up a large leather handbag from the floor and walked along the corridor to the consulting rooms. He noticed she limped.

Once he had held open the door and she'd sat down at the side of his desk, he mentioned it. 'Pain in the hip? Or the back?'

She looked confused.

'Your limp,' he said.

'Yes.' She looked vague. 'I do limp sometimes. I'm not sure why.'

He needed to read her notes.

'So,' he said briskly, 'what can I do for you today?'

'I think I'm very anaemic,' she said.

He felt a twinge of irritation. This was hardly an emergency.

'Why do you think that?'

'Because I get very tired,' she said. 'I can fall asleep at any time. And then I dream. I dream that I am awake and think I see things – people.'

Mentally Daniel cussed himself for getting involved.

'Let's deal with the anaemia,' he said. He looked at her eyes. They didn't look pale. He checked her blood pressure, took her pulse. All normal. Finally he scribbled out a form for a full blood count and handed it to her. 'We'll check up on that,' he said, standing up. 'And about the other – well – I think you should come back and see Doctor Satchel a week after the blood test. She'll have the result by then. All right?'

She looked even more uncertain. 'What if I...? In the meantime, I mean.'

'Perhaps you shouldn't drive until we've got to the bottom of this,' he suggested. 'And avoid alcohol.'

She bowed her head and left the room. She left behind a vague scent of something musty, like old clothes.

Doctors have an instinct for strange people. And the hairs on the back of his neck were prickling. She was weird. Possibly fey, but definitely weird.

Saturday, 22nd April

It never failed to annoy him that Elaine refused to bring Holly on the Friday. After all, he'd argued, again and again, both with the solicitor and with her, in his view Friday was part of the weekend.

But Elaine had stuck to her guns. She was not driving

up the M6, all the way from Birmingham, on a Friday night when the motorway was so busy.

Holly would have spent all day at school and would be far too tired to sit in the car for an hour or more.

Besides, she would have the return journey late at night and what if she was working – or going out?

Wearily, Daniel had offered to drive halfway down the M6 and meet her at the services. It was surprising how very weary divorce made him. Things seemed to take so much effort – especially the ceaseless arguments about access to his own daughter. Finally, in desperation, he'd offered to collect Holly from Elaine's house on the Friday, but Elaine had promptly enrolled her in Friday evening ballet classes, which put paid to that.

Elaine didn't even make the effort to get out of bed early on the Saturday morning. It was invariably around lunchtime that she arrived. Which gave him little more than twenty-four hours with his daughter. She had to be returned early. ('Early, mind,' Elaine was fond of saying. 'She has school on Monday.')

At eleven on the Saturday morning he finally heard her car. Even over the constant buzz of the High Street traffic, Elaine's car was distinctive – huge and noisy, a 4x4 with a bull bar on the front. He heard the slam of the car door and opened his front door.

The huge Honda was parked right outside; she'd already turned around. Elaine had done very well for herself, he reflected. A nice house in Harborne and she was planning on getting married again, so Holly told him. She was to be bridesmaid, she'd announced on her last visit. In pink, her favourite colour.

He'd felt the bile rise up in his mouth and wanted to spit it out.

As soon as he had presented himself on the doorstep the Honda accelerated back down the High Street. Holly was struggling with her Barbie doll suitcase, trying to pull it up the steps on its wheels.

'Daddy,' she said, and the suitcase bumped back down again.

He scooped her up in his arms and buried his face in her neck.

'I was ready at six o'clock,' she announced. 'But Mummy took *ages* getting all my stuff ready.'

'You've grown,' he said, and she giggled.

It was a standing joke between them, that she had visibly grown in the week they had been apart. Neither of them believed it. They just pretended they did.

The moment he put her back down on the floor she pushed past him and scampered up the stairs, leaving him to retrieve the case. 'I want Christabel,' she flung back when she reached the landing.

Christabel was the latest, most favourite doll and she lived here. Like all Holly's teenage dolls, Christabel was impossibly big-breasted, tiny-waisted and long-legged, and eight or so inches tall.

Holly was whispering something in the doll's ear as she descended the stairs, slower than she had ascended.

When she looked up at him her eyes were sparkling with some secret plot.

'What are we going to do this weekend, Daddy?'

'I thought we might go and look for some tadpoles. Didn't you say that you were doing a project at school?'

For some reason he had the impression that he was playing into her hands.

'Yes we are but…' her face fell, 'Mummy hasn't packed my Wellingtons.'

The irritation surfaced again. He distinctly remembered reminding Elaine to include them during his Wednesday evening phone call.

'That's a shame, pigeon.'

She dropped her face forward so her hair curtained her expression. 'I really wanted to get some tadpoles,' she said plaintively. There was a short pause before she said, 'We could buy some. Mine were a bit tight anyway.'

So that was the plan. She'd probably hidden her own Wellingtons. How very manipulative even the youngest of the female species could be.

Now he realised she had worked the entire scheme out – from simple beginning to clever end.

Telling him they were doing a project in school was the first part.

Deliberately forgetting Wellingtons the second.

And the third?

Halfway down the High Street was an upmarket children's boutique called LITTLE MONSTERS. Eccleston was seething with doting grandparents so it did a brisk trade. If he thought back carefully he could remember the window display of a week ago, Holly's last visit. April Showers had been the jolly theme. PVC macs, sweet little hoods, tiny umbrellas and an assortment of decorative Wellingtons – flowery pinks for the girls, frog-eyed Thomas the Tank Engine for the boys. Holly had eyed up a particularly garish pair of flowery pink Wellingtons without saying a word but she must have squirrelled the idea away.

So now he had played right into her hands. 'Neat, little lady,' he said.

Her eyes sparkled. 'Can we, Daddy?'

He wasn't going to be that easy. 'Can we what?' he teased.

'Get some,' she said with just a touch of irritation.

He gave in then. 'OK. I don't see why not.'

The shop was busy on a Saturday morning, bustling with parents and indulgent grandparents focusing all their attention on the children.

Amongst the throng Daniel spotted the local bobby, out shopping with his wife and little daughter. 'Well, hello.'

The wife, Claudine, was French, unmistakably so with a petite chic. The daughter looked the same age as Holly and was very like her mother, which was lucky because Brian Anderton was six-foot four with a broad build to match and a tendency to run to fat. The adults exchanged pleasantries while the two girls eyed each other warily for a minute or two before turning to the footwear display.

They bonded almost immediately over the same pair of bubble-gum pink flowery boots and further gelled when they were measured and found to be the same size. Now chattering happily they unanimously refused to take the beloved footwear off, while the parents flashed their plastic and the Anderton child (Daniel couldn't remember her name except that it wasn't something French) whispered something in her mother's ear.

Claudine Anderton admonished her daughter with an, 'It's rude to whisper in company,' but she turned a laughing face and flashing dark eyes to Daniel. 'I'm so sorry,' she said. 'Bethan tells me you are hunting for tadpoles this afternoon.'

Bethan. Yes – that was it. A Welsh name. Unexpected.

Daniel grinned back at Claudine. 'Yes,' he said, 'we are.

Holly is doing something at school about them.'

Or was it simply a ruse to persuade him to buy the new footwear? He was never quite sure.

He read the eagerness on the little girl's face and added, 'Would Bethan like to come?'

He noted the child's hand tighten around her mother's and the pleading expression on her face. At the same time he noted Brian Anderton's mouth tighten and his forehead crinkle into an ugly scowl while his glance moved between Daniel and his wife, forming some connection.

Either Claudine hadn't noticed her husband's emotion or she chose to ignore it. 'I think she would like to come, Doctor Gregory.' Now she looked to her husband for his approval.

Anderton swallowed. 'Yes,' he said. 'I'm sure *Doctor* Gregory will take good care of our little girl.'

Daniel ignored the sarcasm. 'I'll call round to collect her then, shall I? About two?'

There was no need to ask where the policeman lived. Like the doctor, in Eccleston, *everyone* knew where the policeman lived.

In that same moment, the secret watcher was standing outside the policeman's house. Even though he knew he shouldn't. It was dangerous. What if somebody saw him? But he simply couldn't stay away. From his semi-concealed position, standing against the line of trees, he'd watched as they had set out. What could be more natural than a family outing, shopping together on a Saturday morning? As he'd seen them lock the house behind them, he'd made his plan. He wanted to show her somehow that her garments were appreciated, fussed over, admired. And he had thought of a way to pay tribute to her. He needed to do that because he had noted that today, although the weather was fine and dry, the washing line remained neatly rolled away with no dancing little symbols. She'd left nothing for him. There was nothing for him to look at, to drool over, to touch, nothing to spark his imagination. So she needed encouragement…

She shouldn't do this, deprive him of his stimulus. His mouth tightened. It was that husband's fault. He was suspicious and possessive. He wasn't allowing their relationship to progress, develop as it should in a healthy normal way. He was trying to prevent her from playing with him.

Well – he wouldn't succeed.

Love always won in the end.

He would have to show him. He would give him a jolt. But he must be careful and clever. The police were very smart these days. If he gave her the gift he had in mind, they would be able to get DNA from it. He didn't believe for a moment that the police only kept criminals on file. They had only to appeal to everyone to help *solve the mystery* and all innocent males for miles around would oblige, finally isolating the guilty and all fingers would eventually point at him. That wasn't part of his plan.

No, it must be a sterile emblem.

He smiled. They would soon see how clever he was.

Daniel allowed Holly to wear her new Wellingtons around the house; they were no dirtier than any other new pair of shoes. 'But if they get muddy,' he warned, 'you'll have to wash them. Thoroughly. Or else they stay outside.' He listened to her slapping up and downstairs with amusement.

His weak attempt at discipline failed to wipe the smirk off his daughter's face.

She'd won. She'd got her own way.

He always cooked for Holly. The truth was he enjoyed cooking while his daughter sat on the work surface, directing operations, making comments all the while. The sight of her small form, swinging her legs self-consciously in the new Wellingtons made him as happy as a TV chef. Today he was pan cooking some chicken he had marinated overnight in lemon zest and juice. He fried a few chips and prepared a bowl of salad to eat with it.

Then they sat down to eat while she made comments.

'I think you've overdone the lemon, Dad.'

'Mmm.' He put his head on one side and pretended to consider her criticism. 'Not sure about that, pigeon.'

She giggled. 'I don't know why you call me pigeon.'

He thought about it. 'No,' he said. 'Neither do I.'

She chewed another couple of mouthfuls. 'You were a bit overgenerous with the black pepper too, Daddy,' she said next, severely.

They ate Müller yoghurt to finish and loaded the dishwasher before Holly disappeared upstairs to clean her teeth. This was another trait she had inherited from her mother – cleaning her teeth frequently and with great gusto. Even from the bottom of the stairs he could hear her spitting noisily into the sink.

Like her newfound friend, Bethan Anderton had also worn her Wellington boots into the house. When they'd returned from their shopping trip she'd gone straight upstairs and started texting her school friends. There was no point in owning the latest fashion if no one knew about it. The object was to inspire *envy.* It was an important part of possession.

She was still giggling to herself as she tapped on the keys. Jst cum home frm shopping! Hve pink wellingtons! Luv Beth XXXXXXXXXXX

Soon her mobile was flashing and singing with returning comments. Her favourite was from Saskia. Lcky U!

She saved it.

Brian was sitting on the sofa, fiddling with the TV remote control. He was desperate to watch the opening minutes of a football game. In the kitchen he could hear his wife humming some funny little Edith Piaf café song. She had the same sort of voice as the 'little sparrow', rich, brave, gravelly, cracked. He sighed and closed his eyes for a second. He wished he could banish the demons, that just for once he could stop being influenced by the devils in his past. But the way that doctor had looked at Claudine had made his heart pound with anger. He knew he was divorced and was probably an attractive proposition to women but there was no need for him to look at his wife like that. She was *his wife.*

Brian's attention was diverted by a noise.

Claudine was no hysteric. She didn't scream. She merely made a guttural noise that was part groan, part whimper.

Brian turned his head to make sense of the sound.

'Brian.'

He was at her side in a second. 'What is it?'

She was staring out of the kitchen window, looking over the garden. Disgust had screwed her face up.

He followed her gaze. Through the kitchen window, out into the garden. But Claudine had not hung her washing out to dry this morning. The machine had remained silent, the line coiled up. Not now. It was stretched right across the lawn, from side to side.

And one item was neatly attached to it with a green plastic clothes peg.

'Bloody hell,' he murmured.

It was unmistakably a condom. Pale thin rubber, flopping in the breeze. The bulb on the end had filled with air or—

'I did not even stretch the line out,' Claudine protested. 'It was coiled up. Brian. I didn't do any washing this morning.'

His first instinct was to get it out of his wife's sight. He raced out into the garden. Then stopped. No, he thought and walked slowly back to the house and unhooked his car keys.

Claudine watched him uneasily. 'What are you going to do?'

He stepped out of the front door, unlocked his car and took out a pair of latex gloves and a specimen bag.

'I'm going to find out who's doing this,' he said grimly. 'People can't just come in and,' he paused, 'pollute my garden. Give filthy messages to my wife. He's been stealing your underwear and now he's sending you filthy insults. I'm not having it.'

His silences were the worst. Claudine had learnt this soon after they had been married. His silences always meant something. Whenever he was quiet it was his mind which was busily working things out. And whatever was in his mind was almost always frightening; what he worked out was the product of a sick and suspicious mind. She hardly dared breathe because he was silent now.

Her husband turned his head very slowly to look at her. 'What do you know about this?'

'Nothing.'

His eyes studied her from top to toe, finally concentrating on her face. Then he turned around and left the room.

Through the window she watched him stride across the garden just as Bethan shouted from the top of the stairs. 'Mummy, someone's put a sausage skin on the clothes line.'

She was descending awkwardly in her new Wellington boots. Claudine heard her daughter trip and crash down the stairs. She ran into the hallway.

Bethan was unhurt – apart from her pride. 'Mum,' she said, her face mournful.

Claudine held her daughter to her, smiling now.

Brian was back in the kitchen, peeling the gloves off and throwing them in the plastic swing bin. 'I'm sending this off,' he said, holding the bag up. 'I'm going to find out once and for all what's going on. I'm going to get to the bottom of this, Claudine. He can't get away with it. It's...' He broke off as his daughter clumped into the room.

'...obscene,' he muttered.

He put the bag carefully into his car. He'd take it in on Monday morning.

Claudine had prepared some open sandwiches with Parma ham and some tiny, sweet cherry tomatoes, but as they ate lunch husband and wife hardly looked at each other. Finally Claudine put her sandwich down. 'Is it because I'm French?' she demanded. 'Because I'm a foreigner?'

Bethan tugged at the bread. 'Is what?' She could sense the atmosphere and like most children she worried that she was to blame. 'Is it me? Were my Wellingtons too expensive?' She looked anxiously from mother to father.

Her father stroked her long hair then gave it a playful tug.

'Absolutely not,' he said.

'Is it the sausage skin?'

Husband and wife exchanged glances.

'Yes.' Brian Anderton finally answered her query. 'Someone's been playing silly, rude jokes. If you see someone – anyone in the garden or watching the house – I want you to come and tell me.'

'Yeah. OK,' the child said slowly, not understanding.

They continued eating in silence, chewing their food without enjoying it until Claudine lifted her head. 'I think I hear a car,' she said.

Bethan was ready to go in a flash. In fact, as she tore down the path, Daniel had the impression that she was relieved to be going out. He decided to leave the car outside the police house and walk, with the two girls, through the gate at the back of the garden and across the field, then down to one of the tributaries of the river. They armed themselves with nets and two large Tupperware containers complete with lids. The girls ran on ahead, shouting and laughing and Daniel had to run to keep up with them. The breeze was cool in his face, the sunshine bright enough to make him squint through the trees dappling the light. At the bottom of the slope he could see the sharp glint of Perle Brook. He met one or two dog walkers and a courting couple who giggled and flushed as they greeted him.

He sighed. Today he was off duty. He didn't want to think about anyone – not Anna-Louise or Chelsea or Cora or even Maud Allen. He only wanted to think about his daughter, her friend, spring sunshine and the tadpoles they were sure to catch.

Chapter Four

They were back at the police house by four o'clock, the girls chattering excitedly as though they had been friends for years.

Claudine looked at Daniel, hopping around on the doorstep, his hands still occupied with the Tupperware containers and their wriggling contents. 'Why don't you and Holly stay for supper, Daniel?' she suggested as the girls scampered upstairs. 'It's nothing special, I warn you – just some chicken, but I'm sure Holly would enjoy it and I expect you enjoy being cooked for.'

He had the feeling her 'nothing special' was on a different plane than his and he couldn't deny it, he would love to be cooked for. Not just Mrs Hubbard's left-outs but properly cooked for. It is something married men value cheaply but once home cooking is gone they quickly miss it.

He read the warmth in her toffee-coloured eyes behind the invitation and just as clearly he sensed that PC Anderton wasn't quite so keen on the idea.

Perhaps his wife picked up on it too. She swivelled around to challenge him. 'We do want them to come, don't we, Brian, and I always cook too much. I can't bear the thought of being short of food.'

It would have been very churlish for the policeman to say no, and yet Daniel sensed that the word was on the tip of his tongue. Since his divorce he was beginning to realise that, whereas females found him an amiable challenge, males sensed something predatory about his single status and wanted to lock up their women. Inwardly he gave a wry smile. He wasn't *that* attractive or Elaine wouldn't have walked out on him. He knew he was average-looking, a bit on the bony side. He wouldn't have minded being a couple of inches taller and he tended towards round shoulders from spending his youth poring over books.

So he eyed the policeman warily and waited. Failing to meet his glance, Brian gave a grudging nod and Daniel accepted.

So that was that.

His eyes moved from husband to wife, careful to address them both. 'Actually,' he said, 'it would be really nice. I'm sure your cooking's better than mine, Claudine.' Now was his chance to reassure Brian Anderton that he wasn't chasing after his wife. But he breathed in her fresh, clean scent, oranges mingled with sunshine. If she was single, he added mentally, it would be a different matter.

He gave himself a cop out. 'Perhaps I'd better just check with Holly, see if it's OK with her.'

'Don't worry, Daniel,' Claudine said, her foot already on the bottom stair. 'I'll go and ask her myself. Brian, why don't you put the tadpoles in the kitchen then pour Daniel a beer?'

'OK. Yeah. Sorry.' The policeman was obviously abstracted. 'Lager OK?'

'Yes. Thanks.' Daniel nodded. Brian Anderton disappeared,

returning with a couple of cans of Stella and pint glasses. He handed one of each to Daniel and they settled comfortably into the sitting room armchairs.

Daniel looked around approvingly. *A woman's touch*, he thought, noting the simple clean lines of the furniture, the vase of purple tulips on a low coffee table.

'How did you meet your wife,' he asked, purely as a conversation opener, but quickly realising he'd made a bad choice talking about Claudine.

Anderton was eying him suspiciously. 'Holiday, mate,' he said. 'I was with a few buddies of mine, camping in the south of France. She was there on holiday too.'

'There's something about French women, isn't there?' Daniel winced. *It was an even bigger faux pas.*

'I thought so,' the policeman said testily. 'That's why I married her.'

Right on cue Claudine put her head round the door. 'It's all settled,' she said. 'The girls are going to help me to cook and lay the table. You two men just talk.' She aimed a brilliant smile into the room and closed the door behind her.

At first the two men drank in silence. Everything Daniel thought he could say seemed to have a double entendre.

Avoid comments about his wife, his home, his daughter even. Daniel was stuck for conversation so merely fixed a pleasant, consultation-room, neutral smile on his face and said nothing. Then Anderton set his glass down heavily on the table and cleared his throat. 'I wanted to ask you something,' he said gruffly.

'Go on.' With a sinking heart Daniel knew it would be something medical.

Chest pain, bowel trouble...impotence?

He waited.

Anderton didn't get straight to the point but meandered thoughtfully. 'I'm well used to crime,' he began slowly. 'You know – plain theft, drunken assaults, burglary, that sort of thing, but some crimes, to me, are…' he was frowning, 'inexplicable.' He took a deep swig of lager, frowned into the can. 'I just can't follow them. I can't understand the motive. I mean…' He leant forward, his elbows resting on his knees. 'Why would someone steal a woman's knickers off a washing line?'

'Claudine's?' It was out before he'd thought.

Anderton nodded grimly, took another angry swig out of his lager can and waited for an answer.

'It could be…' he couldn't think of a way to say this without sounding voyeuristic. 'Perhaps her underwear is expensive? Tasteful and someone's simply stolen them.'

Anderton looked almost bored by this explanation,

'But usually,' Daniel continued warily, 'it's stolen by someone inadequate. The act is done for sexual gratification because they can't get it normally. But surely,' he couldn't help himself, 'not here? Not in Eccleston. It's not that sort of place. We don't exactly breed people with sexual fantasies.'

It was a stupidly naïve statement and he knew it.

'We do now,' Anderton said grumpily, 'right in my back yard. Someone's been stealing my wife's underwear from the washing line. And then this afternoon.' He got up, agitated, gripping his can so hard Daniel thought it must crumple and spill lager over the pale carpet. 'This afternoon,' Anderton repeated, 'a condom was pinned to it. Someone – I assume it's a he – had not only pulled the washing line out – it's a retractable one,' he explained, 'but they'd pinned a ruddy…'

Upset he couldn't continue. 'For goodness' sake, Daniel, what sort of a man would do such a thing? A perv? And how far will he go? Claudine was asking me for answers. "Is it personal? Is it because she's French?" Is this rotten weirdo trying to get close to my wife – because if he is I swear I'll…' His face was contorted with anger. 'Is this the start of serious stalking?'

'It could be but—'

The policeman butted in. 'I was involved in a case that began like this a few years back in Birmingham,' he said, his hand stealing round the cigarette lighter in his pocket. 'He began by pinching underwear. "Bloody saddo," we thought. We didn't get too worried. But – well, let's just say it escalated.' He broke off, his face hard, lips pressed together and an angry fire lighting his eyes. Daniel waited for the inevitable eruption but Brian gripped the can of lager tighter until it did crumple in his hand. Luckily it was empty. Hardly noticing he stared, with brooding anger, into the gas fire and said nothing. Daniel knew better than to speak. Anderton must tussle with these demons alone.

At last he looked up and Daniel was shocked to see the hatred on his face. 'He started really stalking this woman. Watching her house, following her to work, shopping, that sort of thing. He'd ring her number and hang up the minute she answered. This went on for nearly three years. We kept trying to get court injunctions but it all took time and in the meantime this poor woman had no life. Her marriage broke up; her children went to live with their dad. She stayed in the house but only because she couldn't bring herself to show people round and sell it. She was too frightened he'd turn up on a viewing.'

'In the end?' Daniel asked curiously.

Anderton turned his gaze back towards the dancing flames. 'He topped himself,' he said bluntly.

And now he was summoned back to his nightmare, knocking on the door of the house in Sparkbrook for what must have been the fiftieth time, already angry, frustrated by the law which was confining him, recalling his promise to protect the vulnerable woman, watching the man taunt her as she stared out of the bedroom window, screaming. He recalled the man picking up a can of petrol, the smell of it even which today, years later, still evoked the dramatic, hysterical scene, a taste and nausea and the scent of burning flesh.

'Go on then,' he whispered as the man held a yellow Bic cigarette lighter out. 'Go on. Go on. Go on.'

He had heard the voice urging the man to do it, goading him even, challenging him that he didn't have the nerve. He had thought that he had muttered the words only to himself. Later he had realised that he had screamed the words at the top of his voice. Seconds later there had been the terrible explosion, the roar of flames that had illuminated the dull day like a scene from a Catholic Hell, burning martyrs, hands beseeching, the sound of flesh crackling like roasting pork, the inhuman screams and then the sickening stink of human flesh burning.

And silence.

He came to. 'Sorry mate.' Anderton looked across at Daniel. 'I was the officer on the scene,' he said. 'There was the most almighty explosion. The fire brigade were there. They doused the flames out but he'd…' Anderton closed his eyes and his face slackened. 'His skin was like mud. Dark, sludgy mud. His eyes…I don't know what had happened to them. They were staring but he was not conscious. He'd stopped screaming. He'd left a carrier bag a little way away. It was full of letters, all to her. All saying the same thing, how much he loved her, that he would die for her.' He laughed mirthlessly into his lager can. 'You know the funny thing, Dan?'

So he was 'Dan' now?

Slowly Daniel shook his head. He couldn't think that anything connected with this grotesque episode could possibly be called funny?

'She was a real plain Jane,' Brian said, smiling down into his lager can. 'Plump, plain, odd, quiet personality. She worked as a medical secretary in the hospital. Her husband had been a medical engineer. They had two children, girls, fourteen and sixteen, and as far as they could see their mother was just plain nuts. She was quiet, shy, wore glasses, had mousey brown hair that she tied back in a pony tail. She had the most gross dress sense, woolly knee-length skirts, flattish shoes. She was simply nothing. Her voice was like suet pudding. And yet in David Sankey's eyes,' he leant back in his chair, 'she was Jordan and Liz Hurley rolled into one.'

Daniel felt his eyebrows shoot up.

'Last I heard she was receiving long-term psychiatric care. Like a zombie.' He sat up. 'I don't want that to happen to my wife.'

Daniel wanted to say something, that he was blowing this out of all proportion, that surely most episodes like this never escalated to such a horrible crisis. He wanted to say this but he felt he couldn't. Not now.

Instead he tried to lighten the policeman's tone. 'How did they meet?'

'He was a porter at the hospital,' Anderton said. 'She

couldn't even remember when it was that she'd first met him it had been so unmemorable, but *he* did in fine and graphic detail. The cleaners had been mopping the floor. She'd slipped and he'd saved her. He saw it as a Galahad act and it brought out the man in him. He said he'd felt chivalrous and strong, that she'd made him feel like that about himself and no one else in the world either had or could. That was that. The seeds were sown and by golly they bore some fruit.'

'That's all?' Daniel asked incredulously.

'That is it,' Anderton said. He drained his can, went from the room, returned with two more cans, sat down heavily and asked, 'So, speaking as a doctor, why?'

'Lonely, inadequate, disturbed people,' Daniel said hesitantly. 'People with low self-esteem who believe that only this one person can give them status. I don't have much experience of this sort of thing,' he confessed. 'We had a couple of lectures on sexual deviation, that sort of thing. As far as I remember it's usually for sexual gratification. They're normally inadequate men who have real difficulty making and maintaining relationships. They're almost always impotent and I imagine your wife's underwear…' He found he couldn't continue.

'Yes, yes,' Anderton said impatiently. 'Like many women she's fond of nice…' He stopped speaking to look suspiciously at Daniel who could feel his face flush right up to the roots of his hair. Surely he didn't realise he fancied his wife? Something told him that if the policeman did believe this it would go hard with him.

Claudine walked in. Daniel breathed in the gentle waft of sweet perfume that he was beginning to associate purely with her as though, like an animal, he could pick up on her own, personal scent. She'd applied some pale lipstick and exchanged the T-shirt she'd been wearing earlier for a crisp, white, cotton blouse. The material was thin and she'd left the first three buttons undone. He could see the outline of her bra and the top of her breasts. *Stop staring,* he lectured himself and averted his eyes. Claudine flopped in the chair, a glass of wine in her hand, her eyes bright as though she was ready to join in the conversation, but her entry had put an end to it. Daniel felt disinclined to continue the subject in front of her. She must have picked up on their silence. 'It's only got to cook for a little while,' she said brightly. 'I expect you're hungry, both of you. It'll be ready in half an hour.'

There was a brief embarrassed silence which Claudine filled. 'Maybe I should have done some nibbles,' she said doubtfully.

Her husband cut right across her. 'You know I don't like them,' he said. 'They spoil your appetite.'

'Mmm.' She eyed him over the rim of her glass, neither agreeing nor disagreeing.

Daniel set aside thoughts of olives and a bowl of crisps.

'The girls are setting the table for me.' She was still smiling but it was a little less natural, a little more strained. 'I hope they do a good job.'

Brian stretched across and gripped his wife's arm. 'I was consulting Daniel about our little problem,' he said.

'Oh.' Claudine's face became even more strained. 'I didn't want anyone to know…' Her voice trailed away.

'He's a doctor,' Brian said crossly.

Claudine looked at Daniel. 'It's quite horrible,' she said, slowly, 'imagining some strange person touching something so intimate. I feel surprisingly…' she turned her toffee eyes on him, 'violated,' she finished.

Again Daniel felt his face flush like a thirteen-year-old's.

'So why does he do it, Daniel?' Her face was open. He noticed her skin, tanned, very smooth, her mouth, pursed in a typically French way, as though she was about to utter the 'u'.

But it was her husband, not Daniel, who answered her appeal. 'Because he fancies you, apparently.' It was said with venom. 'And he has problems with normal relationships.' He spoke carelessly but his face was grim. Daniel reflected that he would not change places with the petty thief when Anderton finally collared him. He would beat the shit out of him. '*She* thinks,' he continued, mockery pitching his voice higher, 'that it's because she's *French.*' Now there was a distinct note of malice in his voice which was making Daniel feel even more uncomfortable. There is nothing worse than being party to marital disharmony. Made even more poignant by the fact that he could hear the two girls shrieking and playing over their heads in, presumably, Bethan's room.

Claudine flushed and protested. 'I only asked, Brian.'

'You only asked,' he mocked in a fake treble *voce* voice.

Daniel felt sorry for her so he tried to reassure her. 'Brian's right,' he said. 'It is usually some poor inadequate person. Someone who's not having much success with women. They're usually socially gauche. They're not generally predatory, Claudine. I doubt it's directed at you simply because you're French and for what it's worth I don't think you're in danger.' He smiled to give his words credence.

Anderton cleared his throat noisily.

'I've told Claudine that I've had experience of this sort of thing before and that in that case it did escalate.' His words were both a challenge and a threat.

His wife's face was taut. Anderton leant forward towards her, his face mean and hungry. 'I'm not going to let this happen.' He waited just a minute before continuing towards what must be the logical and predictable next step. 'This is a small town, Daniel,' he said softly. 'Your practice is the only one. You must know practically *everyone* in Eccleston – particularly the weirdos. You've had training – some – in this sort of affair.'

It was an unfortunate word to use. Even more when his voice was heavy with menace.

But Brian Anderton blundered on. 'You *know* what sort of person would do this. The type.' He drained the last drops of his second lager. 'You can profile the person, keep a watch out.' Then he hit with his question. 'Can *you* think of anyone like that in this town?'

Daniel pushed the image of Guy Malkin firmly to the back of his mind. He was appalled that the policeman was even asking him to collude with something so patently unethical. 'You can't ask me to make guesses,' he said – perhaps a little stronger than he had meant. 'My patients have an absolute right to confidentiality. I can't start pointing you towards one of them. It's not always easy to tell anyway. What if my guess was wrong?'

Anderton moved forward. 'And if it was *your* wife?'

Daniel felt his face become shuttered and hurt. Too late Anderton realised his mistake. 'Sorry, mate,' he said clumsily, rising to his feet, disappearing and returning with another couple of lagers. 'Sore subject. Didn't mean to tread on corns.' Involuntarily they both glanced down at his size elevens and Daniel reflected that with his big feet and clumsy personality Anderton had probably trodden on a lot of corns in his time.

'I don't think these people are generally violent,' he said, struggling to return to the original subject. 'I think your tragedy, Brian, was an extreme case.' He allowed his gaze to settle on the policeman's hard, strong face. 'But if you like I've got a friend who's a forensic psychiatrist. I could ask her for a profile if you like. Then you'd at least have some idea of what you're up against. At least it might help you identify the suspect.' He smiled. 'Nip it in the bud. In the meantime,' he turned to look at Claudine who was watching him, her slim fingers with their gold wedding band wound around the stem of her wine glass, 'I suggest you dry your washing indoors.'

'That's what *I* told her,' Anderton said loudly, jabbing the air towards her with his forefinger.

Daniel was again flooded with embarrassment.

The silence grew. Daniel glanced across at the policeman once or twice and wondered if he was imagining the chill that was creeping between them. He was relieved when he heard a buzzer sounding from the kitchen and Claudine jumped up. 'Oh, I forgot to uncork the wine. Will you do it please, Brian?'

It broke up the conversation effectively.

As Daniel had anticipated the meal was good, very good: chicken breasts in a white wine sauce, vegetables slightly crunchy, potatoes cooked in garlic, butter and cream. Holly kept smacking her lips and saying it was 'yummy'. She had second helpings and he teased her about being a pig. Bethan, he noticed, ate sparingly, like her mother. Not for the first time he wondered that the best cooks in the world are also the slimmest race. He and Claudine watched the two girls eating indulgently. Brian, he noticed, was quiet and something told Daniel he was feeling alienated from him.

What he had done to upset the policeman he didn't know.

The food was the tastiest he had eaten in ages and that included restaurant food.

It also felt good to be eating in company again. The girls chattered throughout the meal, making the slight awkwardness between the two men less obvious.

Claudine waited until she had served the cheese before asking, 'And how is Elaine?'

Daniel looked up. 'I didn't realise you knew her.'

'Not well,' she said, 'we were just acquaintances.'

She flushed suddenly and looked down at her food which made Daniel decide that she hadn't much liked his ex-wife.

'Doing well,' he replied tightly.

'Mummy's getting married again,' Holly piped up. 'I'm being her bridesmaid.'

'Oh.' Daniel felt Claudine's sharp look at him.

He tried to make light of it. 'Time to move on.'

Bethan piped up. 'When did you know Holly's mummy?'

'Years ago. You and Holly were in the little playgroup together just behind the library.'

Both girls stared at her.

'You won't remember it. You were just small.' Claudine laughed and rumpled her daughter's hair. 'Just a baby.'

Bethan scowled. Like most girls of that age she hated to be reminded that once she had been a baby.

As they finished the cheese course Daniel helped Claudine carry the dishes back into the kitchen, leaving Brian sitting at the table, staring stonily in front of him as though wondering how much longer he had to suffer the intruders.

Claudine stacked the dishes tidily in the sink, rinsing them before putting them in the dishwasher. 'I thought we'd have the cheese before dessert,' she said. 'I hope you don't mind doing it the French way. We can relax and have a little more of the wine.' Her eyes were bright with mischief. 'I hope you're not thinking of driving back, Daniel. My husband is off duty tonight but one of his colleagues might just pick you up and breathalyse you.' She threw her head back in a wide laugh. 'That really wouldn't do for the town doctor, would it?'

'No. No. We'll walk.'

'That's good. Then you don't have to worry about enjoying the wine.'

Her manner was flirtatious and he knew that she was fully aware of that. Then followed a small embarrassing incident but it consolidated the instinct that the policeman resented his presence. Daniel had stepped aside for Claudine to walk before him through the kitchen door, back into the dining room, but that meant she must squeeze between him and the fridge freezer. Their kitchen was not big.

At the same time Anderton must have fancied a third or fourth lager. He walked in at just the worst possible moment. Daniel and Claudine were pressed together.

Anderton said nothing but his eyes were wary and suspicious.

Daniel spoke. 'I'm sorry.' For one brief second he had felt the curve of her buttocks against him and pulled back.

'OK. OK. No problem,' she said, it seemed both to Daniel and her husband.

Wisely, after the satisfying meal, she had prepared a small cheese board with some Comte, a strong Cheddar and a wedge of Shropshire Blue. It was served on a blue and white Wedgwood plate with some oat biscuits and a bunch of grapes artistically draped over the cheeses. Dessert was the best *mousse au chocolat* he had eaten in his entire life and that included lunches at the Savoy when his mother had treated the impoverished medical student to decent food. Since first trying it then it had been his abiding favourite, so he considered himself an expert on the subject.

He shared this with Claudine and took pleasure in her broad smile. 'Thank you,' she said. 'A compliment indeed and from such an authority on chocolate mousse.' She frowned and teased him further. 'Such an extensive subject and one that requires hours of research and a lot of dedication.' She opened her eyes very wide as she spoke. He and the girls giggled with her, trying to ignore the fact that Brian had made no comment but was scowling into his lager can.

They lingered over a last glass of wine but Holly was getting sleepy and it would take them ten minutes to walk home. At ten o'clock he finally stood up, effusive in his thanks. Claudine offered him both cheeks to kiss and Bethan gave her rediscovered friend a hug. Brian merely nodded without looking up.

The police house door closed behind them and they set off for home.

There was a short cut that threaded behind the church, through some new builds, which would shorten their walk home. The night was chilly and Holly started grumbling at having to walk at all but there was no way he was going to risk being banned from driving. It could cost him his job. So they set out. The new builds were still little more than a building site, lit by orange arc lights to discourage theft.

A hooded figure walked towards him and he clutched at

Holly's hand, thinking about Anderton's little problem.

'Evening, Doctor.'

He couldn't be sure who it was. Some patient he had had a brushing encounter with. It started him thinking how very sinister hooded figures could be – from yardies to hoodies, from monks' cowls to the burkha. There is something scary about people who veil their faces against recognition.

He puzzled about the hooded figure's identity most of the way home, then gave up.

Holly was tired. Her eyelids were drooping even as she washed, cleaned her teeth and put her nightdress on. He started to read her part of the *Narnia Chronicles* but she was asleep before he'd got to the bottom of the first page.

A message was flashing on the answerphone. He pressed play and heard his ex-wife's solicitous enquiry about Holly which made him angry. Surely she could trust him to look after his own daughter? Then he realised she was doing it simply to rile him. Elaine had a real talent for selecting the very phrases that would most annoy him.

Daniel banged his finger down to press delete, poured himself another glass of wine and slumped in front of the usual Saturday night dreadful telly.

He couldn't concentrate on the film at all, a weird murder mystery that shoe-horned Martians, flesh-eaters and a cat burglar together with a woman with impossibly pointed breasts into the same one and a half hours. He sat back, his eyes on the TV but his mind wandering through the past week.

He was beginning to realise that a few things had disturbed him recently. Sometimes it took until the weekend to have time to ponder. He was concerned about Anna-Louise Struel.

Recently there had been a plethora of articles in the medical press as well as a graphic television programme which had clearly shown mothers deliberately harming their children. Did Vanda simply fabricate these stories to gain attention or was she really harming her own daughter? He must speak to Caroline Letts, the forensic psychiatrist he knew, and learn some clues that could alert him to the truth. He knew the basics – that situations like this invariably meant some pathology in the mother. Which would put Anna-Louise further at risk. Daniel sighed. The silly film had finished and he was getting maudlin. He knew he was going to have to share his concerns with his partners and they would all have to be vigilant. It was an added pressure to an already busy job. And now there was Anderton's silly story, which was altering his perception of this chocolate-box town. It wasn't simply the minor theft from the policeman's washing line that was troubling him. It was that he knew Anderton's perception of these minor events was coloured by his previous experience. On top of that he was worried that when Anderton caught the perpetrator he would explode.

So now, for him, the town was spoilt – less than perfect. For him Eccleston had always held the magic of a storybook place, almost a film set. It was why he had jumped at the chance to join the practice here. Now he could see that there was something contrived – almost unreal – about it. One of the first things he had done when he and Elaine had moved here had been to seek out the local historians through the library. So he knew that the Georgian façades and prolific hostelry existed because in the eighteenth century Eccleston had been an important coaching post en route to Chester, itself an important city. The decades had wrought their change. But there had been a deliberate attempt to conserve the High Street and now the entire area had a conservation order slapped on it. There was still a butcher and a baker. All, he thought, with a sudden chill, but the candlestick maker. For the first time since he had come to live here he wondered whether this perfection came at a price. The next moment he was telling himself the obvious truth that here, as everywhere else, whatever the superficial appearances might suggest, people were people. Good, bad, clever, stupid, kind, cruel.

Anna-Louise, Guy Malkin, Arnie Struel. These were the *real* inhabitants of Eccleston. Maud Allen's day was well over. The last of her generation, she would leave behind a legacy of a world which had been vaporised.

And so, only slightly disgruntled, he went to bed.

He was woken on Sunday morning by the peal of the church bells from the Holy Trinity. As there was no movement from Holly's room he made his coffee and returned to bed, mug of coffee and Sunday paper in hand, to listen to them. He even opened his bedroom window to hear them more clearly. Wherever you go in the world you will hear specific sounds which relate to the religion of the populace. As the muezzin calls the faithful to prayer in Muslim areas throughout the world, the Buddhist is summoned by handbells, so you hear the call for Christians in a peal of church bells. Inevitably it reminded him of poetry –

'What passing bells for those who die as cattle?'

'Stands the church clock at ten to three
And is there honey still for tea?'

He drank his coffee, scanned the paper and reflected how seduced he had been by village England, how hard he had fought to become the country GP, how very much he had wanted to be the family man, old tweeds, digging the garden. And instead here he was, snarled up in modernism, divorced, an absentee father, plucking up courage to trawl the Internet for someone who would share his dream.

Suddenly he felt like hurling the cup across the room.

Holly overslept in the morning and he fidgeted around downstairs, waiting for her to appear. Every time he put his head round the door she was still fast asleep, breathing noisily. At ten he finally heard her stir and she appeared, tangled-haired, rubbing her eyes, in her pink pyjamas. 'Is it very late, Daddy?'

He was reminded of the White Rabbit. Late. Late. Always late. From the time when he awoke on a Sunday he was aware that the day was foreshortened. Elaine would arrive between four and five and reclaim her daughter, so he resented the lie-in robbing him of precious time with Holly.

He cooked breakfast, aware of precious moments ebbing away like the tide. It was a tradition that he fed her up and she loved scrambled eggs. While he was waiting for the eggs to cook she washed her wellies until they were clean enough to wear round the house and later in her mother's car. At twelve he drove her to one of the nearby farms to see the newborn lambs and he watched her indulgently while she stroked the animals, running from pen to pen, cooing over the calves.

They spent an hour or two there and then they went to the local pub for their Sunday carvery. Everyone there seemed jolly, happy, apart from a couple of old farmers ensconced in the corner, moaning about the dry weather, the cold spring and the late government subsidies. He shot them a sympathising look and received a grudging smirk and a, 'Hello, Doctor' in return.

Holly was invariably quiet when they returned home and he knew she, like him, was clock-watching, seeing the minutes tick away. She had her Barbie case packed and was sitting down, ready. Elaine couldn't bear it if she had to wait – even for a minute. She had always been an impatient woman and some strain showed on his daughter's face as, at half past four, they heard the 4x4 roar up the High Street, Elaine's impatience reflected in the angry sound of the engine.

Holly stood up, hugged him fiercely while he breathed in the scent of her No More Tears Johnson's shampoo.

'Bye, pigeon,' he said. 'See you soon.'

Elaine didn't need to knock on the door. Since she had left she had never once set foot back inside The Yellow House. It was as though she rejected everything about him. These days they barely talked except to argue about Holly.

He waved them off, thinking how very small his daughter looked in the huge passenger seat of the Honda.

Then he closed the door.

The house was a morgue now she had gone. He wandered up to her room, noticing everything with heightened awareness: the tidy way she had made her bed, the toys neatly arrayed on the pillows. The room had an unreal look; it was like a pretend room, a children's bedroom set out in a department store. He felt sad and sat down in the sitting room, thinking. This was a parody of family life as he had imagined it. His wife, the girl's mother, was missing. Just for a moment he allowed himself the luxury of a daydream. He'd wanted a son, a brother for Holly, had even penned the imaginary notice in the newspaper. *A brother for Holly.*

He felt consumed with a sudden, hot fury. Bloody Elaine, he thought.

Chapter Five

Monday, 24th April

Monday morning draws the crowds into a doctor's surgery. Everyone who's suffered and braved it out over the weekend attends, plus a few who simply want to extend the break into the weekdays – the Sick Note Brigade with their vague tales of backache, headache, viruses or anything else the doctor can neither prove nor disprove. The waiting room was heaving as Daniel waded through, hardly registering a single face.

Except one.

The child was ill. He could see that in a minute. Floppy, hardly responding, eyes unfocused and dull. Dehydrated. He felt a prickle of alarm. What had he missed from the previous consultation?

'Take her into the examination room.'

Vanda Struel cradled Anna-Louise in her arms and struggled to move as quickly as he.

The moment they were in the examination room he started firing questions at her. 'How long has she been like this?'

'Since yesterday morning, Doctor. When I woke up and went in her room she was like this, takin' no notice of anything.'

He was already feeling the child's pulse. Thready. Her eyes were sunken, her skin wrinkled like an old woman's.

'Has she been sick, vomiting?'

'Not that I've seen.'

'Has she been drinking all right?'

'She had her bottle when she went to bed.'

'Diarrhoea?'

'Not as I've seen.' There was a quick defensiveness in Vanda's manner.

'I'm just going to prick her finger to see what her blood sugar is.'

5.6. Normal. As usual none of it made any sense.

'She'll have to go into hospital, Vanda,' he said. 'I'll get the girls to ring for an ambulance.'

'It's all right,' she said quickly. 'My mum's outside. She can drop us off on her way to work. We'll be there quicker than hanging around for an ambulance.'

'I didn't see your mum in the waiting room.'

'She waited outside – in the car park. We was blockin' a car in so she didn't dare come in. I'll go and get her if you like.' All was eagerness.

'No, no. That's all right. Get Anna-Louise dressed while I write a letter and ring the duty paediatrician.' He hesitated. 'Perhaps you'd better go and warn your mother that Anna-Louise needs to go into hospital.'

He was surprised that Bobby hadn't realised just how sick the child was, that she had allowed her granddaughter to deteriorate and done nothing for twenty-four hours. The next moment it was himself he was chiding. Bobby Millin was a health care assistant, not a trained nurse. It wasn't *her* job to gauge the severity of an illness. She was untrained in such things. Besides, she worked with geriatrics, not paediatrics. She wouldn't realise how quickly a two-year-old can dehydrate when something is wrong.

But what?

Again he asked himself the question.

What had he missed? The eternal question of a doctor. Nature has fooled me.

How?

None of his formulaic questions had given him any answer as to why Anna-Louise was so sick. The flow chart had failed him.

He picked up the phone and was quickly connected with the paediatrician.

Claudine always went shopping on a Monday afternoon; for things she had run out of over the weekend, he presumed. He watched her leave the house, carrying the big wicker basket. How very French, he thought. Not like an Englishwoman who would have driven to one of the supermarkets, either the Co-op here, or into Stafford or Newport to one of the bigger chains, Asda or Sainsbury's or Waitrose, and bundled her purchases into a plastic carrier bag. Oh no, tidily dressed in navy trousers and a white blouse, Claudine walked, the basket over her arm, a list in her hand, as though she was in a French village, visiting the local shops: the butcher's, the greengrocer's and the baker's. It wouldn't have surprised him if she had returned with one of those long French loaves sticking out of the basket. But apparently she had been converted to English bread. Brian's taste? Guy had seen a large, brown loaf at the top of her basket one day when she had passed him in the street. Occasionally when he had been working at the Co-op she had wandered in and he had served her, hoping she noticed how deft he was at clocking the purchases over the bar-coder.

She had walked straight past him, exchanged pleasantries over the counter. But he had caught the flash of friendliness in her beautiful brown eyes. This unknown, secret intimacy thrilled him.

'I'm sending a little girl in. Anna-Louise Struel. She's two years old.'

Concisely Daniel related the story of the breath-holding attacks, the frequent attendances at surgery, working his way round to the current problem – clinical dehydration with no history of any obvious cause.

The on-duty paediatric SHO sounded tired – already – and Daniel remembered back to bygone Monday mornings, paediatric emergencies and shifts that seemed to go on forever until there was no outside world – only that which existed inside the hospital – sick children, anxious relatives. Pathology – endless pathology. Outside there was no healthy, happy place. Only this inward turmoil of anxiety, unhappiness and worry. To which he added his concern, because he would always doubt that he had unearthed the full story and picked up on every physical sign, and theirs, because they were frightened that their beloved son or daughter would die.

He remembered tiredness and worry, decisions, and the pressing tendency of mothers who were convinced their little darlings had meningitis even when it was patently obvious that the children were perfectly well.

'And now she's clinically dehydrated and very floppy?'

The SHO asked all the same questions that Daniel had already asked himself and which drew all the same answers.

'She's not diabetic?'

He sounded South African.

'Nope. I've done a blood sugar. It's normal.'

Which in itself was odd.

'The mother and grandmother are bringing her up now. They should be there (with my hastily scribbled letter) in about fifteen minutes.' He hesitated. 'I'll be interested in your findings. She's a frequent attender at surgery. In fact she's waiting for an appointment to see Doctor Lewis.'

The South African gave a short, cynical laugh. 'Aren't they all?'

'I'll ring later and see what you think.'

Daniel put the phone down. One of the frustrations of being a GP sending a patient into hospital was that he knew the beginning of the story only – the first chapter of the mystery. It could take weeks to hear the ending. Sometimes not even then. Letters back from the hospital were notoriously slow. And now they were out-sourcing the medical secretaries' work to Bangladesh they would probably get lost somewhere between the Indian subcontinent and Staffordshire. Daniel sighed. In his years of working for the National Health Service he had learnt that government intervention invariably made things worse.

He swaggered up the path, towards the house.

It was the husband's fault, of course.

He had sensed some unrecognised aggression in PC Brian Anderton that must frighten his gentle wife. It was unmistakable, this fury that he couldn't disguise and one day he suspected that the policeman would no longer be able to hold it back.

This he recognised without understanding what had planted the seed in the man's mind. He flirted with it without realising the depths to which the policeman's mind could plummet. Dangerously he thought it was simple jealousy.

He walked round to the front of the house. It was a modest semi-detached, one of a line of six. The Eccleston policemen had always lived in these houses.

The flower pot with its spring bulbs almost danced into his vision in its eagerness to be noticed. It was as good as telling him something was underneath it. He looked underneath and found the key with a skip of triumph. For a policeman, he decided, Brian Anderton was surprisingly careless. Fancy leaving a key in such an obvious place.

And now he had the key in his hand how very easy it was to borrow it for an hour, drive to Newport, to the key-cutting shop. Then he could slip it back.

They would never know what he had and he would be able to enter their house any time he liked. Day or night, morning, afternoon or evening. Any time they were not there.

He had the key to their house.

As he watched the key grinder's machine cut out the grooves and peaks, he felt a sudden skip of pleasure. Tomorrow when she left the house to do her shopping or to fetch the little girl from school, *he* would be able to enter it. He clucked a censorious noise. It would serve the policeman right for being so careless if he had an intruder. No burglar alarm! In his mind he was already wandering through the house, picking up bottles of scent from her dressing table, touching the towels in the bathroom, sitting on the toilet seat, touching her sheets, the pillow she laid her head on, rifling through her wardrobe. He handed over the £3.50 and left the shop, fingering the keys in his pocket and smiling. In his life he had never ever felt quite so happy or in control. *He* controlled *them* now.

Daniel wandered into the reception area at eleven o'clock. The receptionist always made a tray of coffee usually accompanied by chocolate biscuits – gifts from grateful patients or bought out of petty cash. It was a good opportunity to chat to his partners.

Lucy Satchel was already in there, munching a huge piece of chocolate cake. 'Marie's birthday,' she explained. 'It's all right, I've added your name to the card.'

Daniel helped himself to a piece. 'I've had to send the little Struel girl in,' he said.

Lucy frowned. 'Anna-Louise?'

Lucy was the archetypal English rose, slim, blonde, late thirties, with a dewy complexion. Daniel had never seen her wear any make-up – not even at the annual Christmas piss up. Neither had he ever smelt perfume on her, which struck him as quite strange. She was married to an engineer who seemed to spend half his life working in the hot spots of the world and the other half loafing around at home. She had two children of school age and a live-in nanny, and lived in a huge, brand new house with umpteen bedrooms and bathrooms in Swynnerton, a small village a mile or two to the west of Eccleston.

'What was it this time?'

'She was dehydrated.'

'What,' Lucy scoffed. 'Mum said she hadn't taken her morning drink or passed urine for twenty-four hours?'

'No, clinically.'

'Just a bit of D and V.'

'Vanda said not.'

'She's always got some sorry story that doesn't quite hang together,' Lucy said, still unimpressed. 'There's something quite strange about Vanda. She's a real misfit. Lucky, really, that she's got her mum so near. Her brother's a psychopath.' She made a face. 'The fact is, Danny, I've been meaning to have a word with you about that little lady. She needs some family therapy.'

The door opened and swung shut. 'Who needs family therapy?'

Sammy Schultz was a complete contrast to Lucy. No one could possibly mistake him for English. Short, Jewish, hairy as a gorilla, originally from New York, married to a local girl who had seduced him with the pretty English town of Eccleston. He had taken a trip over just before they had married and fallen in love with the English village, with its church, Georgian High Street and pubs. In fact he had taken so well to English village life, immersing himself in its cultures and traditions, that he was the real driving force behind Eccleston In Bloom and was to be seen, many a morning, watering the baskets full of geraniums, petunias and busy Lizzies that brightened the High Street through the entire summer. He was also proud to be the one and only American member of The Ecclestonians' Society.

Lucy answered Schultz's question. 'Anna-Louise Struel. Would you believe it, Danny's had to send her in this morning.'

Schultz raised his thick eyebrows, mirroring his partner's look of scepticism. 'Oh, something *really* wrong this time or another false alarm?'

Daniel answered defensively. 'She was ill. Clinically dehydrated. Floppy.' He looked from one to the other. 'She really wasn't well.'

'She's kind of typical of these kids,' Sammy said, his mouth now also full of chocolate cake. 'Mum panics too much, brings the little kiddie down to see the doctor almost every week. And then – all of a sudden – the kids grow up. A miracle or what?'

Daniel started to tell them about the breath-holding attacks and both Lucy and Sammy nodded sagely. They'd seen it all before. Nothing about this case worried them. So they moved on to discuss other patients. Lucy asked about Holly and he heard about her children's impending SATS and her daughter's pony riding lessons.

Marie Westbrook wandered in, then beamed at Daniel. 'Thanks for the card,' she said.

He returned with a 'Happy Birthday.' Surely the card hadn't *only* been from him?

Marie was a tall, pale, slim woman, in her early thirties. He knew little about her but she was a good nurse, patient and understanding, popular with the patients. One thing had struck him about her, apart from her friendliness: she was never in a hurry to go home. If he thought about it, he assumed that she either lived alone or that her home life was not particularly happy. He didn't know which.

Ten minutes later the four of them were back in their surgeries seeing the last of their morning's patients.

There were only two visits. Daniel offered to do one and

met the nurse as she was leaving. 'Happy birthday again,' he said gaily. 'The cake was simply…'

'Blame my mother for that. She thinks I still need a birthday cake. At my age.' Oddly enough she flushed.

'So are you celebrating tonight?'

'I don't think so, Dan.' Her face was shuttered. Another of life's little mysteries, Daniel reflected, as he climbed into his car. He started to realise just how little he did know about the nurse. He didn't know whether she was married or had children. Certainly he had never seen any photographs of them. Her desk was neat, uncluttered and sported no family photographs. He didn't think she wore a wedding ring but he couldn't really remember. She was a closed book.

His visit was to Maud Allen whom he found looking pale and tired, sitting in an armchair which looked directly out over the paddock full of apple trees in blossom and clumps of daffodils.

'So what is it,' he asked, sitting opposite her in a shabby, comfortable armchair.

'I'm so sorry to have called you out,' she said. 'I feel guilty. I know how busy you are but I simply feel washed up.'

There was something anxious yet friendly in her manner. He took her pulse, listened to her heart, peered into her throat. He could find nothing tangible but she did look very tired and a little pale with an unpleasant chalky look to her skin.

'I think you should come down to the surgery,' he said, 'and we'll send off some blood tests.'

'I'll come tomorrow.'

They both looked out over her paddock. 'It should have a pony in it,' she mused. 'Does your daughter like horses?'

'She loves them,' he said. 'Like lots of little girls there's nothing she'd like better than a pony of her own.'

'How old is she now?'

'Seven.'

'And does she like living with her mother?'

He shook his head.

'Then why doesn't she come and live with you?'

'The courts,' he said. 'They almost always come down on the side of the mother.'

'What a shame,' Maud said.

He stood up. 'We'll get the blood tests done, make sure there's nothing underlying your feeling of malaise. Maybe you should have a holiday.'

She shook her head. 'I never leave here,' she said. 'My spirit of adventure, my lust for travel – it's all gone now, but thank you, Daniel.' It was as he was leaving Applegate Cottage that she added, 'I do hope that things improve for you and that your little girl does come back to you.' She put a hand on his arm as she spoke. It gave her words an extra poignancy.

He had backed down the drive and turned out into Kerry Lane before he added the word depression to his observations. Something was troubling the octogenarian.

For lunch he made a quick sandwich at home, sitting at the kitchen table, reading the paper. He had two hours before surgery.

At the police station Brian Anderton was putting the specimen bag down on the desk. 'Do you think you can get this analysed,' he said. 'Get some DNA off it?'

The desk sergeant raised his eyebrows. 'Burglary?'

'Some nut's nicking my wife's underwear off the line,' he said shortly.

'Right-ho then.'

The sergeant's face was impassive but for some reason Brian felt his anger bubbling up. 'You got anything to say?'

The desk sergeant's hand closed over the bag. 'Keep your hair on, Brian. We'll get it checked out.'

But the constable's ill humour hadn't subsided. He grunted a 'thanks' and stomped through into the hallway.

The South African senior house officer, whose name was Leroy, rang Daniel at four o'clock and he could hear the same puzzlement he had felt in the doctor's voice.

'Well,' he said, 'little Anna-Louise was certainly dehydrated. We've put a drip up and rehydrated her with IV fluids. But,' he said, 'and here's the puzzle, though she showed all the clinical signs of dehydration, sunken eyes, dry skin, venous insuffiency, hypotension, her urea and electrolytes were normal apart from a high sodium level.' He stopped. 'Which could, I suppose, just about explain her dehydration but not quite. Her blood sugar was OK, renal function fine. Once we'd given her a drink and pumped some fluids into her she seemed OK. I've discussed her diet with her mum but to be honest I'm not sure just how much got through to her; the grandma seems more with it. We'll keep her in overnight but unless something else transpires she can go home tomorrow morning. I'll expedite the appointment for Doctor Lewis and see what he makes of her.'

Daniel thanked Doctor Leroy for the call and put the phone down.

Puzzles, he thought. General practice was tricky enough

without all these puzzles. He was still pondering the anomalous two-year-old as he worked his way through the evening surgery.

Chapter Six

Thursday, 27th April

Daniel was due to make his weekly visit to The Elms Nursing Home on the following Thursday morning, which suited him well; it would be an ideal opportunity to speak to Bobby about her granddaughter.

The worst thing about resident geriatric homes, he decided, as he pushed the door open, was the smell. It hit him the moment he drew breath inside – a fusty stink of stale urine and old clothes. But the odd thing was that once you had been inside for more than a few minutes you became unaware of it.

Which was lucky.

No one met him at the door so he wandered towards the main sitting room and located Bobby Millin there. He watched her carefully lead an old lady to her chair in the sitting room and tuck a shawl around her legs, fussing over her like a child.

She was a big-bosomed, hefty woman with bleached blonde hair, stocky legs and a very powerful personality. She turned around and straightened up. 'Doctor,' she said brightly. 'I'd forgotten you were coming today.' Her voice matched her appearance, big and booming.

'I always come on a Thursday,' he said. Both ignored the querulous voice behind her asking where her cup of tea was. 'How's Anna-Louise?'

'Fine,' she said, again in the same bright, reassuring voice. 'She's fine. They kept her in for a couple of nights but she's home now. They had to put a drip up, you know.' She spoke with a tinge of criticism in her voice which Daniel thought was undeserved. He had been the one to send the child into hospital. If she'd thought Anna-Louise was so ill she could have taken her straight to the hospital herself – not waited for a GP appointment.

'I spoke to Doctor Leroy.' Bobby Millin had very pale blue eyes around which she had smeared some pink eye shadow, finishing off with a heavy wand of thick black mascara. Her face was completed with a generous coating of orange lipstick. The effect was colourful but clownish. She shook her head at Daniel. 'He wasn't a lot of use,' she said. 'Didn't really have a clue what was going on. And so clumsy,' she said, with a touch of malice. 'I could have taken blood out of the poor child better than he did.' She turned around as an ancient inhabitant approached her. 'Dinners will be here in a little while, Mr Steadman,' she said severely. 'Now just sit down, will you?' She watched as the old man shuffled away, his feet in the wrong slippers, making his walk look clumsy and odd. Then she turned back to Daniel. 'They just said she was short on fluids. Well, any old fool could have told them that.' The large bosom puffed out. 'You don't need a medical degree to tell you when a child is bone dry and needs fluids. Oh – and they said something about a high sodium level.'

Daniel frowned. 'Yes,' he said steadily, 'Doctor Leroy mentioned that. Does Vanda give Anna-Louise a salty diet?'

'Not especially. No more than normal.' Bobby Millin regarded him, her head on one side, the pink eyelids flashing as she blinked rapidly. 'They said it wasn't serious – she just needed to drink more. Amazing how quick she recovered though, with the drip up and they didn't half run it through fast.'

Daniel felt a faint frisson of unease.

In cases of Munchausen by proxy the victims do recover – quickly – when removed from the source of their illness. It is easy to add too much salt to a small child's diet and watch her slowly parch. In fact it is one of the most common manifestations of the syndrome. So what was he going to do about it? Interrogate Bobby as to whether she had ever seen Vanda harm Anna-Louise knowing that the mother would inevitably share the suspicion with her daughter?

It was a dangerous thing to do. He knew as well as any other doctor that once the perpetrator knows they are suspected the assaults against the victim escalate. By speaking to Bobby he could be exposing Anna-Louise to even more danger. There was another pitfall: if he was unable to substantiate his allegations he would have laid himself wide open to a charge of serious professional misconduct. He could even be suspended.

He must be cautious, walk the tightrope of protecting his professional integrity and his patient.

'And so,' he said slowly, 'Anna-Louise is home.'

The words seemed a threat.

The owner of the nursing home, Sister Graves, bustled in then and immediately took charge. 'Oh good gracious me,

Doctor,' she fussed, before speaking to Bobby. 'Why didn't you tell me he'd arrived?

'It's OK,' Daniel said. 'I wanted to have a word with Bobby anyway.'

'Hmm.' Sister Graves was one of the old school who believed firmly in a hierarchical system. Only *she* should speak to the doctor. Daniel felt he had to make it up to her so he forced himself to adopt a hearty tone. 'Now then, Sister, what delights have you got for me today?' She rallied at that and proceeded to talk quickly about the residents she wanted him to see this morning, while Bobby Millin faded away in the background. Daniel spent an hour at The Elms, poking and prodding, prescribing and sympathising, before finally driving home.

The Watchfull Eye

She'd stopped putting her washing on the line. He'd looked for it on Monday and again on Tuesday. The days had been breezy and dry. He would have thought they were perfect for drying clothes but although sweaters and jeans and plenty of the little girl's clothes and Brian's enormous black socks and horrible underwear hung and danced along the line there was none of her pretty, personal lingerie.

He desperately wanted to be inside Claudine's home, to insert his presence there, take something else of hers and leave something of him behind. He knew it must be Brian who had suggested she dry her underwear downstairs but he would get the better of him. Now he had the key he knew his opportunity would come sooner or later.

On Friday morning, the opportunity came.

Brian had already left for work, early he presumed. The police car was not outside. At ten o'clock Claudine left the house too, locking the door very carefully behind her before walking briskly down the road. He knew exactly where she was going, with the basket looped over her arm: to buy the weekend's provisions, and she would be gone for at least an hour by the time she'd queued and gossiped her way up and down the High Street. He was starting work at one, working through until ten o'clock tonight. But she never came in on either a Friday afternoon or evening – unless she'd forgotten something in her routine Friday-morning shop. He had further confirmation of the fact that the policeman must be out because of the way she turned the key twice in the door, double-locking it. She wouldn't have done that had *he* been inside.

He always called him 'the policeman' now because he didn't like saying his *name. Just calling him by his job title depersonalised him.*

He waited until Claudine had turned the corner and was out of sight before he unlocked the door and slipped inside.

Then he started to be clever. He slipped on a pair of latex gloves, which he had filched from a packet of hair dye that had been damaged in the shop.

He stood briefly in the hall, looking around him at the pale walls, the cream carpet, the pictures on the wall. Ahead of him was the kitchen, neat and clean with a stainless steel sink. On his left were two doors, both ajar. He peeped around the first door into a square sitting room decorated in the same pale, neutral colours. The other room was a dining room with dark walls and a mahogany table and chairs. The whole house smelt of her. Clean, fragrant oranges and perfume. She must have given herself a quick spray just before she had left. He breathed her very air in, deep into his lungs, tasted it in his mouth and smiled. He knew Claudine would be gone for an hour but he didn't want her to come back and find him here so, just to make absolutely sure, he had allowed himself only twenty minutes. Twenty whole minutes. No more.

He didn't want to be discovered.

He padded upstairs, noting the cream walls, the tasteful pictures of rainy French street scenes, leant in close to scrutinise one particular framed photograph in gaudy Seventies colours. A little girl, presumably Claudine, about six years old, in a white dress, standing against the whitewashed wall of a French farmhouse, a severe looking, black-frocked woman behind her, her arm resting on the little girl's shoulder. He stood back and wasted a precious moment looking at it. 'Charming,' he muttered. 'Quite charming.'

But of course he couldn't linger. Time was of the essence. He moved on to the landing and found her (he couldn't call it their) bedroom easily. His nose led him straight to it, that waft of perfume leading him on. He stood in the doorway and admired the white, cotton duvet cover, starched pillowcases, the open window blowing the fragrance right through the room towards him. On the far side of the room was a huge piece of furniture even he recognised as antique and French. A sort of wardrobe thing. But he didn't want that. Her personal belongings wouldn't be in there.

They would be in – ah, the chest of drawers.

He tugged the top drawer open and almost recoiled in disgust.

Men's underpants and black socks. Big black, policeman's socks. The smell of shoe polish and feet. He closed it quickly then pulled open the next drawer and immediately smelt the perfume again. Stronger than before. She must spray her underwear. 'The little tart', he muttered under his breath. He removed his glove and put his hand in to touch the beautiful, beautiful things. Pink, black, white and cream. Such a lovely cream brassiere. Satin and lace. He ran his hands over them. The satin felt smooth – almost oily against his skin.

'Sweet satin and lace,' he whispered before lifting out a cream top and French knickers, putting it to his cheek before stuffing them into his pocket.

On the top of the chest of drawers was a small, wooden jewellery box. He lifted the lid and found a pair of pearl earrings pressed into a velvet groove. He put them in his pocket too.

Now he had his trophies he wanted to leave something of himself. But he must remember. Anderton was a policeman, careful, cunning, suspicious. So he had deliberated about what he could leave and be sure that it would remain here, in this house, in this room, near enough to Claudine. It must be something small so that it wasn't discovered, but intimate too. He pulled a hair out of his head and placed it underneath the scented drawer liners, next to the wood. Then he closed the drawer almost reverently.

He was inside.

It was time to go. The sense of urgency was stifling. He went down the stairs, two at a time, his prizes in his pocket, the wires of the bra making him stiffen with anticipation. He let himself out of the front door, rounded the house and crossed the back garden quickly, anxious now to be gone.

Two minutes later he was stepping jauntily across the field, hands in pockets, whistling a tune. With his little secrets nestling in his pockets he felt confident, and so when he met one or two people he knew, he greeted them normally, smiled in their faces and finally reached home. He still had almost three hours before he needed to go to work.

Guy Malkin's home was a bed-sit above the kebab bar on the High Street. His bed formed a sofa in the day with the help of four scatter cushions his mother had given him when he had finally moved out and left her to be alone with her new boyfriend. Guy shared both kitchen and bathroom with another single man named Gerald. Gerald was in his fifties. Guy suspected he was a 'reformed' alcoholic. He was divorced, he'd told Guy, and apart from his drinking buddies in The Bell, he appeared to have no friends.

Gerald was also a bit of a pig in the kitchen and in the bathroom. While Guy wasn't a fussy person he did like to keep his personal space clean and tidy and he'd had a number of rows with Gerald over his untidiness. As he walked past the kitchen he noticed a pile of dirty dishes on the draining board and cursed. Gerald was almost spoiling his moment. He let himself into his room and locked the door behind him.

Now at last he could study his prizes in private. Prizes for being cunning and clever, innovative and brave. He was pleased with himself. His confidence, he knew, was growing.

He laid his trophies out on the bed, the knickers below the top, and the earrings to the side. Filling in the space he could imagine her slim, firm body.

The Silent Tongue

On Friday at around twelve o'clock Daniel was standing outside the ugliest building in a beautiful town. The block of flats where Vanda Struel lived was Sixties concrete, an eyesore, a blot on the landscape.

She lived on the third floor, her mother on the floor above.

Daniel climbed the concrete staircase and knocked on number 37, half expecting Vanda to be out. But the door was opened.

Trouble was, it wasn't Vanda. It was her brother, Arnie, who peered out, bleary-eyed, shaved head, tattoos, a can of lager in his hand. His name wasn't actually Arnie at all. Arnie was a nickname. His real name was Mark. Mark Struel, but everybody called him Arnie after the great Schwarzenegger. It was an appropriate nickname. So appropriate that most people didn't even realise he *had* another name.

He looked as startled to see Daniel as Daniel was to see him. 'Didn't know 'er had called for a doctor,' he grunted.

'It's just a courtesy call,' Daniel said at once. 'I just wondered how Anna-Louise was.'

Struel jerked his finger behind him. ''Er looks OK to me.'

'Is Vanda in?'

'No. 'Er's popped out for some fags.' Arnie gave him a crooked grin. 'I'm babyminding. 'Er's safe with her uncle.'

Daniel felt a physical twinge of alarm.

Safe? The child was just out of hospital, for goodness' sake.

He wouldn't have classed Anna-Louise as safe left alone

with the town's psycho. He felt a quick flash of anger at Vanda who had just 'popped out for some fags', leaving the child with Arnie.

'Your mum not around?'

'She 'ad to go to work today. Somebody's off sick so 'er 'ad to go in.'

'Do you mind if I take a quick look at your niece?'

Struel stepped back. ''Elp yourself,' he said politely.

The fug of cigarettes in the room almost knocked him back. That and what he suspected was the stink of Arnie's feet. His shoes, grubby trainers, were neatly placed side-by-side at the far end of the sofa where Anna-Louise was propped up, her little tongue working, her eyes following him as Daniel crossed the room towards her. Only when he reached her and stood over her did she move her head very slightly. For a split second Daniel had the impulse that this tiny child was trying to convey something to him. The next he dismissed it as pure imagination.

He looked closer at her. There was something, a pleading desperation, a cowed terror. He suddenly felt both worried and powerless. What was going on with this child?

He knelt on the floor and looked up at her. She regarded him steadily, the only sign of movement the small, pink tongue, busily working round her upper lip and chin.

Today Anna-Louise was tidily dressed in a small, full, pink frock with a cream-coloured woollen cardigan, wrongly buttoned, stick legs stretching out in front of her.

Arnie was standing behind him, legs apart, arms folded, looking pleased with himself. 'I thought as she might be cold,' he said proudly. 'So I put 'er the cardie on.'

Daniel took time from the child to swivel round.

He couldn't help smiling to himself. There was something touching about the Beast of Eccleston struggling to dress his little niece in a cardigan.

But, looking back at Anna-Louise, Daniel didn't feel like smiling any more. A toddler of this age should be running around, causing mayhem, getting 'into' things. Living up to the reputation of the 'terrible twos'. Not simply sitting, gazing around passively as though wondering what in Heaven's name the world had in store for her. And what *did* the world have in store for her? Daniel wondered, feeling an iced finger of dread stroke the back of his neck. Anna-Louise's eyes flickered from him to her uncle still without displaying any emotion. The illusion of a plea from the little girl had vanished.

He gave her a full and thorough examination and again found nothing really wrong. She certainly wasn't dehydrated now. He found nothing specific apart from her abnormally passive behaviour. He stood up. The only thing he could do would be to expedite the paediatric referral.

He arrived back at The Yellow House a little after one and made himself a sandwich then sat outside. The garden was slowly coming back to life after a long winter and a cold spring, helped by Atkins, an elderly patient of his whose great love was gardening but who was now confined in a gardenless flat off the High Street. Daniel paid him for his attentions but was conscious of the fact that he was doing the ancient widower a favour. Atkins would often call unannounced, on any fine day, to 'potter', as he called it. It was therapy for him. Daniel was grateful to the old man but having Mrs Hubbard to do his cleaning and Atkins keeping the garden neat he had nothing with which to occupy himself.

He knew what he wanted to be doing with his time – his

family around him. He wanted to be playing football with a son, taking the family on trips, holidays, outings to Alton Towers, Center Parcs. He wanted to swim, cycle, roller skate – anything and everything.

But not alone.

At half past two the telephone rang. To his pleasure it was Claudine Anderton. 'Hello Daniel.' Her voice was bright and friendly. 'Bethan has asked me whether Holly is coming to you tomorrow.'

'Yes,' he said, 'as far as I know.' He was aware of how much he wanted the policeman's wife to invite him to something. Anything – even a simple coffee.

'Then would you like to come to lunch? Brian is working on night duty but Bethan was most insistent. She likes Holly very much.' She gave her light, tinkly laugh.

Daniel laughed too. 'Well,' he said. 'It wouldn't do to disappoint the little lady, would it?'

She giggled. 'Most certainly not, Daniel. What time does she usually arrive?'

'Late,' he said grumpily. 'I'm on call until twelve.'

'Then I shall expect you at twelve-thirty.'

'See you then.'

It was only after he had put the phone down that worms of doubt started to wriggle through his brain. Anderton struck him as a jealous man. Would he mind if Claudine and he were to spend the day together without him?

The next minute he shrugged. She wouldn't have asked him if her husband was likely to object.

Surely?

* * *

Every now and then general practice can be very tough.

Maud Allen stumped in at five-thirty.

He greeted her and she sat down heavily. 'I won't beat about the bush, Doctor,' she said. 'I've found a lump in my breast.'

He took a history, how long she'd had it, was it painful and then followed her into the examination room. Five minutes later his heart sank. He could feel it, hard and unyielding, in her right breast, what he was afraid might be a tumour. Worse he could also feel another hard lump in her neck, over the clavicle. She watched him fearfully.

He asked her to put her clothes back on and she returned to the consultation room.

'We-ell,' he said slowly, 'you know as well as I do that I have to refer you.'

She nodded.

'We have a rapid-access breast lump clinic. They'll take a biopsy.'

'Is it cancer?'

'Maud,' he said, 'we don't know. Not until we have the results of the biopsy.'

Her rheumy eyes looked back at him. 'What do *you* think, Daniel?'

She was asking for his honesty.

He nodded. 'It might be. I'll sort out the referral.'

She nodded. 'Thank you,' she said, 'for not even trying to soft soap me. I've had a long and good life.' She touched his hand very briefly. 'I'm not afraid.'

By way of contrast Chelsea Emmanuel was his next patient.

'Yeah, well. I forgot to take it, didn't I?'

As though it was his fault. Daniel shifted in his seat. This kid was annoying him. He'd given her the pill and now she had forgotten to take it and was requesting the morning after pill.

He didn't need to enquire whether she'd had intercourse recently. The little tart was dying for him to ask her that. She sat in her tiny denim skirt, inches of plump waist displayed, challenging him.

Wearily he tapped on the computer, gave her instructions.

One of these days Chelsea Emmanuel would be wheeling a pushchair down the High Street. He could see her future mapped out in front of him as clearly as though he could scroll down the computer consultations and see right through her entire life. Multiple children from multiple partners. Benefits, plenty of minor health problems from cigarettes, probable obesity, liver and lung disease. He could almost hear her wheezing and coughing her way into the future. And overlying this depressing life would be the thick sludge of depression for which she would, at some point, request – no demand – a tablet.

He tore his concentration away from the future and looked at the girl in front of him. She looked so young. Mrs Gillick may have fought her fight for just such a manipulated innocent as Chelsea Emmanuel.

The girl shifted, parted her legs so he could see to the top of her thighs if he'd wanted to.

'Divorced, ain't ya?' She chewed her gum noisily.

His nod was the briefest of assents.

She leant forward, deliberately displaying her cleavage. 'Was you cheatin' on her then?'

It was none of her business but he still shook his head, signed the prescription and handed it to her.

'She cheatin' on you, was she?' She had a sharp, grating voice and could chew and talk with the skill of a footballer running and dribbling the ball at the same time. She continued, 'Shame that with you bein' such a good lookin' bloke and all.'

It was rare for Daniel to wish for a consultation to end so much that he actually left his chair and held the door open for the patient to leave but he did so now. She couldn't go quickly enough for him.

She brushed against him in the doorway and gave him another clumsy, unmistakably inviting smile.

It was all Daniel could do to stop himself from vomiting into the sink.

Roll on Saturday.

The Secret Heart

He'd finished his evening surgery by six but was reluctant to return home. The evening seemed too long, the house too empty and the consultation with Maud Allen had depressed him. His mother would probably phone and, after criticising his ex-wife, she would launch into a long spiel about Holly before offering to come and keep house for him. He knew it would be the end of things.

Perhaps he could drive out to one of the local pubs. Not in Eccleston but a mile or two out, in Woodseaves. The Plough had a couple of friendly bar women and the food was good. Yes – that's what he would do. But he didn't want to sit in the pub alone.

On impulse he knocked on the nurse's door. Marie

Westbrook was just ushering out her last patient of the day. She turned a tired face to him and it struck him that she was looking drawn and thinner. 'You all right?'

She managed a smile. 'Yes, Dan. I'm fine.'

'Fancy a drink?'

'In this?' She indicated her navy nurse's uniform.

'Stick a coat over it. If I don't mind I don't see why anyone else should.'

The smile she returned was much warmer, genuine. He hadn't seen her look like this for at least a year. 'Yes,' she said. 'I would. I could do with a drop of alcohol after the day I've had.' She unhooked her coat from the back of the door.

'Sorry,' he said. 'Are you overworked?'

She sighed. 'Isn't everyone?'

The Plough at Woodseaves was a traditional pub. Open fires, friendly bar staff, good, home-cooked food. Daniel bought a pint and a white wine spritzer for Marie and they sat down, near to the fire.

'So,' he said 'what's going on in your life?'

She grimaced. 'Not a lot.'

He glanced at her left hand. He could have sworn she used to wear a wedding ring. Now it was bare. She noticed his look. 'It happens,' she said, 'all the time.' She gave a brief, cynical laugh. 'Like you,' she said. 'Divorce.'

His instinct was to ask her whether she wanted to talk about it but somehow he wasn't in the mood for any more tales of woe.

So they stayed and ate, gossiped about patients and tucked in to the food, unable to resist the tempting smells wafting from the kitchen.

He stood up and offered to pay, but, like Maud Allen, she too put a hand on his arm.

'No,' she said. 'Thanks, but I'll pay for myself.'

'OK.' Something prompted him to add, 'We must do this again sometime.'

He was unprepared for the warmth and pleasure that transformed her from a plain woman almost into a beauty.

But as he drove home he was already aware that his open invitation had been a mistake.

Chapter Seven

Daniel was still agitated when he arrived home and his humour was not improved by picking up the two winking messages on his answerphone; both from his mother.

He felt his face tightening. Two. He'd *have* to ring back or she'd do something stupid like sending the police round to check if he was all right or even worse drive all the way down from Sheffield and present herself at his front door.

He dialled her number reluctantly. She picked up on the second ring so he knew she'd been waiting for him to call back, sitting, as she did, hunched on the bottom step of the stairs, eyeing the telephone like a mortal enemy – daring it to ring or not to ring.

She was initially aggressive. 'Well, Danny,' she said. 'It's taken you long enough to return my call.'

The hours of her day must drag.

'Mum,' he said wearily, 'I was at evening surgery. You know I don't finish until gone six.'

'I don't know why you can't sometimes ring in the afternoons. You're not *always* working,' she accused. 'Anyway, Danny,' she said, softening, 'how are you, poor, lonely thing?'

Her pity for him set his teeth on edge.

Without waiting for his reply she ploughed on. 'I did wonder whether to come down and stay with you for the weekend. I haven't got anything special on. Besides – I haven't seen little Holly for months. And she is my only grandchild.' The whine of self-pity irritated him further and not for the first time he wished that his sister would dump her career and have sextuplets.

'Sorry, Mum. Holly and I have other plans.'

'What?' She sounded affronted.

'We're having some friends round to dinner.' Claudine had asked him, but if Brian was on night duty they could come to him for the day. It would leave the house quiet so he could sleep. It was the first he'd thought of it but he quickly realised he liked the idea. Much more than having his mother down.

'Oh.' The exclamation was saturated with rejection quickly followed by curiosity so he responded.

'It's just the local policeman and his wife. They have a daughter the same age as Holly. The two girls seem to have hit it off. They had us for a meal last Saturday. I just thought I'd invite them back.'

'The local *policeman*?' That was another thing to add to the long list of *Things I hate about my mother*: her good old-fashioned snobbery.

But now he had said it he was resolved. That was what he would do. First job of the evening.

Ring Claudine.

'They only live round the corner,' he said.

'How nice for you to have local friends.' His mother's voice was the equivalent of a bad smell under the nose. Which reminded him of something Elaine used to say.

'No bloody wonder our marriage didn't work out. It never had

a chance. Your mother *got in the way. She simply doesn't want you to have anyone else in your life except her. She is – frankly – possessive.'*

Spoken with venom.

It had been hurtful then and he had denied it. But now almost every time he spoke to his mother or heard her voice on the answerphone, always urging for yet another phone call, yet another visit, displaying a total lack of interest in any aspect of his life, he inevitably recalled his ex-wife's words and recognised the truth behind them. His mother could so easily swamp his life with her attitudes, her possession, her vicious snobbery and her total self-absorption.

Yet he was her son.

So he made further small talk, asked, without interest, how her bridge class was going and finally rang off with the usual sense of guilty relief.

A phone call usually bought him two to three days' peace.

Then, straight away, he dialled Claudine's number.

Unfortunately it was Brian who picked the phone up, sounding huffy and defensive. Even more so, Daniel thought, when he extended the invitation.

'I'm on nights all weekend,' he said grumpily. 'I expect Bethan would like to come to you. She hasn't stopped talking about her new friend all week.'

He even sounded resentful about this. 'Hang on a minute,' he said abruptly. 'I'll go and ask her.' He shouted away from the phone. 'Beth-an. Would you like to go to Holly's house?'

'Yeah. Cool.' The words floated down the stairs and into the telephone. They were said with a breathless enthusiasm that lifted Daniel's heart far above the conversation he had just endured with Brian and before that with his mother.

He felt encouraged now and reckless. 'Why doesn't Bethan come over for the whole afternoon? The house'll be more peaceful, Brian.'

'Hmm.' The policeman thought about it. 'I think they said something about going into Stafford to see a film. Maybe you could go together. I'll get Claudine to give you a ring. Actually', Brian confided, 'it *will* do me a favour. I always find it hard to sleep when I'm on nights – even when the house *is* quiet.'

So, Daniel could kill three birds with one stone. Fit in with Brian's plans, please his daughter and best of all please himself.

He felt self-satisfied as he rang off. Now he had Saturday to look forward to.

It was still only eight o'clock and Daniel knew exactly what he was going to do for the rest of the evening.

Something about his life.

He was forty years old. Reluctantly single, although as he tapped in his access code on the computer, he really couldn't imagine being married to Elaine any more. They had been students together but something in her had changed. Toughened, hardened. Somewhere along the line all the fun had gone out of her and been replaced by something else. Perhaps he had changed as well. People did. It had almost been a relief when they had finally split up. The Germans have a name for it. *Lebensabschnittsgefaehrte*. A German friend of his had told him the literal translation was partner-for-a-specific-period-in-time and it described the relationship between him and Elaine. They had grown apart from one another. Like ships in a fog they had collided, spent some time together and moved on. He had no longer been what she wanted and he had been so focused on his new relationship with his daughter that he had not understood that it had replaced the love he had once felt for his wife.

He had no regrets.

Apart from losing Holly.

For a while he didn't tap into any website but sat and stared into the screen without seeing anything but his daughter's face. He missed her more than he could ever have dreamt. He would give *anything* to have her back, living with him all the time, not simply visiting at weekends, struggling that silly pink suitcase up and down his steps.

He sat and dreamt of the fun they could have had together.

He punched his fist into his palm in sudden anger.

Let Elaine marry again. Fine. Let her have another *family*. Again fine.

But *he* wanted *his* daughter back.

He sighed and realised this was getting him nowhere.

He'd never really tried Internet dating before but he knew one or two people who had met partners through it and he wanted another woman in his life. Quite apart from everything else he missed sex. He missed the feel of a woman's body against him, the smell of her, the entire female thing. It was dangerous to search close to home. Practically everyone from a twelve mile radius would turn out to be one of his patients – or, at his age, had been married to one of his patients. The local doctor is too well known.

So.

He started typing in his details.

'Forty-year-old male.' He cupped his chin in his hands.

That didn't sound very enticing. 'Forty-year-old *professional* male. Divorced.' Again he frowned. He needed something different. 'Staffordshire,' he typed. 'Romantic and tenacious but not a bulldog. Interests: country walks, theatre, music (eclectic from reggae to Schubert), cycling, books, cinema etc WLTM single woman 30s for...' He wanted to type *sex* but resisted and instead found the word 'relationship'.

There.

Now to look at what was available.

He found plenty of hits in Staffordshire. Rejected all the 'cuddly' ones, all the ones that were overtly sexual – 'for rubber games', 'spanking allowed' etc. Oddly enough, although he had wanted to suggest intimacy, seeing it blatantly advertised on the screen embarrassed him. The thought of not meeting up to their sexual needs made him squirm.

He scrolled down the list.

As often happens one particular entry caught his eye. He read it through twice. This sounded like his cup of tea.

'Professional woman, mid-thirties, unattached, slim, sporty, with interesting outlook, WLTM man for walks, evenings out (anything from a night at the opera to a greasy spoon café), possible long-term relationship.'

She sounded the woman for him.

He clicked on the picture and screwed his face up.

It was hard to say what she looked like. Much of her face was hidden by a thick curtain of dark hair. Her lips were very pink and pouting. He made a face. Now he wasn't so sure.

Well – there was only one way to find out.

He typed in his details, paid his enrolment fee, obtained a Box Number, sat back and smiled. It was as simple as that.

He felt he had made some progress, gained control.

What he was forgetting was that we do not have control of our lives at all. The entire roller-coaster, from cradle to grave, is a series of events, each one leading to a destiny of its own. We can turn and twist, but our fate will find us somehow.

He allowed himself a beer or two, watched some football on the TV, still with the smug, self-satisfied feeling, and dreamt.

His mother had always called him a romantic, using the word as an insult. And he knew he was. To use one of today's favourite clichés, *he was a man in touch with his feminine side.* In his mind's eye he was already picturing the woman of his dreams. The woman of the photograph, subtly altered. Smiling, not pouting, with clear skin and a positive, chirpy personality. Someone like...Claudine.

'You don't mind, do you, Brian?'

He was suddenly, unaccountably truculent. 'And if I do?'

'Come on, *cherie*,' she appealed. 'Be reasonable.'

The policeman nodded and dropped his head, almost in an apology.

His wife took it as such and they watched Bethan play with her dolls, dressing and undressing them in one outfit then another, always, Brian noted, taking great care to fold the clothes and coordinate the bags, the shoes, the trousers, the tops. As she played with the doll she muttered to herself.

'I don't think I'll wear this...It's far too cold for shorts...I never did like that handbag. I shall throw it away.'

Mother and father smiled at each other.

Which made Brian feel awful.

Why couldn't he have kept his temper?

His mind flicked back eight years to the girl who had come into the station, begging for his help to free her from the man who was so convinced she loved him he could not leave her alone. *His* help she had sought and he had failed her. She had been so vulnerable. While he had riled against the law which allowed situations to progress too far before it intervened, he had promised he would help, that he would defend her and that she could trust him to protect her.

To the death.

He had searched her face and seen terror. Not simply fright but an abject and paralysing fear.

He had wanted to protect her as had all the other officers in the station but it had been to *him* that she had turned and he had puffed his chest out.

He would have to beat the little shit up. Burn the bastard, he had thought.

Chapter Eight

Saturday, 29th April

It was his turn to attend the Saturday morning surgery. Vanda Struel was distraught, hopping from one foot to the other as she displayed her daughter, almost shaking the child in Daniel's face. 'Just look at her leg. It's a mess. Anyone can see it's an infection. She needs antibiotics.' There was anger in her voice, as well as the frightened question, what is wrong with my daughter?

'My mum says there's summat really wrong with her that you lot aren't pickin' up on.' Vanda's blue eyes appealed straight into his. 'But what can I do except keep bringin' 'er down? I aren't a doctor, am I?'

Daniel could not answer her question but turned his attention to the child.

For once Anna-Louise was showing some emotion. She was in pain and she was frightened. She was always a still child but this morning she was rigid, hardly breathing, her eyes fixed on his in a terrified, frozen stare. Even the little tongue hardly moved. Yet yesterday she had been all right.

When Daniel reached out to her she gave the softest little

whimper. He had worked for six months in the paediatric department of his teaching hospital and to see a child frightened and in pain still upset him. Not for a moment had he ever entertained the idea of staying in paediatrics. He simply wasn't tough enough. And fathering Holly had finally convinced him that he had made the right choice – to veer away from hospital work into general practice – so he could spend more time with his family. He felt his lip curve into an ironic sneer.

'Let me take a look.'

Hardened medic as he was, he found it hard not to exclaim when he looked closer at her leg. There was a reddened area as big as a marble which had the classic signs of infection. He remembered the words from medical school. *Rubor, dolor, calor.* Redness, heat and pain and from his own observations and the way the child flinched when he touched the area he had no doubt that this was all three. Antibiotics was the simple answer. Amoxycillin or one of the other common, broad-spectrum drugs. But now he was beginning to suspect something deeper. Why was the child both retarded in development and prone to this plethora of complaints? Was it as he had suspected – that her mother had a hand in it? He took a syringe from the drawer. 'Vanda,' he said. 'I'm a bit worried about Anna-Louise.'

Her eyes fixed limpidly on his. Her anger was spent. 'What do you mean?'

'I think your mother might be right. It's possible that she may have something else wrong. Something underlying. I'm going to do some blood tests to try and find out what it is.'

Most mothers panic at this. If a doctor even hints that a child may have something sinister the matter with them the mother flips. Straight into hysterics.

Not Vanda Struel. She merely stared back at him, unflinching, unblinking. Unexpectedly he picked up on a family resemblance – for the first time he could see a hint of Bobby in Vanda's eyes and some of Anna-Louise in her calm acceptance of fate – some passivity in her face too.

'Whatever,' she said, casually shrugging.

All doctors verbally walk you along the procedure, as though a patient has no eyes. 'I'll have to put a tourniquet around her arm.' He was watching Vanda very carefully, searching for the return of emotion. He found none. 'Can you hold her still for me, please?'

Anna-Louise didn't flinch when he inserted the needle into the vein. Neither did she scream or struggle. She was completely passive, her dark eyes dry. Not a tear or a whimper escaped from the child. She blinked once when she felt the prick of the needle then she looked away, disinterested.

Daniel put the bottles in the fridge. They'd missed today's collection and would have to wait until Monday. He prescribed some antibiotics and told Vanda to bring her back on Monday morning if she was no better.

Brian Anderton was in a bad mood even before he arrived home. The night had ended badly. The High Street had come to a standstill when two huge pantechnicons had met face to face and, like battle lines drawn up in days of old, both had flatly refused to reverse, prepared, if necessary, to fight to the death. Both drivers sat obstinately in their cabs, arms folded, trying to glare the other one out while behind them the traffic built up making the situation even more impossible. Soon the entire town had been gridlocked with car drivers driven by frustration to keep their hands on their horns, which had made his job worse. He had spent more than an hour reasoning with first one driver and then the other, had directed the traffic himself and finally sorted out the chaos. He'd had a good mind to book the pair of them for obstruction, as well as all the car drivers for causing a disturbance. But it was no use explaining to a Polish lorry driver chinning up to a Liverpudlian that an eighteenth-century High Street had catered for horse-drawn post chaises not cars, let alone lorries. The morning had been warm and afterwards he had sweated in the police van, fuming for twenty minutes after the gridlock had cleared.

And now he had another two shifts ahead of night duty, which he hated, particularly over the weekend. Bethan might be an only child but she could be very noisy, however much Claudine tried to quieten her. He felt his mouth tighten. But then, he thought, Bethan would be with her little friend this weekend, the daughter of single, attractive, predatory, *Doctor* Gregory. he felt his temper getting even worse. He didn't trust the little squirt as far as he could throw him. And then on top of that some perv was stealing his wife's lingerie as a bloody sexual trophy. And that, in turn, had resurrected memories he'd been trying to bury for eight whole years. The memories were wounding him even now, humiliating him. She had asked for his help. He'd promised he would but his hands had been tied by the law which had mocked him and failed her. It didn't matter how often he tried to shift the blame, it always seemed to come back to him.

He buried his face in his hands but it was no good. He could still see the flames burning orange into his eyes, still feel the awful heat, hear the terrible screams, and worst of all, smell the stench of roasting human flesh. Even now the smell of roast pork could make him retch. He'd asked Claudine never to cook it, saying it didn't agree with him. It didn't, but he'd never told her why.

So PC Anderton had plenty to put him in a bad mood.

He banged the garden gate open and slotted his key into the door, then went straight into the kitchen, hoping his breakfast would be on the table but it wasn't, and when he glanced through the kitchen window and caught sight of Claudine's underwear pegged on the line again he lost his temper.

'Claudine,' he shouted up the stairs.

She appeared at the top of the landing. 'Brian,' she said. 'You're early. Your breakfast isn't nearly ready. I'm just washing Bethan's hair. Someone had nits in the classroom.' She giggled and that further inflamed him.

'Get down here. Now,' he said, through clenched teeth.

She hadn't picked up on the anger in his voice. 'A minute, please.'

'Down,' he bellowed. 'Claudine. NOW.'

She got the message then, came tripping downstairs in tight jeans and a white, cotton shirt. He noticed she was not wearing a bra.

'What is it, darling?'

He took her by the arm and shoved her through into the kitchen. 'What's that?'

She followed his gaze. 'It's my washing,' she faltered. 'You know I hate to dry it in the tumble dryer. It doesn't smell as nice. The heat of the dryer weakens the elastic and it was such a nice day.'

Images of the burning man raced across Brian's mind so he

was hardly aware of bringing his hand up. It was as much of a shock to him as to her when he heard the slap.

She gasped with the pain, tears starting to her eyes. 'Brian?'

'There's no need to encourage him,' he said, dragging her in front of the window. 'Look at it.' He forced her face upwards. 'Look at it,' he said again. 'Dancing. Enticing. Exposing. What sort of a woman are you, Claudine?'

She couldn't stop the tears now. 'What sort of a man are you, Brian?' she sobbed. 'You never did this before. What is the matter with you?' Puzzlement made her voice low and troubled.

'You're a flirt,' he said. 'Someone who leads men on, *pretends* they can have sex with her. Oh yes. You love to walk down the High Street, your basket over your arm, smiling at men.'

'No,' she protested. 'No.' Then. 'Who are you, Brian? I don't recognise you.'

He was still glaring at her when Bethan ran in, her hair still dripping. She looked from one to the other, her mouth a round 'O'. 'Mummy, Daddy.' As she studied her parents she met something she did not understand. 'Is everything all right?'

Both parents struggled to reassure her but the expression on Claudine's face gave the game away. Bethan's shoulders drooped.

'Go and dry your hair,' Claudine said quietly. 'Breakfast won't be long.'

Bethan ran from the room.

Bobby Millin was struggling to get Vanda to realise. 'Look at her. She ain't right, is she? Did you tell the doctor what I said? I may not be medically qualified, my girl, but even I can see there's something wrong with that kid. I don't know why they're being so blind. Doctors,' she finished scathingly.

But it was no use. Vanda's attention was all on the television. 'Doctor's seen her,' she muttered, without shifting her gaze from the TV screen. 'He isn't worried about her.'

Bobby moved in front of her to block her daughter's view of the television set. 'They don't know everything, Van. That's what I'm tellin' you. Don't you ever listen to me?'

Reluctantly Vanda's eyes fixed on her mother for the briefest of moments. 'Doctor Gregory's gettin' her to see a specialist. He's put her on antibiotics.' She gave her mother a fierce look. 'He took some blood from her. He's going to send it to the lab. They'll soon see if anything's *really* wrong.'

'It could be too late by then. Look at the state of her.'

Anna-Louise was sitting on the floor, surrounded by plastic toys but she was not playing. She was sitting very still, her eyes flicking from her grandmother to her mother and back again.

'Take her back to the surgery,' Bobby urged. 'Tell Doctor Gregory she needs to see the specialist *now.* Not in a week or a month. Now.'

'You take her.' Vanda flicked her cigarette ash carelessly into an ashtray. Worthington's – nicked from the pub. 'She's your granddaughter.'

Bobby Millin was incensed. 'She's your *daughter* for Heaven's sake. Don't you care about her?'

Vanda's answer was another dismissive shrug.

Daniel was struggling with his surgery. Spring had had its effect on him. He desperately wanted some sort of excitement in his life. The surgery seemed dreary, the patients uninteresting. He saw one after the other then pressed the buzzer for the next one, almost groaning when he saw who it was. *This* he didn't need.

'I've got a pain in my tummy.'

Today Chelsea was dressed in some loose-fitting trousers which slung low on her hips, revealing a plump stomach, and a brief, low-cut T-shirt that barely covered her breasts.

Daniel asked the usual questions: where exactly was it? How long had she had it for? Did she have any other symptoms? The questions drew all negative answers.

'Did you take the pill I gave you?'

He already knew the answer from the evasive look which came into her eyes. 'I might have forgotten it.'

'When was your last period?'

Another vague look.

'I'd better examine you,' he said reluctantly. 'I'll call in the nurse as a chaperone.'

'Don't need one.' The T-shirt was already pulled over her head exposing plump, bouncing breasts.

Daniel halted the progress of her undressing. 'You'd better go into the examination room.' He handed her a sample jug. 'Could you manage a sample of urine?'

Chelsea looked bemused.

'Wee,' he said. 'Piss. Urine. Could you manage a sample of it into the jug?'

The girl giggled. 'I could try,' she said jauntily.

When he joined her in the examination room the girl was naked. Without a word he handed her a towel to cover herself. Her legs were wide open, he noted, a look almost of invitation on her face. She licked moist lips.

He had been worried she might have an ectopic pregnancy which could rupture the fallopian tube. It was a serious condition – potentially fatal; but he found nothing to support this. Just a slight twinge in the left inguinal fossa. He told her to get dressed and return to the consultation room. Then he took the sample she'd provided to the nurse's room and watched as Marie tested it. It was negative.

He advised her to take some painkillers for the discomfort and to come back or even call out the emergency doctor if she had continuing problems. He watched her go with an uncomfortable feeling that he'd missed something, some vital sign. He pushed the thought right to the back of his mind. These niggles could drive a doctor mad. He resolved to forget about her – it was probably nothing more serious than irritable bowel syndrome – and concentrate on the rest of his surgery.

To his surprise his last patient of the morning was Maud Allen, suddenly looking her age as she sat down stiffly. She gave him a weak smile. 'I wasn't feeling too good,' she said. 'To be honest I'm having a bit of pain here.' She indicated the edge of her breast. It didn't surprise Daniel that she was experiencing some pain. He'd almost anticipated it.

'Mrs Allen,' he said. 'Have you got your appointment through for the clinic?'

'Oh yes,' she said brightly. 'It's on Tuesday but…' Her voice faltered. 'I'm having a problem sleeping.'

'It's natural,' he said. 'I expect you're worried.'

She simply nodded.

'But there are…' He'd been about to say, all sorts of treatments, but she stopped him with a look.

'I don't want an operation at my age.'

'Mrs Allen, it almost certainly won't come to that. It can possibly be treated with one simple tablet a day.'

'I'll believe that when I see it,' she said. 'I watched my husband fade away as they injected him with God knows what.'

'Medicine's advanced since then.'

'No, thank you,' she said. 'The only thing I want from you, Daniel, at the moment, is adequate pain relief and something to help me sleep.'

He nodded, typed out a prescription for morphine and a sleeping tablet and handed it to her. She didn't even glance at it but smiled. 'Thank you, Daniel,' she said.

He mused for a while after she had gone. She'd only started calling him by his Christian name recently. Previously she had maintained formal address. She had been widowed more than twenty years ago, way before he had joined the practice. Her husband had been a lecturer in Wolverhampton, she a teacher in the secondary school in Stone, Alleyne's. She lived in one of the ancient cottages up Kerry Lane. He loved the place. Quaint and full of character and original features, arched Gothic windows and with its own apple tree orchard, which did beg to have a pony grazing in it. It would probably be up for sale before long, he mused. Had he, Holly and Elaine still been the happy family he had anticipated, he would have considered buying it and letting Holly have the pony she had so wanted.

But then the centre of Birmingham was not a suitable place to have a pony and Holly had stopped even mentioning horses soon after her mother had left. She appeared to have transferred her interest from the real thing to some poisonous pink plastic creature called My Little Pony.

Another dream shattered by the broken marriage.

He walked into the reception area, still a little depressed and reflective, both about Maud Allen and the fallout from his divorce. Marie Westbrook was busy, reading her mail.

'You look down,' she commented. 'Fancy a coffee?'

'That'd be nice.'

She bustled over to the kettle and mugs then handed him his drink.

'So what's got into you?'

He told her about Maud Allen and she gave him an odd look. 'But she's eighty-six,' she said. 'Surely you don't still get sentimental about timely death?'

He felt wrong-footed. 'Never quite got used to it.'

She flashed him a wide, friendly smile. 'Well, there you go,' she said. 'Who would have thought it?'

A moment later she clapped her palm to her forehead. 'I almost forgot,' she said. 'Bobby Millin asked if you'd ring. She's at Vanda's place.'

'I wish you had forgotten,' he said. 'I bet it's about Anna-Louise.'

She handed him a slip of paper with the number on and gave him a look of sympathy.

'Here,' she said. 'Get it over with, eh?'

He dialled the number and listened to Roberta's gravelly voice cataloguing all the reasons why her granddaughter should see the paediatrician without delay. He let her speak without pausing as the minutes ticked away.

'I've taken some blood,' he said. 'I should have the results by Tuesday. Remember she has been an inpatient and they didn't find anything.'

'She's not right, that child,' Bobby Millin said forcefully. 'I don't need a medical degree to tell me that even if you do.'

'Has anything happened *since* I saw her this morning that would make me change my mind?'

'No-o.'

'Look, Bobby,' Daniel said reasonably, 'I'll see Anna-Louise any time. You know that, but sometimes…'

She butted in. 'Don't start calling me an anxious granny,' she snapped. 'Something is wrong with that child. I can sense it. I've always had an instinct for this sort of thing and something is very wrong with my granddaughter and I shall hold you responsible if anything happens to her. I'm fed up with watching her sicken and you doing nothing about it.'

Daniel felt tired – defeated. Threats like this were every doctor's nightmare. 'Bring her in to my Tuesday evening surgery,' he said wearily. 'I should have the results back by then and it'll give the antibiotics a chance to work.'

Bobby Millin gave a loud snort and put the phone down, leaving Daniel feeling terrible. Some minutes later he was aware that Marie was still hanging around, a pleasant, empathic smile on her face, which for some reason made him feel awkward. He had the uncomfortable feeling that she was hoping he'd suggest they call in at the pub again but he didn't want to.

So he said nothing and the silence grew as she bustled around in the reception area. Eventually she left. He could hear a tinge of disappointment as she wished him goodbye. Thank goodness for the long weekend.

* * *

He was stroking the lace, which felt surprisingly sharp against his fingers, unlike the satin which was as smooth as her skin. He fiddled with the pearl earrings, imagining them threading through her ear lobes.

He would make a collection. This was just the start.

Chapter Nine

Brian was watching his wife, sitting at the dressing table, blow-drying her hair. She was wearing a satin dressing gown in a pale blue shade. It was open at the neck. He could see the hollow of her throat, follow it down to the sternum, towards the swell of her breasts. She had small breasts, uptilted and pointed. He had thought that after Bethan they might start to sag but they had not changed, even though she had breast-fed Bethan until she was four months old. Claudine was watching him from the corner of her eye, well aware that he was watching her. She always knew when he was watching her.

She tilted her head back, slowly drying the strands of hair, arching her back. The action reminded him of the day he had first seen her wearing only the bottom half of a pink bikini. No more than a pair of knickers, really, he'd thought in his prudish, British copper's mind. She had been a graceful, flirty young thing. He could still visualise her sitting on the beach, breasts pertly exposed, pretending to chat and laugh with her friends, throwing her head back, showing a mouthful of white and perfect teeth. But he had been well aware that her attention was not on her chit-chat or on the smoothing of the suntan cream up and down her arms but diverted surreptitiously towards him.

She had sensed that he was watching her from the shade of the beach bar. Full of holiday audacity and Dutch courage bestowed on him by the hot sun and the cold beer he had kept his eyes firmly on her, willing her to turn round and look directly at him. But she hadn't – at least, not then. Not until she had started to pack her things into the pink and yellow beach bag, slipped into a scrap of a dress and sauntered past. *Then* she had met his gaze boldly, with a message so unmistakable in her own dark eyes that his three friends had immediately started to tease him. He knew they were simply jealous.

She had been a coquette then; she still was.

Brian felt a sudden rush of hot jealousy. *She was taking great care with her toilette today.* The little worm bored information into his mind.

Daniel Gregory was a wealthy, professional, divorced man and Claudine was very attractive.

Like most men he couldn't really gauge whether Gregory would be attractive to women, but he guessed so – if only from the way his wife fluttered her eyelashes at him.

And he was letting, no *encouraging* his wife to spend half the day and the entire evening with him.

Was he mad?

When he had first taken Claudine home his mother had warned him about her flirtatiousness, at the same time pointing out that he had a jealous and possessive nature. Hadn't he followed an ex around after she had ended the affair? Hadn't he threatened the boy she had taken up with?

'That French girl,' she had said with bitter venom, 'will laugh at you behind your back one day. Watch her. You'll see.'

So had begun an enmity between mother and daughter-in-law which had never mellowed into anything better.

But then, he argued, in defence of his wife, his mother was a sour and cynical woman ever since her husband had found himself a newer, younger replacement. Brian never saw him now but he knew his father was happy and had a new family, twin sons who must, by now, be teenagers.

Good luck to him, he thought – when he thought about him at all.

But he was well aware that his mother's dark predictions, lurking in his subconscious, were not helping matters.

Claudine finished drying her hair, replaced the hair dryer in the top drawer and was rooting around in her underwear drawer. She stood up, frowning. 'Brian,' she said slowly, 'have you seen my new cream lingerie, the lacy ones, that I bought last week?'

He was tired. He simply wanted to go to bed and sleep. Last night had been long and tiring. He felt a sudden irritation. For goodness' sake. She had a drawer full of the stuff.

He gave a loud, stagy yawn and lay back, closing his eyes. But she wasn't going to let it go. She rifled noisily through the drawer for a few more minutes then stood over him.

'You know,' she insisted, 'the cream bra and pants. They're gone.'

He felt another sting of jealousy. Why should she care about wearing her best underwear when she was simply going to the pictures with slimy Gregory?

He didn't like the answer his imagination was supplying.

But just to please her he opened his eyes, sat up and gave a cursory glance at the pile of filmy underwear. There seemed so much there. Piles of it. He couldn't even be bothered to look. So he lay back again. 'Are you sure?'

'Yes. Perfectly sure.' She turned to give him a half-smile. It was an intimate gesture, designed to be so. 'You know I am careful about such things.'

He grunted.

'Something else is missing,' she went on, 'my pearl earrings.' There was a note of hysteria in her voice. 'They are not here either.'

Brian Anderton grunted. Now what did she think he would do with a pair of earrings?

Claudine was still rummaging around in her dressing table drawer, frowning. Then she stood back, hands on her hips. 'Something is different here. Things are not quite as I left them.'

She opened the other two drawers, still frowning.

'Someone has been going through my things.'

'Probably Bethan.'

Claudine opened the bedroom door and called through. 'Bethan. Bethan. Come here.'

Bethan appeared in the doorway, holding her doll.

'Have you been in my drawers, looking through my things?'

'No.'

'Have you seen my pearl earrings, the little ones that belonged to Grandmama?'

'No, Mummy.'

Brian looked from his wife to his daughter. Bethan did not

lie. They had made a great virtue out of telling the truth and as far as he was aware she always had.

But then neither was Claudine in the habit of being mistaken – not about her personal possessions. She was a very particular woman, careful and fussy and those pearl earrings were her only heirlooms from her grandmother who had been a Parisian beauty at the time of the German occupation. She had been propositioned by an SS officer and when she had refused to cooperate had been briefly imprisoned for a trumped up accusation of working for the Resistance. In Claudine's eyes she was a heroine – as was anyone in modern day France who had stood up to the Germans – and this made those pearl earrings precious beyond mere money.

Jeanne Voisier had died an old woman, a few years before Brian had met the coquettish, yet demure, French girl on a beach in the south of France. He had been a shy and inexperienced youth of nineteen, a junior police cadet who had found Claudine's foreignness and sexual openness intensely exciting, unbelievably exotic. She, on the other hand, had teased him about his English starchiness, his sexual inhibitions and his inability to look at her sunbathing topless without blushing.

'Oh, Brian,' she would say. 'You are truly an English suet pudding.'

To him the miracle had been that she could possibly love him. He adored her.

And this made him vulnerable.

Claudine grumbled and fumbled, finally finished her preparations, planted a kiss on his cheek and left. But having wanted to rest so much he found he could not sleep. He mulled over the two innocuous incidents, stringing them together to make something as frightening as a noose out of a simple piece of rope.

One: personal items of his wife's had been audaciously stolen from their own back garden.

Two: further objects were missing from the house. Claudine was meticulous and careful about her own possessions so he knew that when she claimed a set of underwear and a pair of pearl earrings were missing it was true.

But how was it possible?

After tossing and turning for an hour or so he rose and opened the front door, picked up the geranium pot and found the front door key. But his policeman's eyes picked up other minor details. He always placed the key right in the centre. But here it was, carelessly dropped at one side. He knew it had been moved. It could have been Claudine or Bethan. That was what it was there for. But he did not think so. Bethan was always with her mother and Claudine was careful. He had never known her to lock herself out. In fact, even had she done so, she would almost certainly have forgotten the key was there at all.

So he picked up the key very slowly, seeing in his mind's eye, not his wife's nor his daughter's hand, but another hand pick it up. Maybe even take it to a shop and have a copy cut.

When does one start to panic?

Never, says the stoic policeman.

Always, replies the husband and father, because a family brings with it a responsibility to protect and in Brian Anderton the instinct to protect was particularly strong. Perhaps it was the fact that his father had simply dropped out of his life when he had been only fourteen and his mother had turned the full force of her vengeance and dependency on him. Maybe that was the reason that his wife and daughter evoked a fierce sense of duty in him. He turned the key with its plastic fob over and over in his hand very, very slowly and again he asked himself the same question.

Was it possible someone was invading their house as well as stealing clothes from the washing line, or was he allowing his suspicious policeman's mind to invent a situation? Maybe the explanation was both logical and simple, that Claudine had used the key herself and replaced it.

He must ask her before he started jumping to conclusions, or started changing the locks, but he disliked unexplained puzzles. He made his decision then. It wouldn't hurt to fit a few more bolts inside the doors and persuade Claudine to consider safety, if not for herself then for their daughter. And he didn't replace the key underneath the geranium pot. He had always felt uneasy about it being there but Claudine had persuaded him that Eccleston was safe and with his experience of the town he had given in.

But now…

He could always fit a CCTV camera to watch the house while they were out.

The Watchfull Eye.

Daniel, Claudine and the girls had arranged to meet at The Yellow House so they could travel in one car to Stafford and the multiplex cinema. Daniel had offered to drive.

The two girls were initially shy until Holly dragged Bethan upstairs to look at her latest Barbie doll outfit. It was a particularly gaudy affair with spangles shaped into a fish tail and a two-shell top and it transformed Barbie into a mermaid. What exactly happened to Blaine on these occasions, Daniel was not quite sure. He'd certainly never seen the blond boogie-boarder dressed as a merman.

What did it matter anyway? They were just dolls.

While the girls were upstairs, playing, he and Claudine sat at the kitchen table, drinking coffee from china mugs. In her direct way she came straight to the point.

'Are you happy on your own?'

He studied her face before answering. He had initially thought that she wore no make-up. But now he could see she did, mascara, foundation, eye shadow and lipstick. But it was so subtly applied it enhanced her natural look, the smooth skin, the large eyes. His glance dropped to her hands cradling the coffee mug. They bore the same stamp: short, shaped nails with clear polish. He felt a powerful attraction stirring.

Why did she have to be married?

'No, I don't really like it,' he said. 'To be honest…' He stopped. Claudine and Internet dating sites seemed a million miles apart. He settled on a half-truth. 'I'd love to meet someone.'

She reached out then and covered his hand with her own. 'Yes,' she said. 'I think you should. Holly would like it.' Her eyes seemed to be stuck on his.

He stood up then. 'Do you want another coffee or something?'

'Oh no, thank you.' She glanced at her watch. 'Perhaps we should go. We can have a drink there.'

It took less than fifteen minutes to reach Stafford, wending along a country road and under the M6, which was suffering from the usual roadworks and resulting traffic chaos. Daniel parked outside the cinema and they headed for the Harvester pub next door. The girls favoured Coke but he and Claudine elected for a glass of wine with their lunch. Claudine turned her nose up at the food but settled for a Caesar salad, while he and the girls gave in to temptation and tucked into steak and chips. He thought he had rarely tasted food so good and knew it was nothing to do with the cooking. It was the company which improved it.

The girls chattered throughout the meal while he and Claudine looked on indulgently. He glanced around him at other families on their outing and hoped that they assumed Claudine was his wife. He smiled at her and wondered if she had had the same idea and, if she had, whether she would like it.

The film was a typical Disney, plenty of big-eyed heroines, cartoon characters, a nasty-looking demon and a handsome prince. The girls sat between them but all the time he was aware of Claudine. Each time he looked across at her she seemed to pick up on it and turned her head to smile at him. Even though she was two seats away he caught wafts of her perfume every time she moved.

Guy was watching the house.

Damn it. Plod was at home all day. The bedroom curtains remained drawn. He had watched her leave with the little girl hours ago and still the curtains remained stubbornly closed. He sighed. PC Anderton must be on nights. What a shame. It would have been an ideal opportunity.

'Denied,' he muttered. 'Access denied.'

He would have to satisfy himself with touching the things he had already salted away so he walked, grumpily, back to his flat, and spread all the underwear on the bed, as though he was packing for a holiday, the entire bed spread with the filmy garments, in all colours: peach and pink, pale blue, cream, white and black. He finished by placing the pearl earrings side by side on his pillow. But it didn't bring him the usual pleasure. He sat up, disturbed. His jujus were losing their power. The scent of her perfume was receding, her presence fading away. He had a feeling of panic. What if he couldn't get any more?

It was no good. He put his feet on the floor. He felt restless and fidgety.

He needed more.

At six o'clock Brian rose, showered and heated the meal Claudine had left for him. He had an hour and a half before he needed to make his way to the police station.

Daniel had prepared dinner before he had left. Lasagne, a bag of green salad, tomatoes sliced with onion, basil and balsamic vinegar, and a tarte au citron he'd bought from Sainsbury's. He and Holly had laid the dining room table – hardly used since Elaine had left. It looked lovely set with cutlery, glasses, serviettes and candles waiting to be lit.

The two girls touched him with their responsibility and he and Claudine watched them indulgently as they put a match to the candles' wicks.

He opened a bottle of wine – French claret – in her honour.

'I am so enjoying this,' Claudine said as she raised her glass to her lips. 'This is just lovely. It's such a shame that Brian…'

He guessed she would say that it was a shame that Brian couldn't be with them but she didn't. Instead she returned her glass to the table. 'It's a shame,' she said again, 'that Brian finds it hard to enjoy such a night. Such simple pleasures as fine wine and good company. He is a…' She stopped, lowered her eyes as though she knew she had gone too far, that she had committed the sin of being disloyal about her husband. So instead she fell silent, smiled, and they all helped themselves to some salad.

He watched her dainty dinner manners, admiring the cool way she dished out the salad with a flourish, obviously enjoying the food, chewing each mouthful slowly, savouring every morsel. Halfway through she looked across at him. 'I don't know why,' she said, laughing, 'but I didn't expect you to be such a good cook.'

Daniel didn't even affect modesty. He beamed at her and muttered something about it being a pleasure to cook for company. Appreciative company, he added.

He'd never cooked for Elaine. She had put meals in front of him (usually convenience stuff from Waitrose at Newport) with a sulky, almost martyred air that had made him feel guilty for having put her to so much – any – trouble. He beamed at them all and thought how happy he felt.

The girls chattered easily and noisily throughout the meal, hardly pausing their conversation to eat. Perhaps he should have scolded them for talking with their mouths full but the truth was he felt too happy. He hadn't enjoyed a meal like this, around his own dining table, for ages – possibly ever. Maybe in his entire life. The animation of the two girls, the still elegance of Claudine, in her simple black dress, the jacket carefully hung up in the hall. The whole ambience of the evening made him feel so happy he could have sung.

He wished it wouldn't end.

* * *

Brian was watching some Saturday night television, sitting in his dressing gown. He fingered the lighter in his pocket. It was usually kept somewhere on his person, often in his trouser pocket. It gave him a feeling of power, of being in control of his own fate. Claudine had found it there on more than one occasion and asked him, 'Why do you keep a cigarette lighter in your pocket when you don't even smoke?'

He'd snatched it away from her. It was his and he never would tell her its story. He had mentioned against parts of it to her – the bits he didn't mind her hearing – but the details were his to chew over when he was alone. He fingered the lighter now and knew that deep down he still possessed all the hatred and fury that had welled up inside him on that bright, September day.

The girls vanished upstairs as soon as the meal was over leaving him and Claudine to clear the dishes, load the dishwasher and tidy the kitchen. Then they went into the sitting room and chatted idly – mostly about the girls and their idiosyncrasies. At nine o'clock she rose. 'We should go,' she said. 'It's way past Bethan's bedtime and I don't like her to be too late on a Saturday night because we have Mass early on Sunday.'

She was, he decided, a creature of habit.

'Where is she?' Bobby Millin had arrived at Vanda's flat to find her sitting with Arnie, watching television. Of Anna-Louise there was no sign.

Vanda jerked her head towards the door. 'She was sniffling. I think she's got a cold so I dosed her up and she's gone to bed. I haven't heard a sound out of her since. First bit of peace we've had all day.'

Bobby stood in front of her daughter, blocking her view of the TV screen. 'Have you checked up on her?'

It was Arnie who answered. In spite of his bulk and his naturally aggressive personality he was still in awe of his mother. It didn't do to cross her. When riled she could be more scary than Godzilla.

'I looked in on 'er half an hour ago, Ma. Sleeping like a baby.'

He and his sister giggled over the silly joke.

'Well – she is a baby,' Vanda said, trying to extend her neck so she could still pick up on *Strictly Come Dancing*. 'Move it, Mum.'

Bobby Millin didn't answer but disappeared into the tiny bedroom where Anna-Louise slept.

She was in there minutes before she returned, carrying the limp child. 'She's not breathing again,' she said.

Vanda yawned.

'She isn't breathing,' Bobby said again, shaking the child.

''Ere. Let me 'ave 'er.' It was Arnie who tried to take the toddler from his mother. 'Give 'er 'ere.'

Bobby was blowing into the baby's mouth. 'Got to get 'er back,' she said, between blows. 'Got to revive her.'

'Shall I call an ambulance?' Vanda had finally realised what was happening. 'Give 'er 'ere, Mum.'

There followed a bizarre fight in which each of the three tried to grab the child but Anna-Louise remained unresponsive. She lay in Bobby's arms, pale and floppy, while Arnie dialled 999 and Vanda hugged herself, wailing. 'My baby. Has she gone, Mum? Can't you bring her round? Come on, little thing.' She smacked the child's head. Bobby was making a clumsy attempt at mouth-to-mouth.

* * *

When the ambulance arrived minutes later there was no doubt about it. They found three hysterical adults and one dead child.

They took Anna-Louise from Bobby's arms gently but firmly, knowing exactly what they should do. They lay her on the floor and gently blew breaths of air into her lungs. They put their fingers on Anna-Louise's chest and pressed over her sternum to try and get her circulation restarted. But they were getting no response. The other paramedic had connected the child up to a cardiac monitor. But there was only a flat line, the only flicker a response to the cardiac massage. After half an hour of their valiant efforts, with Vanda watching, feeling helpless and hopeless, they said they were transferring Anna-Louise to the hospital. All the time they didn't stop in their effort to resuscitate the child but they were despondent. However great their efforts, they knew they had lost this one. When they reached Stafford General the doctors and nurses were waiting for them. One of the nurses took the child in her arms. The double doors swung closed behind them and Anna-Louise was gone.

Vanda was stunned. 'What's happening?'

Bobby put her arm around her daughter. 'I expect they're still trying to resuscitate her,' she said. 'There's lots they can do these days.'

Her daughter moved away. 'Bring the dead back to life,' she said scornfully. 'Who are you trying to kid, Mum?' She stared at the doors, still now. 'There must have been something wrong with her. She was always ailing. Always a bit strange, wasn't she, Mum?'

Her mother nodded. 'Yes, love.'

Arnie was standing apart, fingering an unlit cigarette, his mouth half open. It gave him a gormless, simple look, transformed him instantly from a thug to an object of pity.

It seemed like hours later that a doctor came out and told them what they already knew.

The three of them looked at each other, stunned. Vanda opened her mouth then closed it again, the only sign that she had heard a loud sniff and tears rolling down her cheeks.

The doctor continued, still in the same quietly controlled voice, that the coroner would be informed and that they would be carrying out a post-mortem to ascertain the precise cause of death.

It was something that assisted Guy, the fact that she was a creature of habit. She always went to church on a Sunday morning. The Catholic church in Stafford. He'd followed her all the way there, early one Sunday morning. She hadn't realised the little red Daewoo was following her. He'd pulled up outside the church and waited for almost an hour, until she came out again. Then he had pulled away, not wanting to chance it that she might realise he was there. She always went to morning Mass, taking the little girl with her. Never her husband. Brian did not seem to be a Catholic. Perhaps the house would be empty. So he rose early and walked the short distance to the field, crossing the stile, noting, with pleasure, that no one else was around. He was earlier, even, than the dog walkers.

He prowled at the back of the garden. No washing was hanging out today. He wondered if the policeman was in. If he'd been on nights he'd be back by now, probably in bed.

The house looked deserted. The bedroom curtains were

open but he sensed that the policeman was there, inside. The trouble was that the impulse to acquire something more of Claudine's was strong. He *had* to have something more. Never mind what. Something of hers that she had touched recently. He stood and scanned the back of the house for a long time, his pulse quickening in time with his breathing as he saw a pair of Wellington boots, pale blue, plain and very clean standing neatly, side by side, on the back doorstep. Obviously they were not Brian's. And they were far too big for the little girl so they must be *hers.* He could feel his excitement mount as he focused on them. He imagined her slipping her dainty feet into them, one at a time, ready to go for a walk, or do some gardening. He closed his eyes and dared himself to walk the few steps. Brave the lion's den even though the lion was in his lair.

Brian was in the bath. It usually helped him to sleep but today he was too disturbed with his horny, thorny problem. He could feel hatred welling up inside him for the person who was inching his way into his home. His life. His wife.

Bethan had left her cardigan behind so Daniel bundled Holly into her coat to walk the few hundred yards to the policeman's house. Brian would probably be asleep, in bed. Claudine and Bethan would be at Mass. He wouldn't disturb the household but would leave the cardigan in a plastic carrier bag on the front doorstep where it would be found when they returned. He'd penned a short note of explanation.

But it was Brian who found it, walked around the house just before he realised that something else was missing.

Chapter Ten

Tuesday, 2nd May

As the Monday had been a Bank Holiday Holly had stayed for an extra day. They'd spent Sunday clearing out her bedroom, making up a charity bag of clothes she had outgrown and toys she no longer wanted, as they were too 'childish'.

Daniel loved everything about even this routine chore: Holly's reminiscences about where she had worn the numerous T-shirts and jeans, skirts and blouses, a couple of thick sweaters and a puffer jacket that she declared she 'wouldn't be seen dead in'. Daniel seemed to recall that she had begged him for it a brief year ago – as she had begged him to buy the pink wellies last week. To the pile she added half a dozen Noddy books and a few Beatrix Potters – until she changed her mind about the Beatrix Potters and said they were still 'sweet'. The bedroom tidy, the Sunday meal eaten and cleared away, and the manes of her collection of My Little Ponies washed and dried, he'd had the rare luxury of snuggling up to her after her Sunday night bath and watching a wildlife film on the television, breathing in the wholesome scent of Pears Coal Tar soap. In some ways she could still be quite unsophisticated.

But the extra day tacked onto the weekend would bring its own penalty. It was even harder to see her leave on the Monday afternoon.

And surgery was always doubly busy on the Tuesday after a Bank Holiday.

In spite of the low he always felt after Holly had gone, Tuesday began well for Daniel. He rose early, showered, dressed and checked his emails. Instant luck. Amongst all the spam, adverts for Viagra and jollies from friends there was one from *her*, his 'match' from the website. He felt an instant hit of excitement. He had no time to savour it now, much less respond, so he closed it down, knowing it would be something to look forward to all day long. He would know it was there right through the inevitably busy surgery and long list of visits and then tonight, over a beer, he would read it and decide if she was a woman he wanted to meet. He felt a little skip of the heart as though some doe-eyed lovely was waiting in the wings. Waiting especially for him.

He was walking along the High Street, pausing to look in the shop window of LITTLE MONSTERS, wondering what treat Holly would want next, when he sensed someone behind him. He half turned to see Maud Allen standing behind him.

'You look happy,' she commented.

He couldn't but agree. 'My daughter's been staying for the long weekend,' he said. 'I don't get to see her enough.'

'That's a shame,' she said. 'I suppose she stays with her mother.'

'In Birmingham. I wish she could be up here. She's only

seven and she'd love it. Especially if she could have a pony of her own.'

Her blue eyes looked shrewdly into his. 'You've no room for a horse where you are, have you, Daniel?'

He shook his head. 'Not a chance unless I can persuade a local farmer to rent out a stable and a field.'

She laughed. 'You'll be lucky.'

He would have asked her how she was, commented on her healthy appearance, but at that moment Arnie Struel planted himself in front of him.

'You're a bloody useless doctor,' he sneered. 'You heard what happened to our Anna-Louise?'

Daniel shook his head.

'She died.'

'What?' Daniel was stunned.

Arnie nodded in a slow, threatening way, his chin jutting out and his dark eyes flashing with fury. 'We lost her,' he said, 'Saturday night. Our little angel.'

Daniel felt his face contort into a frown. 'What did she die of? Septimcaemia? What happened?'

'Same as before. She stopped breathing. They don't know yet exactly what her problem was.' He moved a step closer. 'But I can promise you, Doctor, we'll be wantin' an enquiry.' He sneered in Daniel's face. 'You'd better speak to your lawyer, mate.' He shoved his face even closer so Daniel breathed in nothing but cigarettes and beer. 'You're goin' to need 'im.'

Daniel made to walk past him but Struel hadn't finished with him yet. He put a hand on his collar. 'You oughta be suspended. That's what.'

For a while after Struel had marched away Daniel stood stock still. He could feel his reputation, his career, his entire future ebbing away into nothing. The question was, what had Anna-Louise died of? Had it been preventable? How culpable was he and, overlying that with a thick sludge of misery, what could he have done to prevent her death? The questions rolled round and round in his mind while at the back of it was the dreadful certainty that, whatever the two-year-old had died of, her family would hold him responsible. Whatever the verdict of the coroner, the Struels would never forgive him. And in a small town a vociferous family could ensure that his life and career were made impossible. He was vulnerable and would be judged an incompetent doctor who had failed to save the life of a child, and that reputation could well mark him in this town as a failure. Patients would refuse to see such a doctor. They would lose confidence. The partnership would be dissolved and he would be a ruined man. His instinct was to run fast and far back to the safety and privacy of his house, but it was Maud Allen's wrinkled old paw that prevented him. She smiled into his face. 'Surely, Daniel' she said, 'you're not allowing that bully-boy to threaten you?'

He shook his head. 'Anna-Louise, his two-year-old niece, has died,' he said. 'He's angry – naturally. He holds me responsible. I was the last doctor to see her.'

The old lady's eyes followed Arnie swaggering up the High Street, people shifting out of the way for him. Then she turned back to Daniel. 'Your life will change,' she said, almost prophetically. 'Soon.'

Had he not been so distracted he would have asked Maud Allen about her hospital appointment, or at the very least checked when she was next coming to see him, but his mind was busily running through every consultation he had had with the little girl, hunting for some hidden clue that something serious had really been wrong. But even in the labyrinths of his mind he found nothing and when he stopped thinking about Anna-Louise and returned to the present he found that Maud Allen had gone. He couldn't even hear the tap-tap of her walking stick. He peered along the High Street but she had vanished – probably into one of the numerous shops. Hardly aware of moving forward he found himself in the Co-op, a bottle of wine in his hand, Guy Malkin patiently waiting for him to hand over £4.35. He didn't remember selecting it or picking it up. He knew then that his day was ruined.

He gave Guy the money, watched him flush as their eyes met. He put the bottle inside a plastic carrier bag and proceeded to the surgery.

Whatever had happened he had no option but to be professional, disassociate himself from what had been said and try to concentrate on his patients. But however many times he delivered this lecture to himself he kept having doubts. His one reassurance was that the hospital doctors hadn't been able to find anything wrong with Anna-Louise either. He couldn't be *that* bad.

Lucy Satchel met him outside the surgery with a bright smile. 'Morning, Dan,' she said.

She hasn't heard, he thought miserably.

He told her about Anna-Louise and watched her face harden. 'When did you last see her?' she asked, her face moving from friendliness through various phases, settling finally into suspicion. She even moved back half a step.

Have you ever noticed how quickly people detach themselves from you when you are under suspicion?

Most people, at least.

'On Saturday.' He watched her face change again into the frosty, polite stare of a stranger.

'And how was she?' Her voice was formal.

He drew in a deep breath. 'She had a nasty boil on her leg,' he said, 'I gave her some antibiotics. But there was nothing else I could put my finger on. I expedited her paediatric appointment. She would have seen the paediatrician this week, I would have thought.' He appealed to her then. 'But you know what she was like, Lucy. She was always here at the surgery. She'd been in and out of hospital virtually all her life.' He could feel his anger rising. 'She'd had every bloody test under the sun. Not one of them was significantly abnormal. No one ever found anything.'

She looked disturbed at his anger. 'But you say she died.'

His anger increased. He'd *tried,* for goodness' sake.

Lucy nodded slowly, the constraint still making her face a strange mask. 'I'm sorry,' she said and left it at that.

Daniel felt frustrated. He'd expected Lucy to at least back him up, show him some loyalty.

He regretted that Sammy was on holiday, back in his native New York, visiting family, so he couldn't speak to him. He wandered into his surgery.

Somehow he got through the day and out the other end. He had booked a few minor surgery cases in the afternoon so didn't even go home for lunch. He hadn't fancied running the gauntlet of the High Street anyway, possibly running into Vanda or Bobby or even Arnie all over again. By the time he had finished for the day he felt weary, exhausted and worried. Every time the phone rang he expected it to be the coroner with the results of the post-mortem, but no one contacted him, which left his questions unanswered. *What did she die of? Was it preventable? Could I,* should *I have prevented it?*

When he left the surgery he noted that Lucy Satchel's car had already gone and he felt alone, deserted and isolated. Marie Westbrook was on holiday this week so he couldn't even confide in her or go for a swift drink. Head down, he walked the short distance home.

The four messages on his answerphone from his mother wondering why he hadn't been in touch over the Bank Holiday just about put the lid on the dustbin. He sighed. He couldn't face talking to his mother. Not her. Not now. Not tonight.

He hardly had the heart to open the email, but sat, for a while, staring into the screen, reflecting how very different he felt from this morning. How his optimism and hope had so completely evaporated.

But finally he did.

'Hi, I'm M. It was nice to get your contact.' He liked her breezy tone. 'I'm a professional woman who lives in south Staffordshire and am divorced following a short and very unsatisfactory marriage. I have no children though I'd love some, especially a daughter. I'm 34 years old and have no ties. My family are from London. I enjoy a wide variety of activities: dancing (Salsa especially!), country walks, music Classical and folk, some Pop. I also love reading – mainly modern novels, crime, romances and anything with a historical interest, and of course eating, in particular Italian food and even more when it's served with a good bottle of red wine.

'I'd love to meet you. Soon.'

Daniel read the sentence twice. She'd *love* to meet him.

That sounded good. He felt himself cheering up. It was like coming home to a friendly wife. She sounded ideal – and available. Claudine might be his fantasy woman but she had a policeman husband which to the local doctor was a serious impediment. He read on with quickening interest.

'I enjoy cooking. Now then.' Her tone had changed. 'You must be wondering whether I'm attractive. Well – I don't think people are generally sick when they see me but even I can't pretend I'm a showstopper. I'm five-foot ten inches tall and quite slim, have medium brown hair cut round my face (medium length and straight). So why don't we meet for a drink? Next week would be great. Just suggest a pub, Dan, and I'll be there!

'Yours, M.'

Daniel read the entire email through twice before hitting the reply button. No point in hesitating.

'How about Wednesday?' He named a pub on the outskirts of Stafford. Eccleston was far too public a place to meet someone on a blind date. Particularly now when his reputation was under threat.

In spite of downing almost the entire bottle of wine and yet another spat on the telephone with Elaine about the coming weekend, he woke the next morning feeling buoyant – bullish even. He would sit this one out.

He had a day's grace.

He had been waiting for the coroner's office to contact him about the death of Anna-Louise but it was the pathologist who eventually rang. Even though Daniel had anticipated the phone call he could still feel his hand shake when the receptionist rang through. He spoke into the telephone, deliberately making an effort to make his voice sound confident, deep and fully in control. 'Doctor Gregory here.'

The pathologist introduced himself as Doctor James McReady, briskly informing Daniel in a rich Scottish accent that he was a locum filling in for Michael Gray. The fact that Daniel didn't know him increased his unease. At least Gray was familiar ground.

'I'll be frank with you, Doctor. The cause of death of the little girl is by no means certain or clear.' He was choosing his words with precision. 'Bu-ut…' There was a wealth of meaning in the strung out word. 'I have my suspicion that this was not a natural death.' He proceeded to give Daniel a tutorial.

'Sudden Infant Death Syndrome is well known amongst the general public.' Daniel gave a confidant murmur of agreement.

'Reye's Syndrome is a similar sudden death in older children.' Like a good professor he paused for his student to absorb this fact before hurrying on. 'Certain characteristics led me to suspect this diagnosis.' Another pause. 'According to her mother, Anna-Louise had a history of apnoeic attacks?'

'Yes.'

'Reye's Syndrome frequently follows a viral infection such as coryza.'

Why couldn't he just say a common cold?

'The incidence of Reye's Syndrome is also greatly increased if there is a history of aspirin ingestion. I spoke to Anna-Louise's mother on this matter and she admitted she had given her daughter half an adult aspirin, i.e. 37.5 mgms, two hours before the child's death because the little girl was snuffly.'

Daniel felt a familiar irritation. *Don't they just love the sound of their own voices? Simply half an aspirin would have done.*

'But, you understand, the features of Reye's Syndrome are quite distinctive.'

Why didn't he just get on with it?

'However...'

Daniel fingered his pen impatiently. He was finding his colleague's tone intensely irritating.

'...I found none of the usual findings consistent with Reye's Syndrome, the pâté de foie gras liver, an oedematous brain and so on. Therefore I would have been unhappy to have made this connection without firmer pathological evidence.'

Another pause.

'The police removed some of the bedding of the child. She slept without a pillow, which is common practice these days. Amongst other items found in the child's bedroom they also removed a small, embroidered cushion from a chair. This was found to have traces of the child's saliva on it. I further removed two tiny fibres from one of the child's nostrils that looked superficially the same as the fibres on the cushion. Of course we will have to wait for microscopic comparison analysis.'

In spite of the gravity of the situation Daniel could not resist a smile. Pathologists are the perfect, indistinguishable mix of lawyer and doctor. A scientific policeman.

'I have discussed this matter with the police and we are of the opinion that there is a very real possibility that the child was smothered using this cushion, and the finger inevitably points towards the mother. The mother is the usual perpetrator of such an assault. Was there any history of illness or pseudo-illness induced by the mother?'

Daniel felt ice seep up from his feet, slowly permeating through his body as though he had been drinking a glass of hemlock. Something – life – happiness – trust – or a belief that he had a future as a doctor – was draining out of him. If this turned out to be infanticide, he would feel morally responsible but that was preferable to them finding something physical that he had missed through incompetence.

He was honest enough to admit that his feeling of guilt was because he had had his suspicions but hadn't acted on them. He'd sat back and done nothing. Waited for some proof or indisputable evidence. Now he had it and he was indirectly responsible for the child's death. He'd never involved the Social Services, even though he had been suspicious that all was not well between Vanda and her silent little daughter whose tongue had merely reddened her chin and cheeks without uttering a single word. He should have protected the child. It was part of his job. His duty. Instead he'd waited and now it was too late.

He'd failed her. 'There was a history of repeated illnesses,' he replied lamely. 'She'd been admitted to hospital on numerous occasions but nothing concrete was ever found.'

The pathologist hesitated before continuing smoothly. 'We-ell, you obviously know the family better than I. So I wondered what your opinion is of this theory. Of course it's possible that little Anna-Louise slobbered over the cushion on some other occasion, bu-ut the presence of the particles in her nostrils appears quite damning. Can you answer me these questions: Is Miss Struel capable of smothering her own child? Had you any prior suspicion that all was not well between Vanda Struel and her daughter? Is there anyone else in the picture who might have been involved? The police told me the child's uncle was resident with them and was in the house when Anna-Louise died. Have the Social Services ever been involved with the family? Have you had suspicions on other occasions of non-accidental injury? We took the precaution,' he added quickly, 'of x-raying her entire body and failed to find any old fractures, which tends not to support my theory. Also there were none of the other signs of traumatic smothering – bruising inside the mouth, etc. The lungs were congested but there are other causes of that and I cannot give a cause of death with any certainty on that sign alone.'

Daniel couldn't remember what exactly he muttered in response. The questions he could answer honestly he did: that the Social Services had not been involved in the case; that he had toyed with the idea that Vanda might have been capable of causing her own child's illnesses; that there was a question mark over whether mother and daughter had truly bonded but that he had never sensed any ill feeling on Vanda's part towards Anna-Louise – rather an indifference; that Vanda lives with her brother, who is an aggressive drunk who pumps up his body with exercise and anabolic steroids which are well known to shorten the fuse of their takers. 'But I've only ever seen him display a certain…' His mind drifted to the image of the tiny child propped up on the sofa, her cardigan wrongly and clumsily buttoned, 'tenderness towards her.'

He ignored the pathologist's snort of doubt. But he hadn't seen the two together, the town thug and the tiny, vulnerable two-year-old. He had.

Other questions he could not answer. Was Vanda capable of harming her own child deliberately?

He didn't know. How can a family doctor make this

judgement when all their training is to trust what their patient tells them?

He needed time to think before he started making rash statements. He fobbed the pathologist off with something about needing to search through his records, tagging on the fable that he would ring him back later.

Anything to get him off the hook and give him time to stew through his thoughts.

But his bad luck was far from over.

Ill winds were gusting around him.

On Friday, as his mind was busily planning the menu for the following night, Christine, the receptionist, met him in the corridor. 'The coroner wants you to ring him after surgery,' she said.

It rang no alarm bells. He assumed it would be a further enquiry about Anna-Louise.

There is nothing unusual about a telephone conversation with the coroner in general practice. Any unexplained death is referred to him. As it is often the GP who has vital information about the patient he is frequently the first port of call so the lines are open between the coroner's office and the doctor's surgery.

When he had seen his morning's patients Daniel dialled the number.

Tom, the coroner's assistant, answered. 'Oh yes, Doctor Gregory,' he said. 'It's about an old lady, Mrs…' Daniel heard him shuffle through some papers.

'Allen.'

Daniel felt initially puzzled, then, as Tom proceeded in his slow Staffordshire voice, he began to feel upset. 'What? I only saw her yesterday. She looked well. I hadn't expected…' His voice trailed away as his foreboding increased. 'What happened?' he asked sharply.

'It looks very much like an overdose of some medication, Doctor. Tablets were found at the side of her bed. You'd prescribed some tranquillisers?'

Daniel felt a snag of concern. 'She was naturally anxious and was having trouble sleeping,' he said defensively. 'But she was too lucid a woman to take the wrong dose of tablets.'

'Well…' Tom paused. 'There was a note. The relatives say she'd been a bit distracted. Apparently she'd recently been diagnosed with cancer.'

'We-ell.' Daniel was finding it difficult to know what to say. 'Not exactly. I'd had my suspicions and I'd referred her for an opinion but I hadn't had the results back yet from the hospital so the diagnosis hadn't been confirmed.' He felt bound to add something more. 'But she was an intelligent woman. I think she knew she had cancer and probably realised that I suspected it had spread.'

'Right.' Tom's voice leaked no emotion. 'Well, I shall relay this to the coroner and in all probability he will request a post-mortem and some toxicology reports. That's all then, Doctor Gregory – for now.'

Daniel put the phone down with a growing feeling that something here was not quite right. In his mind he revised his physical findings, together with the initial prescription. Then he sat down at his desk. She had asked for the sleeping tablets, he realised now, not because she was having trouble sleeping but because she intended to take her own life. He recalled their final encounter, outside the supermarket, her vote of confidence in him.

He put his head in his hands and remembered her interest in Holly. He felt a stab of grief for the passing of yet another from that brave, resourceful and inherently decent generation. Even the way she had elected to take her own life rather than allow the cancer to destroy her inch by inch, little by little, reflected her character, her dignity. She had known how cruel this disease could be.

What he did not yet understand was how this would affect him.

Chapter Eleven

Monday, 8th May

The weekend with Holly did something to allay his anxiety. He heard nothing from Claudine and as though Holly sensed that something was not quite right she didn't even mention her new friend. But his problems were only beginning.

Monday morning brought further trouble.

The day began badly with a telephone call from the pathologist who had performed the post-mortem on Maud Allen. Dr Gray was back.

Such specialists frequently adopted a condescending manner towards their colleagues in general practice and Doctor Michael Gray was no exception. Although he'd known Daniel for a number of years he cut straight to the chase without preamble.

'I understand that you had made a diagnosis of breast cancer which had metastasized to the lymph gland and the spine.'

The back of Daniel's neck felt suddenly hot. 'No I hadn't,' he said defensively. 'Not exactly. I'd examined her and found a breast lump which I felt to be suspicious. She was complaining of backache and I also found an enlarged lymph node in her neck. I'd done some blood tests and referred her to the rapid-access breast lump clinic. That was what I'd done.' He was tempted to add, *Have you got a problem with that?* but knew there was no point in antagonising his colleague.

Michael Gray cleared his throat noisily and Daniel just knew he was building up to something. 'Well – for a start I did find a *cystic* lump in her breast,' he began slowly. 'It was quite large, about the size of a golf ball. I've taken a section and sent it for histology but I'd bet my bottom dollar that it wasn't malignant. It looked perfectly innocent to me.' His tone was smug.

It took the wind out of Daniel's sails. He felt his face contort into a hostile scowl.

'Well, of course,' he finally spluttered, 'you had the advantage on me. You actually *saw* the wretched thing.' He thought how peevish and petty he sounded. '*I* didn't.'

The pathologist took absolutely no notice but ploughed on – with increasing malice. 'I also understand from the relatives that you suspected that the lump in her neck was a secondary deposit from this primary.' It was a statement not a question.

'It was a natural assumption.' Daniel winced at the resentful tone in his own voice.

'Oh.' The pathologist pulled out his trump card. 'Well – it looked like an old fractured clavicle to me. The relatives tell me that Mrs Allen fell off her horse when she was about fourteen. She broke her clavicle and it was badly set. She'd had a lump there for years.'

'When I touched it,' Daniel said, 'she didn't say anything.'

He could already guess where this was heading.

'But of course Mrs Allen didn't die of misdiagnosed cancer, did she?'

'Come on.' Daniel felt bound to defend himself. 'I couldn't possibly have anticipated that she would commit suicide on the back of my findings. I made my examination and acted on it. I referred her. I was doing my duty as her GP to give her the best possible chance of life. When she said she couldn't sleep I naturally prescribed what I thought was appropriate treatment for her.'

'It's very unfortunate that you prescribed opiates *and* sleeping pills after planting the seed in her mind that she was terminally ill.'

There was not a trace of sympathy in the pathologist's voice.

So Daniel had enough to worry about to make him forget about the threats from Arnie.

It was Sammy Schultz who collared him on the following afternoon, looking uneasy and serious. For no reason at all Daniel's heart did a little flip.

'Sammy?' he said.

His partner was holding a piece of paper in his hand, held at arm's length as though he wanted no part of it.

'Umm, can we go into my room?'

Daniel felt the same way as when he had thrown a snowball at a school window and the headmaster had found out who it was and summoned him to his office for a caning. Meekly, he followed his partner into his consulting room and felt a further snatch of alarm when Sammy Schultz closed the door very deliberately behind them.

'I don't know how to say this, Dan,' he said.

Daniel gave a humourless laugh. 'Spit it out, Sammy,' he suggested. 'That's the best way.'

Sammy sucked in a deep breath. 'Why don't you sit down?'

Daniel sat.

'We've had a complaint.'

Daniel frowned. 'What sort of complaint?'

Sammy Schultz was practically wringing his hairy hands. 'Oh, Dan,' he said. 'I don't believe a word of it. Not a goddam word.'

'What sort of complaint?' Daniel repeated quietly.

'The very worst sort.'

Daniel waited silently for the axe to fall.

Sammy couldn't even look at him. 'Sexual harassment,' he muttered. 'Inappropriate examination. Intimate fondling.'

'What?' He was so shocked it was all he could do to stop himself from grabbing the letter out of Sammy's hand.

He didn't need to. Sammy handed it to him, a look of intense sadness – almost grief in his manner.

'I know things have been difficult since Elaine left.'

Daniel was horrified. 'What are you saying?'

He scanned the piece of paper twice. It was badly written, in childish writing with numerous spelling mistakes but there was no mistaking the accusation.

'I toeld the doctor I ad a pain in my tummey. E got me to liey down in a littel cubikcle with nuthing on and he tuched me up. All over. He's a perv and I don't want him for my doctor no more.'

It was signed *Chelsea Emmanuel (Miss).*

Sammy's eyes were on him, waiting for an explanation.

'I take it you have examined the young lady in question recently?'

Daniel nodded.

'Surely you had a chaperone?'

'She refused one. She said she didn't like the practice nurses so I asked Marie to wait outside the door. By the time I got into the examination room Chelsea was starkers.'

Sammy looked resigned. 'You should have insisted, Dan. The girl is only fourteen years old.'

It was on the tip of Daniel's tongue to point out that Chelsea was no innocent. She was a sexually precocious tart. But that wouldn't help his cause so he listened meekly to his partner.

'This may cost you dearly, Dan. And it's terribly bad for the practice – particularly on top of the little Struel girl's death. In a small town like Eccleston it doesn't do to gather such publicity. I take it we're still waiting for the verdict on that.'

Daniel nodded. *And they didn't even know the full facts that surrounded Maud Allen's suicide.*

He felt very alone and very afraid. It was hard to disentangle these events. He stood up, his resignation on the tip of his tongue but Sammy Schultz slapped his shoulder in a sudden display of bonhomie. 'Weather the storm,' he said, 'but I advise you to contact the Medical Defence Union.'

The Medical Defence Union were helpful – sympathetic even – but he couldn't mistake the underlying seriousness of their tone.

'Well, Doctor,' they said, 'this is unfortunate,' before they advised him to write down his recollection of the entire consultation, exact times, words said, precise examination details. They asked him to fax his computer records through and his personal details. He heard a distinct and regretful 'Hmm' when he said he was divorced.

* * *

He spent an hour gathering information on the consultation from the computer and composing his fax to the MDU and left the surgery with a burning feeling of indignation. He didn't need anyone to tell him how potentially serious this could be. No matter that *he* knew he was innocent. It wouldn't make any difference to anyone else – not the townsfolk, his patients. The allegation was enough.

He felt dejected, defeated and helpless, paralysed because there was no way to fight back. He felt a sudden fury against her. It struck him then that he had lost his one ally – Maud Allen – who had believed in him. She had abandoned him when he could have done with her.

As he walked along the High Street he felt paranoid. He felt people were watching him because he realised that if Sammy Schultz had his doubts, then how much more so would all these other people who knew him only slightly – as a doctor – and not as a man?

His partner should trust him. Surely? Sammy knew him better than his patients did. He'd known Elaine and Holly. Their families had once mingled. And he thought him capable of deriving sexual satisfaction from touching up that grubby little…?

He walked on, meeting no one's eyes. He knew now what it was like to walk down the High Street, feeling conspicuous because all eyes were on him.

As he stepped down the street the words of the Medical Defence Union rep rang in his ears: *'No chaperone, Doctor? Her word against yours. We suggest you don't continue to see female patients alone but insist on a chaperone being present at all physical examinations. For your own protection, Doctor.*

At least until this mess is sorted out.' Brief pause. *'And, as you know, these matters can take some time.'*

Daniel felt unbelievably paranoid. The eyes were on him.

As luck would have it Arnie suddenly planted himself in front of him.

Daniel held his breath.

'You've bin touchin' up a little kid, haven't you?'

So – the news had spread. Mouthy little Chelsea had told her story, gained an audience. Of course – now he worked it out – Chelsea Emmanuel and Vanda Struel were friends. He'd seen them a couple of times together, strolling down the street, Anna-Louise in her pushchair, watchful and wary as ever. Sharing her experience with Vanda was as good as putting it in the cards in the window outside the Post Office. Arnie was taking his revenge. And already Daniel sensed that the town would swiftly polarise – those who believed her story and the others who would surely trust him? He felt an air of desperation.

It was all conspiring against him. More. What chance would there be of having custody of Holly with all this hanging over him? Mistaken diagnoses and now this.

He felt terribly tired and depressed. His life was unravelling in front of his eyes and he was powerless to stop it.

The policeman had finished his stint of night duty and was vigorously digging the garden, working manure into it with real gusto. Guy was watching him from the shelter of the rim of trees. With Brian working as lookout he couldn't enter today but he'd be back again and again. One of these days the house would be empty again. And then...

He smiled. Just knowing the power he held over them was enough.

Brian stopped digging for a moment, straightened up and looked around. The neighbouring gardens were empty. Everyone was out at work. He scanned the field which appeared empty. He stood very still for a long moment, staring out towards the lake and wondered. Was he imagining a movement in the trees or was it the wind, teasing him by lifting branches and dropping them again, whispering tunes in the rustling leaves? He wasn't sure but now when he resumed his digging he had a cold feeling down the back of his neck and knew that it was from that line of dark trees that eyes had observed him. Not only him but Claudine and Bethan too.

Wednesday, 10th May – evening

Distracted by all the events of the past weekend and work, Daniel had almost forgotten about his date with 'M'. The pub he'd chosen was in Stone, a market town five miles away: far enough to trust he would not be recognised. It was an old-fashioned place, near the canal. He'd been there a couple of times with Elaine, in their early, settling years in Staffordshire, in happier days, when they had still been convinced this would be their joint and permanent home. She'd grumbled, he remembered, at the house white wine, making a face as though she was being given vinegar.

He settled himself with a pint of beer, in a corner seat, facing the door. He could spot the mysterious woman the moment she walked in and decide. He had a great belief in physical attraction forming relationships.

He sneaked a surreptitious glance at his wristwatch. Ten minutes past eight. She was late.

Maybe she wouldn't come at all. It was perfectly possible that she'd lost her chirpy confidence and was going to stand him up.

What humiliation – to be stood up on an Internet first date at the age of forty.

This was worse than his real first date – at the age of sixteen with a classmate he'd always fancied. Like many first dates it had been excruciatingly awful, the pair of them blushing and tongue-tied.

Fortunately, he mused, subsequent dates had been worlds better.

The door opened and a woman walked in, glancing around as she did so. She was wearing a shiny black Mac with the collar pulled up and had long, shining, straight brown hair.

So far so good.

The woman scanned the bar and he had an impression of a lot of black make-up around the eyes, red lips and a certain vague familiarity that he had met this woman before.

Her eyes reached him. She smiled. He drew in a deep breath. Oh no. This couldn't be happening. Not on top of all the other sheer awfulness. It was a mirage. 'Hello, Daniel,' she said, walked straight up to him and sat down in the seat opposite.

It was Marie Westbrook, his own practice nurse, and he felt as acutely embarrassed as on that very first dreadful date.

'I did wonder,' she gave a self-conscious smile, 'if it would be you and then I thought, no, it couldn't be. Too much of a coincidence.'

He stiffened and wondered how he could get out of this one.

She looked very different from when she was at work. For a start her hair was always pinned up in a sort of plastic bulldog clip thing. She wore no make-up. And her clothes. At work she wore the regulation navy blue dress and sensible shoes. But as she slipped her coat off he caught a glimpse of a generous cleavage, a short leather skirt, stiletto shoes and a great deal of jewellery. She flashed her teeth at him and he tried to focus above her breasts, onto the swinging silver earrings.

'Well,' she said archly, 'aren't you going to buy me a drink?'

He gaped at her.

She crossed her legs, deliberately revealing a shapely thigh.

'Well,' she said, 'I'm here now. We may as well make the most of it. No point just going home.'

There was something desperately brittle in her voice and manner. Daniel's embarrassment was replaced by sympathy.

'You're right,' he said. 'What can I get you?'

'Red wine,' she said, 'please.'

He was glad to escape to the bar and make his plans. What the hell was he going to do now? He didn't want to go out with the practice nurse. It could only lead to further difficulties. And yet. He turned to smile at her from the bar. There was nothing wrong with her. She was in her early thirties, more than passingly attractive.

The truth hit him like a thunderbolt. He simply didn't fancy her. Why not? Because he fancied Claudine. And as he had decided when he had parked himself facing the pub door, physical attraction is all.

Therefore the evening would be a waste of time, as would any subsequent dates with anyone except…

The barman was waiting.

'Pint of Titanic and a red wine.'

'Large or small.'

'Small,' he said then felt instantly guilty. 'No, make it a large.' The barman grinned at him.

Daniel fished out some money and reflected. It would just about finish his reputation: divorced, wrong diagnosis, allegations of sexual harassment in the surgery, failing to find out what was wrong with the Struel child, having an affair with the practice nurse and the fixation in Brian Anderton's mind that he was trying to bonk his wife. It was hard to believe that a few short weeks ago he had felt practically unassailable.

'Six pound thirty, please.'

He handed over the money and weaved through the tables back to his seat.

'Thanks,' Marie said and flashed another smile at him.

He didn't know where to start. Chat up and small talk never had been his strong point.

Luckily she was not tongue-tied. 'I know you're divorced, Dan,' she said.

'And you?'

'I'm not *actually* divorced. Separated. In fact Mark and I have been apart for years but we've never quite got around to severing the knot.'

'Children?' he managed.

'No. We started falling apart within months of being married. It would have been folly to have started a family. I was only twenty-nine when we split up. Lots of women aren't even married by then – let alone have children. I sort of hoped that I could make a fresh start but…' She took a long draught of the wine, 'the years start slipping by.'

'Have you had many relationships?'

She sighed. 'A few. But it's quite startling how… Oh I don't know. It's hard finding someone who's the right age, lives within ninety miles, has the same sort of aspirations, interests, intelligence even. I went out with the man of my dreams for about eight months but he turned out to be married, busily cheating on his wife. I dropped *him* like a hot coal.' She laughed. 'He's still got the nerve to ring me from time to time. To see if I'm all right.' She made a face.

'And are you – all right, I mean?'

'Yeah,' she said casually. 'I miss having a partner and I wouldn't like to think I'll never have children, but all things considered it's better than being unhappily married. What about you?'

'Nothing really since Elaine blew out of my life.'

'No dates?' she asked incredulously.

He was thinking about Claudine as he shook his head.

The evening passed strangely. He felt unreal every time he looked at her face and remembered who she was.

She offered to buy him a drink and it would have seemed churlish to refuse. He had a half pint, thinking about the drive home. A drink-driving offence on top of everything else would finish him. She said she lived within walking distance and returned with his half and another large red wine.

As soon as he could he stood up, wondering if he could get out of driving her home and refusing a coffee.

In the end he decided not to offer her a lift. He had no wish to prolong the evening. The feeling of relief when he finally reached his car made him practically euphoric. He didn't relish facing her at work tomorrow.

Chapter Twelve

Daniel spent the rest of the week studiously avoiding any of the public areas in the surgery: the kitchen, the coffee room, even the reception area. Instead he stuck to his consulting room like glue, hoping he wouldn't bump into Marie. He was relatively successful at it and trusted that they could continue to work together without embarrassment. He heard nothing about either of the coroner's cases or from Chelsea Emmanuel. And so he was in a limbo which might last a long time. The wheels of coroner's courts grind as slowly as police investigations and are equally as thorough. Though all was quiet there would be a frenzy of police activity. This then was the calm before the storm. He knew he would face criticism over Maud Allen's death. The suggestion of the wrong diagnosis and his resultant prescribing had led to her suicide. What he didn't know at that time was that there was another factor.

And as for the fiasco over Anna-Louise's death he couldn't even begin to guess what his contribution might have been. It seemed that there had been no pathology – no hidden sinister illness. But there might have been pathology working around her which he had failed to act on.

The Medical Defence Union also kept ominously quiet about Chelsea Emmanuel's clumsy allegation. He just knew their lawyers would spend some time chewing over the salacious details before any action was taken.

On the Friday evening he was delighted to receive a friendly phone call from Claudine. 'Daniel,' she said. 'I am so sorry I haven't been in touch. We have all been very busy. How is Holly?'

'She's fine,' he said, enjoying listening to her voice with its slight accent so unmistakably French.

'I felt I must speak to you,' she continued, 'to tell you that I don't believe for a moment any of the things they are saying about you in the town, that you missed finding something wrong with little Anna-Louise. The Struel family are malicious. I am sure there is an explanation and that you are not to blame for the child's sad death.' Without realising that she was, in a way, talking about the same subject, she moved on. 'And I was so sad when I heard about Mrs Allen. I can't understand why she did it. She was such a – survivor. Like my grandmother, she was a brave woman and I am sad that she died like that. Oh, Daniel,' she said, 'and that horrible girl spreading rumours about you. It is awful. Such a small, nice town and so much happens here. I just can't understand it that you of all people are having such a bad time. This is when you need your friends most.'

He couldn't but agree.

'I don't know what has happened to this town,' she said sadly. 'When I came here I was so happy to be away from Paris, here in England in such a pretty place, but it has changed. It was not like this when we first came here. Now…'

'You haven't had any more…' he didn't quite know how to put it, 'trouble, have you?'

'No, but Brian is so suspicious. He imagines the person who

stole my lingerie from the washing line is now getting into our house and stealing things from my drawers. Not just lingerie but jewellery. Some earrings that I must have lost. ' There was a note of sadness in her voice.

Daniel was appalled. 'And what do you think?'

'Oh, Daniel, I don't know.' She sounded weary. 'I don't know what to think any more. Brian is…I don't know, different. Changed. Something is wrong with him, in his mind, I think. He is very strange sometimes. He imagines things. Even…' She hesitated, 'about you. You know? He has changed the locks and is fitting extra bolts to the doors. He has told me to keep the doors bolted when I am inside. He's very angry, Daniel, and very suspicious of everyone.'

'You're not in any…'

They both knew what he meant.

'No. No – of course not. He wouldn't hurt *me.*' Her emphasis on the last word was subtle but unmistakable. And they both knew what she meant by it.

Privately Daniel wanted to tell her to be careful, to come to him if she felt threatened but he could say none of it. He fell silent and waited for her to suggest an outing with Holly and Bethan over the weekend but she didn't. He took the hint and after a few more pleasantries she said goodbye.

He hung up.

So now he had no one. 'M' had turned out to be his practice nurse and he wasn't starting a relationship with *her*, and the friendship with Claudine which had promised so much had come to an abrupt halt because her bloody policeman husband was suspicious of his motives.

Daniel's face twisted. Maybe Brian wasn't so deluded – merely perceptive.

* * *

He and Holly spent most of Saturday cycling along the disused railway which ran between Stafford and Newport. It had been made into a gravelled flat track, popular with joggers, dog walkers and cyclists with a pub halfway along. They stopped and drank a J2O, from the bottle, with a straw, in the garden, sitting at one of the wooden tables underneath a Racing Green umbrella. As usual he had had to pay the penalty of kitting Holly out with the right clothes, in this case padded cycling shorts, but as they pedalled along the track he forgot about his multiple problems and simply enjoyed the warm sunshine and Holly's chatter.

They cooked Sunday lunch together and Holly grew quiet towards the end of the afternoon. When four o'clock came she suddenly put her arms around him and burst into tears. 'I don't want to go back to Birmingham,' she sobbed. 'I want to stay here with you. Please let me. I want to live here and see Bethan and have a pony and stay in my bedroom. Why can't I?'

He felt the familiar pain in his heart. This was so hard. He could almost have joined in her tears. Instead he sat her on his lap. 'Now listen, pigeon,' he said. 'Life here isn't always such a bowl of roses as you think. We wouldn't have fun every day, having little adventures and doing things together. I wouldn't be buying you clothes every time I saw you. I have to go to work, like Mummy does.'

'I know that,' she said, almost angrily, 'but even doing boring things with you like tidying out my bedroom and cooking, seems like fun.' The tears were rolling down her cheeks. 'I want to stay with you, Daddy. Please let me. Don't send me away.'

He stroked her hair, staring at the kitchen wall. *Should he have tried harder with Elaine?*

Right on cue he heard the 4x4 roar up the quiet street.

Monday, 15th May

This was to be the day of the calm before the storm, the false promise of peace, of settlement and serenity.

Sammy Schultz met him in the car park. 'I've some news for you,' he said. He glanced around at the trickle of patients parking and entering the surgery. 'Let's go into my office,' he suggested. 'We can't talk out here, there's no privacy.'

Daniel knew that it would be something about Chelsea Emmanuel and followed his partner again feeling like a boy trailing the headmaster to his office after a misdemeanour. Sammy closed the door behind them then turned to face him. 'Sit down, Daniel,' he said. His face was grave.

'I've spoken to Chelsea Emmanuel,' he began.

Daniel waited with baited breath. He noticed that Sammy was not meeting his eyes.

He waited.

'I explained to her what the usual procedure was in cases like this,' he said, 'what the repercussions would be, that she'd be questioned, that your career was on the line.'

The silence was thick enough to be cut with a knife.

'I don't think she'd thought,' Sammy continued, 'beyond the letter. 'When she did she withdrew the allegation.'

Daniel's first emotion was one of relief. Quickly followed by anger. Pure, furious, white hot anger.

'They were lies anyway,' he managed.

Sammy wafted a piece of paper in front of him.

'The result is that Chelsea Emmanuel has written another letter to say that she was mistaken, that she supposes it was your job to examine her and that she's sorry if she's caused any trouble.'

Daniel gritted his teeth. Cause trouble? How dare she, the little tart, make those allegations, put him through hell for a week, endanger his reputation. How bloody dare she? He wanted to run round to her grotty little couple of rooms and shake her until her eyeballs fell out.

Sammy was watching him anxiously. 'Dan,' he said.

'The little b—,' Daniel burst out, his anger patently obvious to his concerned friend. 'How dare she.'

'If you want my advice,' Sammy said cautiously, 'you'll put the whole thing behind you. Forget about it, Dan. No harm's done.'

'No harm,' Daniel said. 'No harm?'

Sammy put his hand on Dan's shoulder. 'Drop it,' he said. 'No good will come if you pursue this matter. More people will get to hear about it. The gossip'll continue. People have short memories.'

Daniel said nothing for a minute or two then he faced his partner. 'Tell me,' he said, 'in the States, if this situation happened, what would the doctor do?'

Sammy looked uncomfortable. 'Hard to say,' he said.

'Stop bullshitting, Sam. What would they be likely to do?'

'They might talk to a lawyer,' he said reluctantly, 'try and get some recompense for the allegations. False allegations,' he substituted quickly.

'Yeah. I thought so,' Daniel said.

'But listen. A word of the most friendly advice,' Sammy said. 'This isn't New York or Chicago or some other huge American city. This is a real small town in Middle England. It's a place where gossip spreads like a forest fire in Australia. Hot and quick. Please, Dan,' he pleaded, 'don't make the biggest mistake of your life.'

'I'll tell you what I will do,' Daniel said. 'I'll sleep on it. Have a think. As soon as I've decided I'll let you know. That's as good as I can give you.'

He was conscious, as he left the room, that he was leaving behind one very apprehensive man.

General practice, he reflected, as he walked along the corridor towards his own consulting room, was supposed to be undramatic. The calm end of medicine. No crash calls or open-heart surgery. No dramas, collapses, heart attacks or such like. He stomped along angrily. It didn't help meeting Marie in the corridor with a come-to-bed-smile. 'Morning, Doctor,' she said.

His reply was, he reflected later, an impolite, uncivilised grunt.

Shit, he thought, as he slammed the door behind him.

He was losing it.

Brian was peering out of the kitchen window. 'OK, you bastard,' he muttered, 'come here. Just come here. I'm ready for you.' He clicked the cigarette lighter once, twice, three times, held the flame up to the window. 'See here,' he shouted. 'Have you got the guts?' He scanned the line of trees. 'No. I thought not. You haven't got the balls. So leave my wife…'

'Brian. What on earth are you doing?'

He whipped around. 'Protecting you,' he snarled.

She touched his shoulder timidly. 'But I don't need protecting.'

'You do, Claudine, you do.' His hug was too tight. She wriggled away from him.

He eyed her suspiciously. 'By the way, Claudine…' She knew that tone and was on her guard. 'Who were you speaking to on the phone on Friday night when I got back?'

'Daniel,' she said. It was useless to lie. 'I wanted him to know that we are behind him, that we believe in him. Terrible rumours are circulating.'

'And why?' he demanded. 'He's been touching up a fourteen-year-old.'

'That is a lie.'

'Is it? Well – the rumour that's circulating the town is that he'll be suspended.'

'No.' She couldn't hide her upset. 'Surely you can see that the girl is lying. Look at her. She's a little slut.'

'Why are you so bothered? What's he to you?'

She felt her face flush.

Lucy Satchel was thawing. She brought him a coffee when she'd finished surgery and gave him one of her wide, open smiles. 'I can't tell you how relieved I was that the girl's withdrawn her allegations. They were malicious,' she said firmly, 'but they could have caused untold harm.'

Daniel was glad of the olive branch. 'Well – thanks,' he said.

But it was difficult to have any extended conversation in the surgery. There was a knock on the door and Christine popped her head round. 'There's an extra asking to see you.

Cora Moseby. Never makes an appointment,' she grumbled.

'OK, I'll see her,' she said.

Lucy waited until the door had closed behind the receptionist. 'Now there's a woman with a problem,' she said.

Daniel recalled the woman who had turned up before, again without an appointment. 'Oh?'

'She's had a trauma in the past. Won't go into details but she's still very disturbed by it. She's had some psychotherapy but still suffers from nightmares. I'm trying to keep her off medication but…' She held her hands up in a gesture of defeat. 'One of these days I'm going to give in to her and prescribe something. She has trouble sleeping. I don't know much more about her other than that she's divorced with a couple of kids. I don't think she ever sees them. From what she says they think she's a nut and her ex-husband doesn't seem very supportive. I feel sorry for her. She's another born victim. Oh well.' She gave another of her rare smiles. 'Off I go.'

It was around lunchtime, two days later, as Daniel was grilling some cheese on toast a favourite midday standby of his – that his telephone rang. He picked it up, returning to the grill, hoping and praying that it wouldn't be his mother. He wanted a peaceful lunchtime and she was capable of spoiling it only too easily.

His wish was answered. It wasn't his mother but an unfamiliar, haughty voice. 'Doctor Gregory?'

'Ye-es?' He was casting around his memory for a clue. A hospital colleague, patient?

'My name is Richard Snape,' the voice said. 'I'm a solicitor acting for the late Mrs Allen. I wonder, could I trouble you to call in to our offices on the High Street at some point?'

Daniel was bemused. What on earth would Mrs Allen's solicitor want with him?

'Yes. Yes – of course.'

'When would suit?' the polite voice asked.

'I have a half-day tomorrow.'

'Would two-thirty be all right then?'

'Yes. Fine.'

Richard Snape gave him the address of his office and Daniel hung up.

He didn't have much time to reflect what Maud Allen could possibly have to say to him from beyond the grave. Could it be a letter? An explanation, an accusation? Something exonerating him from her suicide? Or a reproach? The phone call left him with a very uneasy feeling. He had an instinct that trouble was brewing from some other quarter now. Yes, Chelsea Emmanuel had withdrawn her allegation so the worry had been defused. But not the anger. He had known all along that she was making it up. It was others who would have continued to doubt him. But this was different. It wasn't like his bodged diagnosis on Maud Allen and its tragic consequences. He couldn't shake off his responsibility in that. He'd got it wrong and she had died believing he was right. She had trusted him – misguidedly as it had turned out.

His afternoon was spoilt by a visit from the police who seemed to be trying to corner him into making a statement about Anna-Louise. Not Brian Anderton but a CID colleague from Stafford who had nasty, suspicious eyes that darted around the room as though he was searching for clues.

'So, Doctor,' he said, 'tell me about Vanda Struel.'

It was no good using the excuse of confidentiality. The

detective's suspicions grew when Daniel tried to fob him off with that. 'Look,' he finally said. 'I never saw Vanda Struel harm her child. I wondered why it was that Anna-Louise seemed to have such a succession of consultations. Anna-Louise had numerous tests and we didn't find anything wrong. She always recovered in hospital.' Even as he spoke the words he was recalling the descriptions of Munchausen by proxy cases. It fitted the bill too neatly.

He felt that the detective would never be able to prove anything.

Daniel arrived at the solicitor's a little late. He'd had a last minute call which had taken longer than he had anticipated. He started apologising but the solicitor, who was a youthful, balding man, seemed impatient to move on. 'That's all right, Doctor Gregory,' he said, leading him into a small office lined with shelves groaning under thick files. Snape gestured to a chair. 'Do sit down,' he said.

'Now then.'

He opened a file and steepled his fingers together. Cleared his throat. 'We acted for the late Maud Allen,' he said pompously while Daniel waited for the familiar twinge of guilt.

'My client,' the solicitor continued smoothly, 'made a new will a few weeks before she umm…' He seemed embarrassed. 'She left her estate to her niece apart from the cottage.' He waited for maximum effect. 'The cottage, Doctor Gregory, has been left to you.'

'What?'

'Applegate Cottage,' the solicitor eyed him over his rimless glasses, 'together with the acre of land which adjoins it.' He smiled comfortably. 'The paddock.'

Daniel sat back in his chair. He should have still felt guilty. He had played a part, unconscious and accidental, but still a part, in Mrs Allen's death. Yet the guilt was overshadowed by happiness. The paddock could easily house a pony for Holly. She would come and live with him now. Not in the centre of Birmingham. He could move in, sell The Yellow House. He would have spare money, for holidays, for school fees, for fun. He visualised the pretty, ancient place then looked up to see the solicitor watching him carefully.

'I had no idea,' he managed, hoping the solicitor hadn't read his pleasure at the news. 'She didn't tell me. Not anything.'

'I feel I should warn you,' the solicitor added, 'that it is possible that Mrs Allen's niece might just contest the will.'

Daniel felt startled. 'What?' It was as though someone had offered him a bag of sweets only to snatch them away before he had had the chance to taste one.

'The trouble, is,' the solicitor said, 'that...umm...'

Spit it out. Accuse me.

'Well,' the solicitor said. 'Mrs Allen believed she was terminally ill.'

He was avoiding even looking at his client.

'And of course, this belief led, we would imagine…'

Oh they were so careful, these legal people.

'…to her suicide.'

There were a few more formalities, papers to sign, and the solicitor squared up the papers and promised to be in touch while Daniel tried to rid himself of the conviction that the solicitor was unsympathetic. Finally he left and drove slowly back to Eccleston, almost screeching to a halt when he saw Guy Malkin and Vanda Struel walking, arm in arm, down the street. He couldn't believe it. Yet there they were. Brazen and comfortable with each other. He could even have sworn that Guy met his eyes and gave him a malicious, triumphant smile.

He garaged the car, reflecting. Why is it that odd and dangerous people seem to hook up with each other when their relationship seems guaranteed to bring out the worst in them?

Chapter Thirteen

Friday, 19th May

And then the storm broke, flashing and crashing around his ears, raging through day and night.

It began in a suitably spectacular way, with a hammering on his door early on Friday morning.

His initial thought, just before he swam into consciousness, was very like his panic reaction as a newly qualified houseman. Someone was in trouble. A medical crisis. Heart attack. Haemorrhage. A stroke. A major incident.

It was none of these but an even worse nightmare.

When he opened the door his mother stood there.

'Don't look so thrilled, Daniel,' she said dryly. 'An expression of untainted joy would have done nicely but then…' She sighed and stepped forwards.

He was speechless as she pecked his cheek.

'They do say,' she said, marching around him, 'that if Mohammed won't go to the mountain then the mountain must go to Mohammed. So here I am, Daniel dear.'

He picked up the *large* suitcase with a feeling of panic.

What is it about mothers?

His second rogue thought, which caused a surreptitious smirk, even through his dismay, was that his mother truly did resemble a mountain.

She had always been a big woman, a size sixteen, with an ample bosom which projected far forward, seeming to defy the laws of gravity – and age. There was not the hint of a sag about his mother.

She always dressed as though for a bridge party, in tweed suits, summer and winter alike, the only concession being that in summer she wore a silk blouse while in winter a sweater completed the ensemble.

Wondering who, in Eccleston, had witnessed the arrival of *his mother* he shot a glance up and down the road, grateful that at this time of the morning it was deserted apart from Guy Malkin who was either on his way to work at the Co-op or lurking with intent. He looked furtive enough to be doing the latter. Daniel heaved a great big sigh and closed the door behind them, placing the suitcase at the bottom of the stairs and following his mother into the kitchen where she was already filling the kettle.

His mother was addicted to Earl Grey tea and drank gallons of the stuff. What good health she confessed to she attributed to Earl Grey – himself. Daniel didn't mind how much of the wretched stuff she drank. His only objection was that without even asking him what he would like to drink she handed him a mug of the offending tea – which he couldn't stand. He thought it tasted of dust. Ancient dust.

She sat down at the kitchen table, looking around her with a critical eye. He braced himself for the inevitable criticism of the décor, the lack of cleanliness, the untidiness. Anything. Any perceived shortcoming in his home would justify her moving in but she sipped her tea innocently enough then turned her eyes towards him without speaking.

It was left to Daniel to open up the conversation. 'You haven't driven all the way down here, surely. Not just to…'

His voice trailed away as her face tightened. 'Of course I have, Daniel,' she said severely. 'As I said. If you won't come and visit me, well then. It's up to me, isn't it? Or I shall lose contact with my one and only grandchild.'

Cognitive Behavioural Therapy.

It was the new answer. The new buzz word. The current way forward in medical circles. Daniel drank his tea very slowly and wondered whether he dared. It was taking quite a risk.

He made his decision. 'Why is it, Mother,' he said abruptly, 'that whenever I see you or talk to you I instantly feel guilty?'

Unlike a patient his mother wasn't in the least bit fazed. 'Perhaps it's because of the appalling way you treat me, Daniel,' she said.

He might have known it wouldn't work with her.

He sighed again, drank the tea, and felt deflated.

'I take it Holly *is* coming in the morning?'

He nodded.

'So what plans *did* you have for the weekend?'

He didn't like her use of the past tense. The truth was that he hadn't made any plans. He *had* sort of hoped that Claudine would suggest something – or that something exciting would occur to him – or that the local paper would suggest some event or special entertainment they could attend, but nothing had come up. In fact the weekend stretched ahead a little bleakly. He could be honest and say that to constantly plan some little treat, weekend after weekend, was hard work. But that would imply boredom with his own daughter.

And yet he *knew* how very unnatural it was, that all their time together, this father and daughter, who loved each other so much, should be spent as 'treats'. It left little time for simply *being* together, to become familiar with each other without the sparkle of a treat. It was, in a way, a strain, an effort. Too much effort when all that he wanted was normality.

An ordinary existence with his daughter.

The worst thing was that buried deep he knew how he could achieve it. Weighted by the promise of a pony and her newfound friend, Bethan, Holly would elect to live with him. And if her daughter really insisted, Elaine, with her new husband, would surely agree. Holly was a persistent little thing and once she had set her mind on something she was practically impossible to divert.

He allowed his mind to drift on. He and Claudine, doing all sorts of family activities, almost like husband and wife.

His mother was watching him suspiciously. 'I hadn't really made any definite plans,' he said.

Brian and Claudine were facing each other in the kitchen over breakfast. He was making a pretence of reading his paper but really he was watching his wife intently out of the corner of his eye. He had opened the conversation innocently enough, with a casual question. No point in arousing her suspicions too early. Best not to put her on her guard.

'Did those earrings ever turn up?'

Claudine frowned. 'No,' she said crossly. 'They didn't. I can't think where they can have got to. I have looked everywhere.'

Brian lowered his paper so he could read her face better. 'And what about the underwear?'

She gave a typical Gallic shrug: shoulders raised simultaneously with a pursing of the lips. 'Those neither,' she said. 'I don't know what happens in this house sometimes.' She giggled, walked behind her husband and put her hands on his shoulders, massaging them gently. 'It swallows them up.'

'You might try bolting the front door and leaving through the back.' But he was aware that he was speaking without conviction. He wasn't sure he believed in this phantom intruder who left no evidence, simply slipped into the house, took personal items of his wife's and slipped out again. In fact the more he thought about it he could thread it all together. Daniel Gregory and his wife. His wife was having an affair and sometimes she left belongings at his house – earrings, the odd pair of knickers, trophies he could gloat over after she had gone. Claudine was planning to leave him. She was trying to pluck up courage to break the news. The two little girls had been deliberately introduced to each other to make Claudine's flight easier. Did they think he was a fool? That he didn't realise? Brian Anderton smiled. Well – they would learn one day. It might take weeks or even months but he would confront them with his knowledge of their guilt.

Claudine flashed him one of her wide, innocent smiles unaware that her husband was deep in his own dark thoughts.

Don't fall for this, Brian. She's playing you along. Don't trust her. She's laughing at you. Look at her. She's laughing at you. Look at her eyes, twinkling with fun achieved at your expense. Don't let her make a fool of you.

He wished he could laugh with her as he used to in the old days. He sat, wooden, at the breakfast table, staring ahead of him, his shoulders tense. Claudine finally got the message. She stopped rubbing his shoulders and flopped into the chair opposite. 'Hey, serious,' she teased.

His resentment flared into anger. He scowled at her.

'Brian?' she asked uncertainly.

He wanted so much to trip her up.

Expose her.

'If someone's stealing your things,' he said slowly, leaning forward into his folded arms, 'at first they simply took them from the washing line. Your underwear. But… Well – let's just say it's escalated. How do you think he could have *found* your earrings or the underwear?'

'You're imagining it,' she said, pouting. 'You're just trying to scare me. Frighten me. I *must* have made a mistake. Been careless, mislaid them. There is no other explanation.'

He'd had enough. 'What about the key you leave in the most obvious place in the world?'

She grew panicky then. 'You think he's been *inside*?'

Slowly he nodded. 'I do, Claudine,' he said.

'But surely nobody would dare,' she said uncertainly. 'You are the policeman here, Brian.' She reached and stroked the back of his hand. 'Please say it isn't true, that you're making it up. It can't be. This is a peaceful town. Law abiding. Someone would have seen a person getting into the house.'

'Perhaps someone did,' he said. 'I shall be making enquiries.'

'But, Brian,' she said nervously, her eyes wide. 'I'm here for most of the time.'

'Exactly.' She would have liked to ignore the menacing tone in his voice but it was impossible. She stood up, retied her apron around her waist and stood in front of him. 'I think you're just trying to scare me,' she said. 'I don't think *anyone* is watching this house, stalking us and stealing things. I think, Brian, that because you are a policeman, you are suspicious and see a criminal around every corner, behind every tree.' She bent to empty the dishwasher and Brian felt a hot flame of fury shoot through him. If she'd seen what he'd seen, watched terror grow in a woman's eyes, seen fear paralyse her until she could no longer breathe. If she'd seen a woman terrorised until she was no longer able to leave her home, do her job, care for her family. If she'd seen the evil that men can do without laying a finger on the person then she would be frightened too. She wouldn't mock him then, but appeal to him to help her.

But maybe she liked it. Perhaps she wasn't a reluctant victim but a willing participant. There was always another side to every story.

He was searching for a sign – any sign that she was being unfaithful to him. Had she been making up to the Doctor? What if…? The little voices were insistent. She was alone in the day, when Bethan had gone to school. Gregory had free time in the day too. The surgery was closed in the afternoon. Plenty of opportunity.

His fingers closed around the cigarette lighter and he fumbled with the flint. One click, two clicks and it fired. He watched the flame flicker. Flames could grow into…He squeezed his eyes shut but he could still hear the screaming, see the human torch, smell the burning flesh.

He knew exactly how it had all started. She liked to flirt, to tease, to plant little seeds in his brain. Well – maybe she had better take care. People could be pushed too far.

* * *

'Please, Constable, sir, Sergeant. Help me. Surely the law protects?'

His face was sneering. The law protect?

The law gives jobs to people, learns how to argue that black is white, mistrusts those it should lean on and always, always, makes excuses, for the blacks, the Asians, the drug pushers, the single parents… The list goes on and on.

'Brian?'

And she had no idea.

He stared at her, flung his paper down onto the table, knocking over the milk jug, and left without an apology, muttering something about going to work and slamming the kitchen door behind him.

Seconds later Bethan peered round. 'Daddy's in a bad mood,' she commented cheerfully.

Brian stopped off to buy some cigarettes. He didn't really like smoking and Claudine forbade it in the house but today he badly needed to rebel. He wanted to do something. Anything of which Claudine would disapprove. And so he bought the cigarettes, stuck one in his mouth and lit it with the lighter. Guy Malkin was strolling down the street and grinned at him. 'Didn't know you smoked, Constable Anderton. Bad for your health, you know.'

'I don't normally,' Brian said through clenched teeth and was annoyed with himself for feeling so stupid.

He puffed on the cigarette with a feeling of wonderfully sinful rebellion. He strode up the High Street, passed Francesco's hairdressing and beauty, and the library and the millennium clock. When he reached the mini roundabout he crossed it and strode towards the police station.

It was his belief that cigarettes had only caught on because they were banned. It was the fourteen-year-olds behind the sheds at school who started and then found themselves unable to stop. By the time Brian Anderton was standing in the police station car park he was completely sick of the foul taste in his mouth. He dropped the end, stubbed it out with his foot and reached into his pocket for a peppermint. As he stood and looked around him he felt his dislike grow for the new supermarket they were building, almost wrapping itself around the tiny police station as though to assert its superior size.

He heaved a great big sigh and walked inside. Time to face another day shift.

Not only did Daniel have to run the gauntlet of his mother cooking an inadequate lunch of spaghetti on toast but lunchtime brought another unwelcome telephone call from Richard Snape. Snape caught him at home just as his mother was stubbornly rinsing all the dishes before putting them in the dishwasher. A pointless exercise in his view. The habit infuriated him because he could have had the kitchen tidied up by now and be sitting in front of the computer screen renewing the search for the woman of his dreams. Someone who *wasn't* married and didn't bloody well work for him so could waylay him in the corridor.

He simply *couldn't* have a relationship with his practice nurse. Romance in the surgery might work in the soaps but real life was another matter altogether. Besides – the truth was that he didn't fancy Marie Westbrook one little bit. He found her just a little bit intrusive. His tastes led in another direction completely. A direction he was just beginning to sense could lead to dangerous waters. No – he was much safer surfing the net for another pretty fish.

'Doctor Gregory, it's Richard Snape here,' the solicitor said in a suspiciously hearty tone. 'Do you have a moment for a very brief word?'

Why is it that any contact with a solicitor fills you with foreboding? Daniel gritted his teeth.

'Certainly.'

'I did mention to you, I believe, that Mrs Allen,' he experimented with a tentative joke, 'your benefactress, to put it in Dickensian terms,' a little snigger, 'had a niece.'

Daniel's heart sank. He knew what was coming next.

And he was right.

'I believe I did also mention the fact that she *may* decide to contest the will.' Sly Snape waited for Daniel to confirm.

'Yes,' he said tersely. He could almost feel the jaws of the trap snap shut behind him.

Snape continued. 'Unfortunately she has taken this business one step further. She is claiming some measure of coercion in the redrafting of her aunt's will. Particularly in the light of the very *peculiar* circumstances surrounding her aunt's very tragic death.'

Thank you, Lord. You giveth and you taketh away.

Daniel could feel the cottage and more importantly his dream slip-sliding away from him. He felt panicked into impotent protestation. 'She can't think that I *engineered…*' His voice faded. 'I shall take legal…' He reminded himself he was speaking to legal advice.

'There will be no need for that.' He was like a nanny consoling a child with a grazed knee. 'I'm sure it'll come to nothing,' the solicitor said, 'but I felt you would want to know.'

'Yes,' Daniel said flatly, the wind taken right out of his sails. 'Yes. Yes, of course.'

The solicitor spoke again. 'You won't, of course, need to answer these allegations. I thought I would draft a reply and we could revise the text together. How would that be?'

'Fine. Just fine.'

So his dreams of the pretty little cottage, My Little Pony and a permanent existence with his own daughter, Claudine popping in and out, faded and were replaced by yet more finger-pointing.

Daniel felt a quick surge of resentment. When he had first joined the practice in Eccleston, The Yellow House had seemed the obvious choice for the GP of the town. In fact three or four doctors had lived there before, ever since it had first been built more than two hundred years ago. But the truth was that he was sick of stepping out of the front door straight into a consultation room because whoever was passing was invariably one of his patients and they always wanted to ask him something. He had no privacy. At first it had been a novelty. He had felt part of the town, a real country GP. But now it was a drag. The thought of the isolated, lovely cottage, with its own field, waiting for a little bay pony, had been more than simply a means to secure his daughter; it had been an escape from the intrusion of his patients and now the chance that had been dangled in front of his eyes was under threat. He could not bear to see it slip away.

His mother was watching him like a hawk. 'Everything all right, Daniel dear?' Her yellowed teeth seemed wolfish and predatory.

'Fine.'

* * *

Guy had watched the policeman walking down the street, puffing amateurishly on a cigarette like a sixteen-year-old, trying to look nonchalant. His eyes followed him all the way down, past the jeweller's and the chocolate shop right up until he crossed the road. Then he turned the other way.

An hour and a half later, Claudine, the little basket over her arm, tripped down the road.

But this time Claudine had done as Brian had instructed her. She had bolted the front door and left through the back door, locking the mortise and tenon lock and pocketing the new key so his own key was useless. He inserted it, felt the resistance and cursed, feeling a sudden rage against her. Didn't she know what he took he took out of love, to evoke her, conjure her up? He needed her.

Didn't she know that if he had nothing new of hers she might fade?

At the back of his mind was fear.

He was on to him.

The policeman was on to him.

So when he was on the late shift at the Co-op and Anderton presented himself at the till his hand shook. 'What can I get you?'

'A bottle of whisky,' Anderton muttered.

Guy Malkin took it down from the shelf and handed it over.

The policeman snatched it from him, gave him a twenty-pound note, didn't even bother to check the change and disappeared through the door. Even then Guy Malkin was shaking.

Chapter Fourteen

He was sitting in the surgery with his head in his hands. He didn't want to go home to an evening spent with his mother. Minutes passed before he was aware that someone else was in the room with him. He didn't look up and the next moment he felt fingers running through his hair.

'Poor Danny,' she said softly. 'Poor little Danny. Something's upset you, hasn't it?' She bent and kissed the top of his head, straddled her hands along his shoulders, massaging them gently. 'Do you want to talk about it?'

He felt as though he was in a trap, tried to jerk his head away.

I do want to talk but not with you.

He swivelled his head up specifically to meet her eyes and deliver that negative but she mistook the movement, fluttered her eyes closed and planted her lips on his in a gesture which should have felt romantic but succeeded in feeling insincere and stagy. She tasted of chocolate and coffee and all he could think of was Claudine.

Marie Westbrook even *smelt* wrong. Of antiseptic and

penicillin and underlying that an unpleasant, cloying perfume. He managed to push her away. 'No.'

The nurse faced him with a hard look in her eyes. 'Sure, are you, Danny? You don't want the shoulder I'm offering you?'

There was something ominous in her voice so Daniel felt he was in the presence of some hostile being. He struggled to regain something of their previous friendship.

'I like you,' he said. 'But maybe I'm not ready for another relationship just yet. Things are tricky here at work.' It felt lame.

Her returning stare was cool and appraising. He feared she would say something cutting but she didn't. She simply stared for a long minute or two, her face now impassive. Then, without saying another word, she turned around, left the room and closed the door softly behind her.

Daniel broke into a cold sweat. For a reason he could not put his finger on he wished very heartily that he had never had that accidental Internet date with the nurse.

Or was it accidental? He had always thought it was too much of a coincidence. He tried to think back to the time when he had decided it was the way forward. He had found a leaflet, assumed it had either been left by one of the patients or one small piece of the hundreds of pieces of junk mail that bombarded the practice every single day it was open. It took the receptionists more than an hour each weekday morning to sift through it. Why wouldn't an Internet dating site put a leaflet in a doctors' surgery when it was well known that people in trouble flocked here, the unhappy, the recently divorced, the bereaved, the simply lonely and anyone with an entire myriad of problems which might put off a prospective partner. What better than to surf an Internet dating site?

He had a feeling he would regret this for months to come.

But Marie running her fingers through his hair had set up a hot chain reaction. She had sparked off a desire in him to speak to the French woman, to listen to her cool, accented English. The desire was so indestructible that after surgery he drove straight round to the policeman's house.

It was only as he pulled up outside the modest semi that he took time to think. What would he do if Brian or Bethan opened the door?

In fact it was Claudine who opened the door, her eyes wide open and startled when she saw who it was. At the same time she must have recognised something strange in his face because her brow wrinkled with concern almost at once.

'Daniel,' she said quickly. 'What are you doing here? Is Holly all right?'

He felt silly now. 'Yes,' he said. 'Yes. Holly's fine. Claudine.' He felt helpless now. 'Can we talk?'

'Brian's out,' she said, her hand coming up quickly, almost defensively. Her face looked anxious.

He felt even more helpless now. 'It's you I wanted to speak to,' he said.

She flashed him one of her warm smiles. 'Of course,' she said. 'What am I thinking of? How impolite. Do come in.'

She led him into the cream-coloured sitting room and sat down, opposite him.

He began awkwardly. 'You understand that anything I say to you is in confidence.'

She looked almost insulted. 'I realise that,' she said stiffly. 'You don't have to explain that.'

Then it all spilt out, the allegation of sexual misconduct, his mistaken diagnosis with Maud Allen, and finally, his failure to prevent what would probably turn out to be the murder of a small child.

She sat motionless before crossing the room and kneeling on the floor in front of him. 'Daniel,' she said, looking up into his face. 'What an awful load you carry on your shoulders and you have no one to confide in. No wife to welcome you home from work, to speak to about the daily worries. You are so alone.'

He reached out and touched her hair.

The Victorians have a fine old phrase for it. They call it, with typically sly implication: Being found in a compromising position.

Whatever *we* choose to call it, both eras would nod their heads in agreement. It was the worst possible moment for Brian Anderton to walk in. He took in the entire scene in in less than the time it took him to stride across the room. 'What the fuck's going on here?' he said when he was within punching distance of Daniel. 'What have I barged in on?'

Claudine staggered to her feet, her face sickly white. It was the first time Daniel had ever realised that she was nervous of her husband or that PC Brian Anderton was capable of flashes of violence.

'Nothing,' he said in his best surgery tone, the one he used on threatening patients, the drunks, the sick-note requesters, the cheating drug addicts on the government's pathetically misguided methadone plan.

Claudine took a step back, her eyes not leaving her

husband's face. 'Nothing's going on, Brian.' She too was struggling to recover normality.

Like Daniel, trying to take the heat out of the situation. Only neither of them realised how hot the situation really was.

'Daniel was hoping to catch you in,' she said quickly. 'He has had some very unpleasant problems with patients.'

Anderton visibly sneered, his top lip pulling away from his teeth like a horse straining in a race.

'Well he's keeping *us* pretty busy what with one thing and another. In fact I could spend my days investigating him.' The sentence might have been addressed to his wife but it was Daniel who flinched at their implication.

A policeman can always unearth something bad about you.

Anderton hadn't finished with him yet. He took one heavy, menacing step, towering over Daniel. 'Offload your failings on someone else's wife,' he warned. 'Leave mine alone and don't ever come round here if I'm not here. I've heard about your lecherous behaviour at the surgery – with minors too.' He took another threatening step forward. 'You were lucky to get away with it, *Doctor.*'

Daniel looked at Claudine who gave him the slightest of nods. For her sake he felt bound to raise some defence. 'Look, Brian,' he managed, 'I'm not like that. Those allegations have been withdrawn. Leave it.'

Anderton didn't respond.

So Daniel left the room – and the house – believing he would never go there again.

As he walked up the High Street he was greeted as usual by the 'Hello, Doctor' brigade, but for once he didn't return a single greeting. All he could think of was what he was going to say to Holly when she came for the weekend and pleaded with him to let her play with Bethan Anderton.

He had forgotten all about his mother having arrived for the weekend. He remembered just as he inserted his key in the lock. She'd left it on the latch. For a moment he panicked as the door swung open.

Then he remembered.

'Danny,' she said. 'Darling. You're home.'

It was the last straw.

Chapter Fifteen

Saturday, 20th May

Brian was sitting very still in the dimmed room, his left hand reaching down for cans of lager. The right clicked the lighter, again and again and again. Although his body was still, in his mind there was frenzied activity. He was working it all out in military style. First of all the watching. All soldiers know the importance of the initial surveillance. Now he thought about it Gregory must have been staking out his house for months, watching his wife. Next came the stealing. Perhaps the pilfering of garments from the washing line had been a message meant for Claudine, a reminder of all they were sharing. Then had come the intrusion, cleverly masquerading as an innocent friendship while he, the rat, inched closer to his wife. He thought back to the day they had 'accidentally' bumped into each other at the children's shop. Now he thought about it, it had been Claudine's idea that they should go to that particular shop to buy Bethan a pair of wellies. He would have gone into Stafford. His eyes narrowed. She must think he was *thick.* Anderton took a long swig at his beer, clicked the lighter and watched the flame with something approaching a smile. It seemed completely random – whether it fired or not. Sometimes it would light on the first click, at others it took three or even four. He became fascinated in this careless confusion when so much could depend on it. It only took one small spark from a 90p lighter to explode a bomb or start a forest fire. One small spark. That was all it took.

All the time the curtains remained tightly drawn. He enjoyed the dimness. If Claudine or Bethan so much as opened the door he simply growled at them. So they left him all day and sat together in the kitchen, Claudine aware of a feeling of sick dread.

Somewhere, in a dark, dusty little corner of her mind, hidden beneath festoons of spiders' webs and bat-shapes, she had sensed that there was a dark side to Brian, the door of which he kept tightly shut. In one way, if she was honest with herself, knowing there was this dangerous side to him had made him exciting. But occasionally when the door swung open – as when he had struck her last week, or shouted at her when she had pegged her clothes on the washing line after he had instructed her to keep them indoors – what she glimpsed in the room beyond frightened her. She took a nervous sip of coffee. When she had been a child and she had been frightened she would hide her head in her mother's lap. But her mother was miles away, still in a suburb of Paris, an unwelcome and infrequent guest at her daughter's home.

Claudine looked up. Bethan was sitting motionless, watching her.

Why, Claudine thought, did the underwear business upset him so much? What did it mean to him that it had not to her? After all, it was he who had said it was just someone with odd habits who had stolen the lingerie. A pervert, a man who derived sexual excitement from wearing women's clothes. There was no harm in it, no threat, was there? It was not really personal, was it? That was what he had said – at first. But she sensed that it had begun, at some point, to mean something else – something more frightening, something which had opened the door to his dark side and now he had moved into that area and closed the door behind him. She could no longer access the husband she had known. He had gone from her.

She wanted to speak to Daniel about it. Perhaps she could book in to see him at the surgery and tell him that Brian was beginning to frighten her. That he looked at her as though she was a stranger, spoke differently, acted strangely, had become withdrawn and hostile, that his eyes no longer rested on her with love but with suspicion and something very near dislike. She sat, still and silent, deep in her thoughts until she looked up and realised how very quiet Bethan was being. When the child did speak, even her voice was strange.

'Won't Holly be able to come here and play again?' she asked solemnly.

We all perceive events through our own eyes, from our own perspective and this was her daughter's.

Claudine reached out and touched Bethan's hand.

'I don't know,' she said uncertainly.

'But she's really nice. I liked her.' She looked keenly at her mother. 'But Daddy doesn't, does he?'

'He doesn't dislike Holly.'

'Then it's Holly's dad, isn't it, that he doesn't like?'

Claudine said nothing but listened to the total silence which came from the sitting room. Too quiet, she thought. It was not healthy or safe for him to sit there, drinking lager, alone, in the dark, all day, excluding wife and daughter while his thoughts went who knows where?

Safe?

Why had she used that particular word? What was unsafe about him? Brian was her husband. Surely there was nothing unsafe about him.

Brian was piecing everything together. Sewing it into a recognisable shape, stitch by stitch.

The missing clothes, the jewellery, the personal items. Who but Gregory? Taking trophies.

He didn't reason that it was not in Daniel's psyche to commit such an aberrant, trivial crime. He did not apply logic at all because his own mind was spiralling out of control.

Red mist was forming.

He clicked the cigarette lighter again and again in his fingers. Sometimes it sparked and flamed but other times it didn't. He peered at it, less than an inch from his nose, as though he was very short-sighted, though he wasn't, and tried to guess which times it would work and which times it would fail. After forty or more clicks he realised that it was completely random. He sat up, smiling. So let it *be* random. How it all ended up would be left to chance. He only needed to plan how. Where.

And like the good soldier he could bide his time, pick his moment, wait and see.

Something in Brian still struggled to retain a hold on reality, to separate the two events, the eight-year-old plea for help and the intrusion on his wife, but control was slipping away so he gave up. They were one, and by dealing with *this* in a controlling and decisive way he could merge the two and thus affect a satisfactory ending. He had only done what he must do.

So that was that.

His gaze wandered towards the door. Claudine was helpless. He could see that now. It was up to him to protect her as he had failed to protect that other woman, so long ago. This time he would act earlier.

He would take the initiative.

But the question that burnt in his mind was, was she *innocent or guilty?* How far had things gone? He decided that he would set her various tests to find out. He would know when she was lying and when she was telling the truth. He would return home unexpectedly, check in her purse, read the numbers from her mobile phone. He would follow her to Sunday Mass, check up on her when she was supposed to be shopping. He was a policeman. He could think of hundreds of ways to expose his wife. All he had to do was to pretend to be normal.

At eight in the evening he finally stirred himself, feeling stiff after the hours of inactivity. He flexed his muscles and worked out a plan of action. He clicked the lighter one last, satisfactory time, watched the small flame ignite, splutter and die and then he smiled.

Back in control.

Chapter Sixteen

The weekend passed well for Daniel. Holly and his mother seemed to be forging a better relationship and Holly only mentioned her newfound friend once, suggesting they asked her to join them and when Daniel said it probably wasn't a good idea she did not mention her again.

He tried to ring Claudine just before lunch but no one answered so he left a friendly, neutral message and hung up. They must be on a family outing, he decided and was part relieved and part slightly jealous.

The three of them went for a walk in Doxey Marshes to see the swans and then called in for coffee at Costas, finishing up meandering along the aisles at Sainsbury's to pick up something for supper and tomorrow's lunch. Holly took her grandmother's hand happily, selecting vegetables and fruit with all the enthusiasm and commitment of a gourmet and he found himself relaxing for the first time in ages. Something in Holly's artless chatter seemed to bring out something less selfish, less self-absorbed in his mother, so she listened to her granddaughter, hardly interrupting, her head bent over to one side.

The only slightly bitter note in the entire day was a text message from Marie asking whether he was free over the weekend. She said she was *dying to meet his daughter,* offered to *pop* over and cook his dinner *and then...* He fingered the reply button, trying to decide whether to respond with a polite, *Sorry, I'm busy, mother here!* followed maybe by a friendly, *See you at work next week,* or simply ignore it. He felt awkward. Perhaps that one, accidental date would embarrass their future working relationship. Something told him she was a persistent woman.

In the end he decided to ignore it. Mobile phones can so easily be out of range, he told himself. There is nothing to tell the texter that their message has been read.

Even so, he felt wrong-footed and rude. She was a nice woman who deserved a nice man. But not him.

A heavy shower finally drove them home through dingy streets underneath a distinctly threatening sky but they returned happy and wet. As he walked along the hall he could see the answerphone flashing a message. While his mother and Holly dealt with the shopping he pressed play to hear Claudine's voice unrecognisably shrill.

'Daniel, it's Claudine. Brian is behaving oddly. It's best you don't telephone – please, at least for a while. I think he's having some sort of a breakdown. I'm worried and he seems to think we are closer friends than we are. Please take care of yourself and of Holly.'

The line went dead, leaving Daniel staring at it stupidly.

Something in him was warning him, a red light flashing inside his head, which distracted him from rational thought. All evening it blinked inside his brain, through the extended game of Monopoly, Holly's incessant chatter and a late supper of cheese and biscuits. His mother disappeared upstairs at ten o'clock, muttering something about packing ready for the morning and for the first time in his life he was sorry to see her go. As it was half term she had agreed to drive Holly all the way back to her mother in Birmingham. It would be a huge detour but he had the sneaky feeling that his mother wanted to check up on how Elaine was doing. Infuriatingly she still harboured desires to see them reunited no matter how much they both tried to persuade her that their marriage was, thankfully and irrevocably, ended.

He tucked Holly up, leaving her sleepy, in bed, unable to stop himself from whispering his dream of the cottage, the pony, them being together. He watched her eyes light up. 'Really, Daddy? Really?' She put her arms around his neck. '*Then* will I be able to come and live with you? I shall call my pony Chocolate. Whatever colour he is.' She lay back against the pillow, a smile lighting her face. He closed the door behind her, thinking how very much he wanted this life. His daughter, a home, even his mother. Nearby at least.

Yet, he had a little voice nagging him that Holly thought that life with him would be endless Saturdays and shopping trips with no credit limit, that each and every meal would be either Gary Rhodes gourmet, Jamie Oliver or in a restaurant. He walked downstairs slowly. This weekend pact was so *false.* It wasn't *really* what life was like. As he reached the bottom step he blinked at the vision of hordes of little princesses spoilt by their absent fathers.

But by the time he was back in the lounge his thoughts had turned inexplicably back to his problems at work, to Maud Allen and Anna-Louise. What troubled him about Maud were her last words to him that his life would change. He froze. Surely – surely she would not have sacrificed her life for his elusive dream of having his daughter with him? As much as he rejected the idea it would not go away but left him uncomfortable. She had been a tough, brave, unselfish woman. But surely this had been a step too far just to give him a paddock? And now he had the niece to deal with who would no doubt be hostile towards him – the doctor whose wrong diagnosis had led even indirectly to her aunt's death. And he had benefited.

In the wake of these thoughts was the knowledge that the true story of Anna-Louise's death was as much a mystery to him as it was to the police and the pathologist.

Who had stood to gain by the little tot's death? No one. So it was not gain. The only person who knew the true story was almost certainly her mother.

But when he sat drinking a final malt whisky before turning in, having seen his mother off to bed, it was back to Claudine that his thoughts returned. He was worried about her. Although – yes – he fancied her very much, he'd never touched her. Nothing physical had ever happened. And whatever his personal desires might be he had never had any hint that she felt anything but friendship towards him, her daughter's friend's father. So what was going on in her husband's mind? Daniel had been careful not to expose himself. Brian couldn't *know* that he fancied Claudine like mad, fantasised about her like a fourteen-year-old. He *couldn't* know that. Surely?

He finished his whisky, resisted the temptation to have another and followed his mother and daughter up to bed.

But once there he lay with his hands cupped behind his head, hearing the noises of the night – a boy racer screeching up the High Street, the tinny tone of the millennium clock striking twelve, then one. Something was disturbing him and he knew it was the note of panic in Claudine's voice when she was normally so calm. What was PC Anderton up to?

By one-thirty he was groaning. After the allegation made against him by Chelsea Emmanuel the last thing he needed was for the local bobby to be accusing him of making advances on his wife. No female patient would feel safe again.

He tossed and turned, dozed fitfully for a couple of hours, finally gave in to insomnia and padded downstairs to make himself a cup of tea.

He propped himself up and read an article in *Pulse* on the use of statins to prevent myocardial infarctions. That, finally, did send him to sleep.

Vanda Struel had got rid of Arnie for the night so she could have the flat to herself and entertain Guy. There was something fantastic about him these days, tall and gangly as he was. Almost overnight he seemed to have turned into a sexpot and Vanda wasn't complaining.

Guy was very sure of himself these days.

He leered at her. 'I'm glad you ain't got that little tot no more. We couldn't have had half the fun.'

Even Vanda looked slightly shocked at this. ''Ang on a minute,' she said, 'that's my daughter you're talkin' about. My little girl.'

Guy looked slightly abashed. 'Sorry, love. I didn't mean it like that but…' he glanced around him, 'it's great here.'

She put her hand in his. 'Didn't mean to be so touchy,' she said.

He put one of his large hands at the back of her jeans and pinged the elastic of her thong. 'I'm feeling randy,' he said.

* * *

Daniel woke late on the Monday morning, the scent of bacon frying somehow entering his dreams so he was waiting in a long queue in an American diner. His mother shouted up the stairs. 'Daniel, Daniel. Come along. You'll be late for surgery.' It reminded him of his long gone schooldays.

He pulled his dressing gown on and went downstairs. Again Holly and his mother were in obvious conspiracy. There was a détente between them that he had never noted before. Holly had set the kitchen table with a blue and white checked cloth and a vase of flowers picked, presumably, from the garden. There was a jug of fresh orange juice, sparkling water glasses and a pot of tea (almost certainly Earl Grey) in the centre surrounded by cups, saucers and a milk jug. He stared, first at the cordiality that marked the relationship between his daughter and his mother, then at the table which looked so inviting compared to his usual bowl of cereal eaten hastily from the bowl, straight off the bare pine. Holly and his mother looked at him with the same mix of indulgence and exasperation that most females express when looking at their men.

'It looks lovely,' he said. 'I really appreciate it.'

'Well, eat up then,' his mother responded severely.

So he did. He enjoyed the fry-up and ate with great gusto, which even extended to the Earl Grey and the orange juice. He vanished up the stairs to have a shower, leaving Holly and his mother to clear up. They both kissed him goodbye as he left for the surgery, practically whistling.

His good mood lasted right up until he walked inside and straight away bumped into Marie Westbrook, looking annoyed. 'Morning,' he said, with gusto, instinctively sure that she had been lying in wait for him.

'I'd have thought you would have had better manners than that,' she said crossly.

'Sorry?' He decided to play dumb. It was the easiest option.

'Didn't you get my text message suggesting we meet up over the weekend?'

'Sorry,' he said again. 'I was busy. My phone was switched off in the bedroom. My mother's been up and Holly too.'

'I'd like to meet Holly,' she said.

He ignored the remark.

Why should she meet his daughter?

Her pale blue eyes held his and he knew she was waiting for his response. The moment extended into embarrassment but he was determined not to make any firm arrangement with her.

Finally he mumbled something about having to get on with his surgery and bolted into the consulting room.

His first patient of that Monday morning was Vanda Struel, accompanied by her mother. As she sat down he realised how much smaller she looked without Anna-Louise in her arms. Only half a person, really. He'd hardly ever seen her without her daughter, either holding her or in a pushchair.

'How are you?' He asked the traditional open-ended question as he had been trained.

She stared back at him, mouth and eyes oddly dead. 'How do you think?' she asked truculently. Then blurted out, 'The police think I killed her. They think I killed my own little girl. My baby. Can you believe that?'

Unfortunately, yes.

He held her gaze steadily.

Daniel had little experience of Munchausen by proxy. It isn't a common condition but, from what he did know, Vanda Struel fitted the bill perfectly: single mum; loads of stress; multiple investigations on the child, most at the instigation of the mother with no pathology ever found; dramatic stories, some of which *had* to be untrue; finally – and this was the clincher – recovery of the child when admitted to hospital, away from the mother. He stared into Vanda's pale eyes, hoping she could not read his thoughts. The real problem for him was, what did he do about it?

He could have countered her statement about the police suspecting her of being responsible for the child's death with the obvious, *well, did you?* But no doctor could take that line. What would he do if she admitted it? Break confidentiality and inform the police? He could almost write the complaint it would inevitably lead to.

No. It would be unethical.

Besides, sufferers of the condition rarely do admit it. In fact, it is believed that their minds block out the events so completely that they would not be able to admit it. To them, the acts which led up to their child's death simply did not happen.

But he wished the powerful vision of Vanda bending over her daughter's cot, pillow in hand, pressing, harder, harder and harder still, until the child was dead, would leave him. He gaped and looked at her and simply couldn't find the right words. Not *any* words. All he could see was the child's tongue furiously licking her lips until they were red and sore. But it was a tongue that could not speak.

Vanda must have sensed his confusion. She fixed her stare at a spot on the floor. 'I didn't do it,' she muttered. 'I just didn't do it. Whatever *they* think I couldn't have done *anything* to my baby. I *loved* her.'

Two fat tears rolled down her face as she looked across at him. 'Can't *you* convince them, Doctor? Can't you tell them how much I loved my baby, that I was *always* here, fussing about her, caring for her? Tell them, please.'

And that, he thought, *is part of the syndrome.* They do love their child. There is no doubt about that. But it is a perverse love. They love the attention that their 'sick' child brings them, the sympathy, the admiration. How well they care for a child that is always ailing. It is a terrible condition.

You always hurt the one you love.

He looked across at Vanda and tried to feel sorry for her. He struggled to find the right words to say. He put his hand, briefly, on her thin shoulder. 'It won't make any difference, Vanda, whatever I say. The pathologists make the decision. But if it'll help I have already told them that I never saw you harm Anna-Louise.'

Behind her daughter, Bobby Millin stood, her gaze hardly moving from him. It was as though she was trying to convey something to him. He gave her a polite smile and a nod.

Vanda bowed her head in acceptance. But a moment later she was fighting again. 'And now,' she said with a touch of spirit, 'they won't even let me bury her. The coroner says we can't have a funeral until another specialist has looked at her. What good's that? How many bloody specialists does my dead little baby have to see?'

Her small hands were gripping the side of the chair. 'It's like they won't let my baby rest until they've got me for something.' Two more tears followed the others down her cheek. Her complexion, never florid, was now parchment white.

It suddenly struck Daniel that Bobby was contributing nothing to this consultation. In fact, he was mystified why she had come at all when she was so abnormally silent. He looked directly at her, inviting a comment. She met his gaze unblinking but still said nothing. Her plump face was almost deliberately impassive. Controlled. Her silence bordered on being embarrassing.

She could have defended her daughter, protested her innocence, said how ridiculous the entire question was, but instead she continued to look at Daniel as though she would like to have said something.

What, he wondered, did Bobby Millin know?

He eyed her thoughtfully while he made soothing noises to her daughter, that it was routine, that investigations did not necessarily mean suspicion of guilt, that all would probably be explained satisfactorily. Bobby kept her gaze on him without flinching.

A few hundred yards outside Eccleston, just a little outside the town, on the left-hand side of the Stafford road, is a small, old-fashioned petrol station connected with a workshop, called Claremont Garage. It was there that Brian Anderton pulled up. The owner greeted Anderton cordially. 'Morning, constable. What can I do for you?' He serviced the police cars and was on good terms with PC Anderton and his colleagues.

Brian indicated the petrol can in his hand. 'Fill it up, will you?'

The garage owner squirted a gallon of petrol in, making conversation. 'Waging a bit of war, are you?'

'Sorry?'

'Molotov cocktails? Hah hah.'

Brian grimaced. The joke wasn't funny. He handed the garage owner a five-pound note and told him to put the change in the Air Ambulance collecting box, which stood on his counter. He had a deep superstition about the Air Ambulance, that if he always put spare change in the collecting box he would never have to use it. His face was grim as he climbed back into the police car. It would be sent out for someone though, one of these days. Not that it would do any good. It would be too late for *Doctor* Daniel Gregory by the time either the ordinary ambulance or the Air Ambulance got to him.

His mouth bent into a smile.

Anderton stowed the can of petrol upright in the boot of the car. He intended to plan this assault with military precision, choosing the time, the place, the date, with care. He was not going to rush this. For, like a child waiting for Christmas, a large part of the pleasure would be in the anticipation.

He drove home.

It annoyed him that when he opened the front door Claudine greeted him with a look of apprehension. She should, he thought, look pleased to see him. Very pleased. So he addressed her sarcastically. 'I'm home, darling. Now isn't that nice?'

She shrank back. She actually *shrank.* Recoiled as though he was a spitting cobra.

This inflamed him.

But he managed to suppress it. For now.

'Is my tea ready?'

She smiled at him.

False wife, he thought. *I know your game.*

He buried it, his jealousy and the white heat of his anger. His time would come. That he knew and maybe the false

Claudine would burn alongside her lover. Like a person with a bad habit, a nail-biter or a smoker, his fingers itched to click the lighter. He felt it in his pocket, smiling to himself at the memory of the petrol can safely stowed in the back of the police car.

Ready, he thought.

All was ready.

He just needed to find the right time.

Daniel had finally given in and prescribed Vanda some antidepressants, feeling the usual sense of defeat as he printed off the prescription. Antidepressants were a failure on his part. To have spent half an hour listening to her problems and giving her some simple, practical advice would have helped her so much more. Tablets were simply a panacea for her hurt and an apology from him. He had watched her take the prescription reluctantly, as though, like him, she knew how inadequate they would prove to be. As he'd met her eyes he'd wondered. What was she? Grieving mother? Callous murderess? Or both?

'Come back next week,' he'd said. 'Book a double appointment. We'll talk some more.' He'd tried the cheery bit. 'Maybe they'll have realised that Anna-Louise died from natural causes and you can have a funeral.' Vanda had managed a watery smile and left, followed closely by her mother.

So there had been no opportunity for him to speak privately with Bobby Millin. It was a shame. He was sure that she could shed some light on the death of her granddaughter.

Chapter Seventeen

As Daniel thought about it he became convinced that Bobby Millin held the key to what had happened to Anna-Louise. So a visit to the nursing home was called for. Daniel normally visited on a Thursday, straight after morning surgery, spending about an hour shaking hands with the old ladies (and the two gentlemen), speaking to the staff, issuing prescriptions and changing medication. There was rarely any serious illness to worry about. Occasionally chest pain or pneumonia, but The Elms was one of the better nursing homes. They had their crises but they looked after their patients, nursed them through illnesses serious enough to have caused death in their assortment of frail octogenarians. Yet somehow, however sick the patients appeared, they invariably pulled through. The nurses were skilled and dedicated and when death inevitably removed one of their patients the place was soon filled from a long waiting list.

Once or twice the elderly inmates had had sudden illnesses but in the elderly this was only to be expected.

So three days after the consultation with Vanda he was ringing the bell to The Elms and waiting to be admitted. Before this system of locking the door had been introduced, there had been a tragedy. Four years ago, on a dusky November evening, a male patient who was profoundly deaf had wandered outside. Somehow, unchallenged, he had drifted towards the High Street and then out onto the B5026, the winding road west towards Loggerheads, walking up the middle of the road, oblivious to an approaching car. The unfortunate motorist, turning the corner, had slammed on his brakes when the tall shape loomed in front of him but it had been too late. Humphrey Bladon had died instantly.

Since then The Elms had kept all entrances and exits locked.

Daniel was in luck. It was Bobby Millin who met him. Obviously today she was the one assigned to accompany him on this morning's round. The Sister must be off for the day.

Daniel was restrained. He didn't even mention Vanda or Anna-Louise until he had inspected four residents of the home, each one with a multitude of problems and a stew pot of pathology. Heart disease, depression, arthritis, thyroid deficiency, obstructive airways disease. The list was endless. He listened, spoke, prescribed, sympathised. Three quarters of an hour later he'd finished.

'Bobby,' he said uncertainly as they walked back along the corridor. She turned incurious but perceptive eyes on him.

'Doctor?'

'About Anna-Louise.'

Her eyes flickered.

He pressed on. 'Did you ever see Vanda harm her?' He felt he must ameliorate the implied accusation of the question. 'I'm not suggesting *deliberately,* but in temper or under stress. It can be difficult for a single mother, you understand?'

Her eyes widened but she didn't speak straight away. Instead she began rubbing her fingertips together. 'Umm.'

'It's all right,' he said. 'I shan't take it any further but…' He purposely left the sentence hanging in the air.

Bobby nodded very slowly. 'She did,' she said hesitantly. 'I did see her once or twice. She fed her salt. I know that too much salt can be harmful to a small child. I told her to stop it, but she said it was good for her. Another time I saw her pulling at Anna-Louise's leg until she cried. The worst thing was that she used Anna-Louise's crying to say what a difficult child she was, trying to make me sympathetic towards her.' Bobby Millin's eyes met his. 'I didn't blame her, Doctor. It was only a little tug. To be honest I felt sorry for Vanda, that she felt she needed to play this silly game. Perhaps to justify her own shortcomings, maybe? I saw her giving her rum in her bottle but she said it was to help Anna-Louise sleep better. I knew she was doing wrong things, Doctor, but I just thought she was young and a bit misguided.'

Daniel felt a thud of recognition because he instinctively recognised her words as the truth. 'You didn't say anything?'

'I did to her,' Bobby said. 'I did. I told her what she was doing was wrong. She simply looked blankly at me. Doctor…' She touched his arm. 'I honestly don't think Vanda knew what she was doing. I don't.' There was real distress in her face. 'I can't believe...' she began. 'I can't. She *couldn't* have smothered Anna-Louise. She just *couldn't* have done it. Surely?' Doubt was creeping into her voice as she spoke. Then her shoulders drooped. 'I should have done something more, shouldn't I?'

It would have seemed cruel to have agreed with her but Daniel couldn't disagree.

Yes, he thought. She should have done something, said something more, involved the authorities. But then – so should I.

And now it was too late.

Bobby Millin was standing, looking at him with an expression of fear in her eyes.

'What is it?' he asked, feeling a snatch of fear.

She put her hand on his arm. 'Doctor,' she said. 'She thinks she might be pregnant again.'

Daniel stared at Bobby Millin's face. 'Who?' he asked.

'That goof…' Her face showed clear contempt.

Daniel knew exactly who she meant. Guy Malkin. He recalled seeing the two of them together, walking up the High Street, Vanda's tiny figure trotting alongside Guy Malkin's gangling shape. Oh, no, he thought. This was the worst scenario. Another child would make things worse. If Vanda had failed to cope with Anna-Louise, what would happen now? More abuse?

Daniel felt disturbed as he left the nursing home. And he felt terribly guilty. He had failed. He should have picked up that something was wrong between mother and child, that they were failing to bond, that the relationship was pathological. He could have prevented it by alerting the authorities. The shame was that Vanda Struel wasn't a bad person. Confronted with her behaviour she could have changed – at least been given the chance to. It was her mother's responsibility to speak out, to protect her granddaughter but, ultimately, the fact that the child was dead lay at *his* door. It was his job.

The question now was how to proceed?

He was depressed as he opened his car door.

* * *

Bobby Millin watched him through the window. She had picked up on the fact that he felt in some measure responsible. Her lips tightened. Her gaze slid across the desk to a framed photograph. She picked it up. Anna-Louise, nine months old, in a pale pink dress, still needing to be propped up, gazed solemnly back at her. She stared at it until one of the other health care assistants came up, put her arm around her and said, 'You must be heartbroken.'

Bobby was still crying as she replaced the photograph on the desk.

Although Guy had Vanda now, he still felt he was missing out on something. Vanda was easy game but Claudine – now, she was a challenge. Yes, he had Claudine's pretty earrings, her underwear. But he wanted *her*. He wanted to touch her, to feel her in the flesh. Not just have her *things*. He wanted *her* to look at him with love. *That* was what he wanted.

And he knew how he was going to get it.

Brian was not pleased to be told he would have to do nights again. 'Starting on Saturday,' the sergeant said. 'Hope you didn't have anything special planned with that lovely young wife of yours.'

Brian mumbled a reply. He was formulating a plan. He would do his nights but he would also watch the house. Pretend not to be there and he would see. Then he could act.

Daniel heard nothing from Claudine.

The solicitor made Daniel's day by ringing to say that he had heard from Maud Allen's niece who said that she was prepared to settle out of court for £100,000 and he strongly recommended that he accept.

Daniel said he'd think about it. He felt a certain fury that this niece, of whom he had never heard, should suddenly pop out of the woodwork and claim her right. What had *she* ever done for the old woman?

He sat in his surgery, calculating. Applegate Cottage was worth about £400,000. He could get £500,000 for The Yellow House but, thanks to Elaine, he had a £300,000 mortgage on it. That would still give him £200,000 left minus solicitor's bills and no mortgage. He and Elaine had sorted out all their moneys in final settlement. She earned a good wage as an accountant so he didn't have to give her any more.

He decided quickly and picked up the phone before he could change his mind. Let the niece have her money. In that, at least, he could have finality.

He instructed the solicitor and sat back. What was he really going to do about Bobby Millin's confession? Inform the police? The Social Services? He didn't have her permission. She had trusted him as a doctor and he couldn't break that trust. Without her statement there would be no evidence. If the pathologist could not be certain that Anna-Louise had been smothered the case could not be proved. He knew where his responsibility lay – to ask Bobby to give her permission to go to the Social Services armed with her information.

But at the back of his mind lurked a further fear.

He had sensed that all was not right; he had done nothing apart from referring her, and the little girl had died. It was possible – but only just – that it had been from natural causes. She had certainly suffered from apnoeic attacks – or so the family had said – and the post-mortem had been inconclusive.

The sense of guilt was always floating around, familiar now, but joined by this further fear. What if Vanda really was pregnant again? If he did not do something a second child might follow the path of its dead sister. But what could he do? He was not allowed to speak. Confidentiality is valued very highly. The doctors' surgery is as close as a confessional. Break that and you risk people not being open with their medical advisers. Doctors have been struck off the medical register for not respecting the confidentiality clause. But a child's life was at stake. After tussling with the problem for some minutes Daniel finally did what any doctor would do. For the second time in as many months he dialled the number of the Medical Defence Union.

They, for their part, advised him to ask Bobby Millin's permission to speak to the police.

Their point was clearly made. Vanda Struel needed help as did her unborn infant.

He rang The Elms to speak to Bobby, only to be told that she had gone home for the afternoon.

He tried her home number but there was no answer and he didn't have a mobile number.

He had one last resort. He scanned the addresses on his mobile phone and connected with Caroline Letts. They had been in the same year at medical school, briefly been lovers and parted very good friends. She had never married and currently worked as a child psychiatrist in one of the units in the University of North Staffordshire, Stoke-on-Trent.

She was friendly when he spoke.

'Goodness, Daniel, it's been ages. How are you?'

He told her he was fine, asked about her, and then steered the conversation round to Vanda Struel. She listened, without interruption, before giving her opinion. 'As I see it your problem is, Daniel, proving it. If the pathologist can't be certain the child was deliberately smothered you have absolutely no chance. The only way it can ever be brought to court is if you rig up surveillance on the mother and child and actually *see* her deliberately harming the child. And that is fraught with difficulties as some of my colleagues have found to their cost. But if the little girl is dead…'

Dully he told her that the mother might be pregnant again. Again Caroline was sympathetic.

'Should I let her know of my suspicions? Make her aware that I'm not happy about what happened to Anna-Louise?'

'Absolutely not,' she said with conviction. 'That often escalates the incidents. They are more dangerous when they are suspected. The best thing might be to take the grandmother into your confidence and get her to act as your "spy". Or at least,' she added, 'advise the grandmother to supervise and visit her daughter often and not to be afraid to speak to you if she is at all worried. Give her an open understanding, Daniel, take her into your confidence.'

'I have already,' he said, 'to some degree.'

'Well then – you can but hope that she can protect this second child. And if there are any suspicious illnesses in the new baby it might have to be made a Ward of Court – taken into care and only see the mother under supervision. It's the only way of protecting vulnerable infants.'

It didn't help him much. He made a loose arrangement to take Caroline out to dinner, knowing as he put the phone down that it probably wouldn't ever lead to a definite date.

What was wrong with him, he thought crossly, wanting a woman who was unavailable and rejecting two perfectly eligible women? He felt irritated with himself and meeting Lucy Satchel in the reception area didn't do anything to make him feel better. Her smile was very tight and false. 'Well, Dan,' she said coolly, 'so your little slip up with Maud Allen has borne unexpected fruit.'

He didn't like the acid tone in her voice.

'Yes, it was unexpected,' he said. 'I was absolutely flabbergasted.'

Her eyebrows lifted. 'Really?'

He was well aware that to have pressed home the point would have appeared like the protestation of a guilty man. But what did she really think he'd done? Driven the old woman to suicide? Surely not. He muttered something non-committal and left it at that but it registered that she didn't even make an effort to extend her congratulations.

It had been an eventful day. The weather was clear and chilly. Wearily he decided to leave his car at the surgery and walk home. Mistakenly he thought that the walk would do him good.

It was not to be.

Halfway up the High Street he saw Claudine sitting in the passenger seat of their car. Bethan was in the back, waving at him madly. He could have sworn Claudine had seen him too but she carried on staring straight ahead. He rapped on the window and Claudine turned to face him, a look of complete fear making her look like a character out of a horror movie, both her mouth and eyes wide open. He felt a tap on his shoulder and knew who it was before he turned around. 'Stay away from my wife, *Doctor* Gregory.'

Daniel felt compelled to defend himself. 'Look, Brian,' he

said in a vain attempt at friendliness, 'you've got the wrong impression here. Claudine and I...' He glanced at her. Her eyes were still wide open, her mouth tense and unhappy. He couldn't do any good by trying to reason with Anderton. 'Well you've just got the wrong impression. Come on…' He put a hand on the policeman's shoulder. 'Our daughters are friends. There isn't anything wrong in that.' He felt uncomfortable at the policeman's frozen stare. 'I'm hoping that Holly will be moving up here permanently.'

But Brian was staring right through him. The confidence hadn't thawed him at all.

Daniel knew he simply wasn't listening. He shrugged, gave an apologetic smile at Claudine and Bethan and walked on.

Ten steps later he turned and looked back.

Brian Anderton was still staring after him.

Daniel felt a pricking of anxiety. He had seen that identical stare once before. It had been when he had been studying psychiatry. He had worked for a few months in a secure psychiatric unit where some of the worst cases of violent and unstable mental illness were housed. One evening an inmate had been staring at another patient with the same, identical look that Brian was giving him now. Seconds later the patient had sprung at the man, trying to tear his throat out. Even now Daniel shivered when he thought of it, prising fingernails out of flesh, a swift spurting of blood, the animal snarling. The alarm bells had sounded, five strong male nurses summoned and they had needed all their strength to tear the man away from his victim.

Days later, when the sedation had been starting to wear off, it had been Daniel's job to interview the patient, whose name was Mark Shilling, and try to ascertain what had provoked the attack. Shilling had looked puzzled, almost confused at the question, but he had thought about it before giving what to him was a rational explanation. 'He just wouldn't stop sniffing,' he said. 'It was getting on my nerves.'

Daniel had nodded, shocked at this glimpse into a volatile mind.

So now he quickened his step away from Anderton trying to reason with himself. What was he saying? That the town's policeman had an unstable mind? As diseased as someone who needed to be locked up for their behaviour?

He reached home and pushed open the front door.

Chapter Eighteen

The house seemed empty without either Holly or his mother. It took a while to readjust to the silence that greeted his return home from work. The corridor seemed longer, narrower and darker. He went into the kitchen. The first thing he noticed was that his answerphone was flashing out two messages – the first was from Marie Westbrook. 'Daniel,' her tone was wheedling, coaxing, 'I expect Holly and your mother have left and you're on your own again. I'm on *my* own; you're on *your* own. Why not give me a ring and we'll have a drink together?' She rapped out her mobile number – twice.

He flicked on to the next message. It was from his mother. 'Daniel, dear. Just to let you know, I've left Holly with Elaine. I must say she looks well on all this, knee-deep in wedding plans. I'm sure I don't understand her. The man she's marrying is—' Daniel pressed delete. He didn't really want to hear about Elaine's new man. It wasn't that he still cared about her. He didn't, but the very subject of her 'knee-deep in wedding plans' simply bored him.

He settled down for the evening, searched the Internet dating website but saw nothing he could be bothered with, channel-hopped the television for an hour or two and went to bed early. At eleven o'clock his telephone rang. He stretched out his hand then withdrew it. He couldn't face fending off either his mother or Marie right now. Ten minutes later he was asleep.

It was almost two weeks later that Vanda Struel turned up in his surgery, proudly brandishing a miniature Bell's whisky bottle containing a urine sample. He looked at it with something approaching distaste.

She was almost beseeching him to be pleased for her. 'I've got a new bloke,' she said. 'He's really nice. Good to me and all that. We're gettin' on really well.' Her eyes still met his with that hopeful expression. 'We'd like a kid of our own.' Her gaze dropped to the whisky bottle.

He asked her when her last period had been, then offered to get the nurse to test it, aware that he was unable to share in her enthusiasm. Marie was grumpy when he handed her the bell-shaped bottle. She practically snatched it from him without a word. He watched her perform the test awkwardly, hardly registering surprise when the line turned blue. What did this mean? he wondered. Another child to be harmed at its mother's will? He felt suddenly impotent to prevent it. What could he do? I could counsel her, he thought, take the line of, *Are you ready for another child so soon after...?*

Marie was watching him. 'It was only a friendly gesture,' she said sharply. 'There was no need for you to ignore it.'

He struggled to understand and returned her stare blankly.

'Don't you ever pick up your phone messages?'

'Not always,' he said and left it at that.

He was just leaving the room when she asked softly. 'What do I have to do, Daniel? Go down on my knees?'

He couldn't answer her – not truthfully – so he avoided saying anything, whisked through the door and back along the corridor to where Vanda Struel was waiting.

'Well?' she demanded.

'It's positive,' he said, knowing that this was both a momentous and monstrous statement.

She jumped up. 'Fantastic,' she said beaming. 'Guy'll be over the moon. He'd love a little boy.' There was no mention, no memory, no regret for Anna-Louise.

Claudine was picking up a few things from the supermarket.

'Hello, Mrs Anderton. Nice morning.'

Claudine focused on the gangly youth who frequently served her at the Co-op store. She gave him one of her wide, friendly smiles. 'Hello, Guy,' she responded. 'How are you today?'

'Well,' he said. 'I'm well.'

'Good.'

She was aware that he was anxious to engage her in some sort of conversation, however banal.

'How's Bethan?'

'Oh – Bethan's very well too, Guy. She's looking forward to spending some time in France next month with my family.'

'Oh. Is the Constable going too?'

Claudine's eyes flickered. 'No,' she said. 'We have decided it would be a good idea if…' She started again. 'Brian does not have any time off.'

'Oh,' he said. 'Shame.'

'Yes.' She passed some of her groceries across to him. 'It is a great shame but it'll be good for Bethan's French to be with my mother. I am anxious for her to learn the language and my mother speaks very little English.'

''Course,' he agreed.

He was staring at her rather stupidly, she thought, and handed him a litre bottle of milk.

'I think I'm going to be a dad.'

She looked up, startled. 'Really?'

'Yes.'

'Congratulations.' She couldn't think what else to say. *Who is the mother,* would have seemed inappropriate but she couldn't remember ever seeing him with a woman. He had always been alone. *A loner,* she thought.

There was a brief, awkward silence. She was aware that Guy was watching her expectantly. She smiled at him and at last he started scanning in her shopping.

Elaine and his mother must have worked something out between them. It was his mother who rang him late one Monday evening towards the end of June. 'Daniel,' she said in her usual abrupt, businesslike way, 'I have a proposal.'

He was instantly on his guard.

She continued regardless. 'Elaine finds the school holidays difficult,' she said. 'Her mother has a busy social life and helps in the Red Cross charity shop in Worcester three times a week.' She described Daniel's ex-mother-in-law with more than a hint of disapproval.

'So Elaine and I have had a little chat.'

Daniel waited.

'She's willing to let Holly stay with you for the entire duration of the summer holidays, right up until her wedding in September, provided *I* am around to care for Holly while *you* are at work.' Without allowing him to speak she continued. 'Needless to say I have discussed this with Holly and she is completely thrilled at the idea. I imagine that you had contemplated having some sort of summer holiday with her, in which case I shall return home during that period to check up that all is well at my own house. Well, Daniel?'

She didn't exactly give him much time to think about it but the more he did the more he liked the idea. 'If you're happy with the idea, mother.'

'Of course I am, dear boy,' she said kindly, 'otherwise I wouldn't even have brought it up. Now then…'

She went on to discuss arrangements. She would finalise everything with Elaine, which suited Daniel. He didn't even have to talk to the witch. And another bonus that had occurred to him, even as his mother had been speaking, was that having his mother and daughter stay for the summer gave him the perfect excuse to fend off Marie's advances.

On the third of July Snape rang him to inform him that probate was almost settled, the niece had accepted the £100,000 out-of-court settlement and that he should be able to take possession of Applegate Cottage some time in September. With an eye to drumming up a bit of extra business, he asked where Daniel was intending on living and, when Daniel said that he wanted to move to Applegate Cottage, he suggested Daniel put The Yellow House on the market. But that wasn't what Daniel had planned. He'd decided he wanted to make the cottage absolutely perfect before he and, hopefully, Holly moved in. He asked Snape if he could have the keys and inspect the place. He wanted to look around on his own and decide what he needed to do to it.

* * *

Snape reluctantly agreed to let him have the keys and Daniel finally visited Applegate Cottage on the eleventh of July, the day before Holly and his mother were due to arrive. It was much as he remembered, except a little smaller, a little darker and very obviously the house of an old woman. Everything in the place was old-fashioned and neglected. It smelt fusty and very slightly damp with a background of lavender and the cloying scent of mothballs. Pieces of Maud Allen's furniture were still there, heavy, old-fashioned items that seemed too big for the house. He must ask Snape what should be done with them. They were, he assumed, what the niece did not want. Other items had left marks on the carpet where they had lived for years and no longer did – the small square patch where a grandfather clock had stood, four marks where the feet of a card table had been, a few pale patches on the walls where pictures had hung for years. He opened the french windows with difficulty; the key was stiff and the door swollen with damp. They opened straight out into a small paved area set with a rusty table and four chairs and beyond that the wicket gate, which opened out into the paddock. The sound of birdsong greeted him as he stepped outside and, if he half closed his eyes, he could picture the pony grazing in the field. He closed the doors behind him and went upstairs.

There were numerous small rooms, one with a heavy bed which, he assumed, had been where Maud Allen had finally died. It seemed the niece did not want this either. He stood at the bottom for a while, feeling confused about the old woman's final deed. What had been in her mind? he wondered. Panic? Unhappiness or an acceptance that this was her ultimate act? He glanced out through the window, saw the trees in the orchard and felt a sense of quiet, dignified peace permeate the room. That, he decided, had been her state of mind. She had come to the end of a good life and had wanted to bow out in her own time. He wandered back out onto the landing. The upstairs was bigger than he had remembered. There were three good bedrooms and a decent-sized bathroom and, with a small amount of building work, it would be easy to put in a second shower room, an en suite for him and one for Holly.

He went back downstairs. The kitchen was large but old-fashioned; it had an Aga and another set of french windows which opened straight out onto a second patio. Mossy crazy paving and some pots holding leggy geraniums and a few self-planted weeds. He eyed the kitchen. With some units fitted it could be made very homely. There was easily room for a sizeable dining table, which meant that the second room downstairs could be used as a study.

The house was structurally sound, he'd noted as he'd made his tour – a few window frames were rotten and there was a damp patch in the hall but there was nothing that couldn't be fixed by a good builder. £50-60,000 should fix it, he decided, which would leave him well in pocket.

He was just beginning to feel smug when a grey Toyota pulled up outside and a stout, middle-aged woman climbed out stiffly. She glared through the window at him and his heart sank. He'd hoped he would never actually need to meet the niece.

She stood in the kitchen doorway. 'So you're Doctor Gregory,' she said sharply.

He didn't even attempt to smile.

'I suppose you've come to gloat over your acquisition.'

'Look,' he tried to explain, 'I'm as sad as you are over your aunt's death. I liked her. I did the best I could. You'll have your £100,000,' he added.

'Oh, thank you,' she said with heavy and bitter sarcasm. 'You've done very well out of your mistaken diagnosis, haven't you, Doctor? Well, you don't mind, I assume, if I collect a few things she left me?'

He shook his head. 'Help yourself,' he said, waving her on. 'Please.'

She flounced past him and disappeared into the house. He drove off with a nasty taste in his mouth. He wished his good fortune had come in some other way.

His mother's plan was put into practice. She and Holly moved into The Yellow House in the middle of July, as soon as Holly's school had broken up for the summer, and Daniel readjusted to having the two females living with him. He was surprised at how much he enjoyed it, having two women fussing over him – patronising him even. Holly and her grandmother seemed to almost conspire against him and he often caught them exchanging amused glances across the meal table when he'd said something they found funny or 'typically male'. The house quickly took on a different air. It was bright, noisy, lively and very happy. He took them to see Applegate Cottage one afternoon and revelled in watching Holly scampering through the orchard, chattering to her imaginary pony, galloping, trotting and finally sedately walking. He even went so far as to take her to the riding school, book her in for lessons and make tentative enquiries about a small, Welsh pony which seemed docile and well behaved. He showed Holly the room that would be hers and arranged to meet a builder at the property. He invited Reeds Rains, the local estate agent, to value The Yellow House, basked in their praise for the property, its position and condition and was pleased when they valued it at £595,000 – well over the price he had expected.

'You may have to accept less,' they warned him, 'if you want a quick sale, but Eccleston is a very desirable area. Near to the M6, yet it's retained its air of an elegant, Georgian coaching town.'

He assured them he was in no great hurry to sell, which they countered by telling him that putting a property on the market took some time. There were brochures to be printed and approved, advertising to be organised and so on, and they sent someone round to measure the rooms and take photographs. In this, too, Holly and his mother took great pride, cleaning the rooms, tidying up and artistically arranging vases of flowers, placing fresh towels in the bathrooms and removing the weeds from the garden that the gardener had missed.

It was a busy summer and Daniel hardly thought about Claudine. Holly didn't mention her friend and he barely saw either of them. Once he saw Claudine walking up the High Street gripping Bethan by the hand. He gave a little pip on his horn but if she saw him she did not respond or look up and even Bethan seemed to scuttle away, quickening her pace. Luckily Holly hadn't noticed. He wasn't sure he could have explained to his daughter why her new friend, who had seemed so sweet, had suddenly decided not to acknowledge her.

In August, Guy Malkin served him in the supermarket, which had now relocated to its new position behind the police station, and informed him that Mrs Anderton had taken Bethan to France for the month. Daniel simply nodded as though it was just another piece of town news.

For the first two weeks of August he had a break with Holly, and his mother moved, as planned, back to her house. He and Holly had hired a cottage in a tiny sailing village called Dale, in Pembrokeshire. They spent the fortnight in the traditional way: beachcombing, jumping waves, visiting the local pub for pasties and chips, and preparing meals on a brick barbecue while the waves lapped at the sea wall. It was a pleasant and peaceful time. He returned to some favourable quotes from the local builder with a jokey note that next time he visited the surgery he expected the same VIP treatment.

He had forgotten about Brian.

But Brian had spent the entire summer thinking about Daniel Gregory. He was a little more relaxed with Claudine safely out of the way across The Channel but equally aware that she would soon be back in Eccleston, with Bethan chattering in French, he thought gloomily. Serve him right for marrying a foreigner, his mother responded with typical sourness.

He would never get any sympathy from her.

Plotting Gregory's downfall, choosing the date, hiding the petrol can at the back of the garage ready for use, had returned some control to him but it was not quite enough.

He took a perverse delight in the poetic neatness of his plans but it was nothing compared to the pleasure he would take in the destruction of the man he had come to hate.

Claudine returned on the very last day of August and he eyed her with disfavour. She seemed more foreign than ever. Most of her and Bethan's clothes were new, French, bought by an overindulgent mother who could not believe that he could provide perfectly adequately for his own wife or that the English sold anything of such *chic*. Claudine even *smelt* foreign, of garlic and soap, sunshine, perfume and tart red wine.

Within minutes of opening the front door and calling out that she was home, Claudine knew that Brian was no better. In fact he was worse. Much worse. He was glaring at her with contempt, if not hatred. 'Have a good time, did you?'

She ignored the sarcasm in his tone and gave no response.

'Enjoy yourself, my dear?'

When she failed to respond he taunted her again.

'What – no kiss for your beloved husband?'

Her heart sank.

'And how was your *darling* mother?'

'Well?'

Brian turned his attentions on to Bethan. 'Glad to see me, are you, *darling*?'

Bethan moved behind her mother. '*Maman,*' she murmured.

Brian glared at the pair of them.

Claudine staggered upstairs with the suitcases and wondered when she would be packing them again, ready for her return to France.

On the third of September Elaine got married again and Daniel felt good enough to send his ex-wife and her new husband a wedding present; a dozen Waterford Crystal champagne glasses in a presentation box. Inside he enclosed a *Best Wishes to the Bride and Groom* card.

Sincerely meant. This was obviously what people meant when they used the word finality. His marriage was perfectly and completely ended. A line had been drawn beneath it.

But the product of that marriage still existed.

Having Holly for such a long period had been wonderful. Hard work but such fun. On her last night he sat her and his mother down and asked them how they felt about a new arrangement. Holly stared, round-eyed, at his suggestion that she come and live with him permanently and typically childlike asked, 'But I will see Mummy?'

'Of course, darling, you'll see Mummy. Plenty of her. As much as you like. It's just that you'll *live* in Applegate Cottage with me.'

'And when you're at work…?' his mother put in.

He was silent, knowing she would soon work it out.

She eyed him with some amusement. 'Are you sure you could cope with me living in the same place?'

Holly was watching her grandmother with her mouth open too.

'Granny,' she pleaded.

It was enough to melt her heart. 'It'll take some organising,' she said. 'I'm not sure. It would mean a huge life-change to move down here.' She gave him another look, softer this time. 'I take it you're not suggesting I live with you.'

'There are some very nice flats up for sale on the High Street,' Daniel said. 'It's a gated complex with its own swimming pool and gym. I think one of them would suit you very well.'

He couldn't believe he was doing this, actually inviting his mother to live less than a quarter of a mile away from him but he knew this was a practical solution. It would solve not only his life but his mother's and Holly's too.

She nodded, still looking incredulous. 'It would have certain distinct advantages,' she said. 'Is there a bridge club here?'

Daniel laughed. 'Bound to be,' he said.

So it was settled. Or so it seemed.

The cottage was about to be legally transferred to him, the builders poised to start the renovations. Elaine took a lot of convincing and there were numerous phone calls and not a few tears. But he could tell that her recent marriage had altered the situation. While Holly liked her mother's new husband she preferred to live with her father and grandmother who now spoilt her with unguarded indulgence. It had been decided that Holly should stay with her mother until Christmas and then move up to Staffordshire – whether Applegate Cottage was ready or not. Dan had even had a couple of potential buyers view The Yellow House. Both had seemed interested and the estate agent was convinced it would sell quickly.

Daniel was happy with his life.

But because he was so content, imagining that events were sorting themselves out satisfactorily, he was oblivious to what was happening around him.

Vanda's stomach was expanding day by day, the baby growing nearer to the time when it would no longer be protected by her own body around it. Guy Malkin had moved in with her and his newfound cockiness had made him bold enough to plot. He was working on an audacious plan.

Brian Anderton's mental state was teetering on the edge of calamity.

And Daniel remained unaware of all but his new, happy family state.

Marie Westbrook was skirting around him, sure that at

some point, when the time was ripe, he would pick up the threads of their romance. But she was unconscious to the fact that Daniel was not throwing even the vaguest of glances in her direction.

In that period, as autumn started to shorten the evenings, only one event brought Daniel even near to remembering all that was brewing beneath the surface. Bobby Millin attended the surgery late in October complaining of backache. And when he had examined her, found nothing serious and issued a sick note for a month she gave him a strange look. 'That baby'll be born before long,' she said darkly. 'Then what'll happen, do you think, Doctor?'

He stared at her. He didn't want anything to spoil this new heaven he was busily creating for himself and his mother and daughter. Their weekends were spent supervising the building work, choosing furniture, carpets, curtains and kitchen units, designing and planning. He didn't want this woman with her messy, damaged family ruining his life.

'What do the police say?' he asked sharply.

'They're still investigating.' Her anger made her voice very firm and unfriendly.

'We-ell.' Daniel held his hands out. 'So what can I do?'

She stood up. 'Nothing,' she said and left.

Even the Medical Defence Union seemed to be on his side for once. A very nice woman rang him and in the sweetest possible voice relayed the welcome information that they had completed their investigation and their findings were that he had done all he could for Mrs Maud Allen and that, while the circumstances of her death were regrettable, he certainly had nothing to answer for. Daniel gave a whoop of joy the minute he had put the phone down.

But sometimes happiness is unrealistic. It is certainly transient. All states eventually come to an end and happiness is no exception.

* * *

One night, late in October, Claudine had walked down to the wine shop. Brian had fancied some beer and it wasn't worth taking the car. She was glad to escape the oppression of the house. It was suffocating her slowly as though a snake was tightening around her windpipe. She often felt that she could not breathe the same air as her husband. It was terrifying her so much now that in her quiet, lonely moments, she planned her return to France.

The air was freezing that night, a mystic fog making the High Street look like a set from a black and white film, Sherlock Holmes or a Hammer House of Horror. But she welcomed the icy air and simply walked quickly to fend off the chill.

Bad luck – good luck. Guy Malkin spotted her as he locked the door of the Co-op store. She was going to the wine shop, he surmised. He waited until she came out, her wicker basket heavy on her arm. If he walked a few paces behind her she would not hear. There was always some background noise – a car, music, people talking. But when she turned into the alley it would be quiet and still.

He chose his moment carefully, grabbed her from behind.

He'd watched how they did it on *Crimewatch.* They pull their collars up, their hats down. They make their voices gruff and unrecognisable. They fold their arms around their victim's neck, making them gasp, frightened and compliant. He did all this, now, pulled at her coat, found her breasts, rubbed against her, touched her lips with his fingers and whispered into her ear.

Chapter Nineteen

Daniel had felt fidgety that night. He had been too excited at the prospect of his imminent life-change to merely sit at home and either watch TV or surf the Internet for a female he no longer wanted or needed. So he had decided to visit The Eagle for a pint or two of ale and now he was walking home.

He knew instantly that someone was in trouble. He could hear the gasps, the fright, the panic of the woman and the grunts of the man.

It wasn't until he spoke, 'Hey there. What's going on?' and the youth sped off, pulling up his trousers as he ran, leaving the woman crying inconsolably, that he realised it was Claudine Anderton who threw herself into his arms. He held her until she settled, her sobs became more spasmodic and her shaking stopped, then he asked her who it had been.

'I don't know, Daniel,' she said. 'I don't know, I don't want to know. Some evil monster. Take me home, Daniel, please, take me home.'

What could he do but return her to her husband? The town policeman, who the moment he opened the front door to see his wife in such a state – clothes awry, buttons ripped off, crying inconsolably in Gregory's arms – eyed him with suspicion and loathing.

It was no use for Daniel to protest. 'Come on, Brian, do you think I'd…?'

The policeman glared at him.

Daniel tried again. 'Be reasonable.'

But what he didn't realise was that Anderton was beyond reason. He saw only what he saw: his wife upset, clinging on to Daniel, her clothes in disarray. That was what he saw. And he remembered the story about Chelsea Emmanuel who had claimed the doctor had molested her. He threw a punch which landed squarely on Daniel's nose. Daniel gasped and fell back. Then Anderton grabbed Claudine by the arm and slammed the door in Daniel's face.

Daniel was left on the doorstep, nursing his bleeding nose and knowing he would do nothing. He was in no position to make an accusation against the town's policeman.

He couldn't afford to.

Saturday, 5th November

Remember, remember the fifth of November
Gunpowder treason and plot.
I see no reason why the gunpowder treason
should ever be forgot.

In times past, to celebrate the foiling of the Catholic plot to blow up the Houses of Parliament people used to burn effigies of the Pope. Tagged on to the end of the original ditty is a second verse which few of us chant these days.

A penny loaf to feed the Pope
A farthing o' cheese to choke him
A pint of beer to rinse it down
A faggot of sticks to burn him
Burn him in a tub of tar
Burn him like a blazing star
Burn his body from his head
Then we'll say ol' Pope is dead.

Guy Malkin simply hated the fifth of November. He'd never liked his name anyway. But when the little brats ran after him shouting 'Penny for the guy, Guy,' he could have wrung their scrawny little throats. Something had happened to him since he had met Claudine and hooked up to Vanda. He had changed. But others didn't know that he wasn't quite the passive, ordinary little bloke any more. He had a secret. And that secret made him powerful.

So just let them come. He was ready for them.

Guy knew the whole of the ditty, both verses, and he liked the words. Particularly the first few lines of the second verse. He enjoyed imagining the Pope choking on beer and cheese. He muttered them to himself as he left work that night. He had plans. He was going to go to the bonfire tonight.

Saturday evening began murky. Damp enough for people to need petrol to ignite their bonfires, but not wet enough to stop the festivities.

Eccleston, of course, held its own organised bonfire.

It being the end of half term, Holly was staying for the weekend and his mother, at the last minute, had announced her intention to visit too. She and Holly seemed to have formed an invisible and powerful bond that surprised him. His mother was changing, becoming less self-absorbed, less pitying, happier. He was surprised at how much he liked her.

Daniel had decided that this weekend they would all attend the bonfire. Then, on the Sunday, Holly could have another riding lesson while he would look again at the Welsh pony and see if the school was willing to sell it to him. He liked the animal. It seemed safe and placid. After all – he didn't want anything too skittish or dangerous for his daughter. Just a nice, sweet-tempered beast for his little girl to trot around the local lanes and bridle paths.

Guy Fawkes' night was a nightmare for the two police officers on duty, PC Brian Anderton and WPC Shirley Evans. Shirley was tired. She had an eight-month-old baby who was just cutting her teeth and so was miserable. Her mother-in-law had very reluctantly agreed to have the baby so that Paul, her husband, could take their six-year-old to the local bonfire in Eccleston. She felt grumpy, partly through lack of sleep and partly because she wouldn't have minded being at the bonfire herself. Not in an official capacity but as a mum.

As if that wasn't bad enough, she glanced at her colleague and Brian seemed even more odd tonight. On edge, irritable and downright weird. She heaved a long sigh. She just didn't want to spend the next eleven hours with a moody guy! Tonight of all nights.

'Penny for the guy, Guy.' Vanda called out cheekily, linking her arm in his. He felt his face flush bright red. She was always goading him, teasing him. Well, she'd better watch out. She didn't know, did she? She didn't know he had a secret side to him. A secret heart. She'd have a shock if she knew what he was capable of. The squad car cruised alongside him, Anderton half leaning out. 'Off to the bonfire then, Guy? To see the guy burn, Guy?'

With a loud cackle the squad car slid along the road leaving Guy staring after it.

Again he flushed. *If only they knew!*

Guy continued up the street, Vanda taking two steps to his one long-legged stride.

On this night *everyone* took the piss, called him names, chanted those stupid rhymes right in his ear, made daft comments about putting him on the bonfire. Even the policeman.

Well, sarky officer, he thought, you can mock me if you like. I can't stop you, but from inside *I* am mocking *you*. Because you don't know the first thing about me, do you? He turned around and stared after the car. I've got your wife's knickers spread out on my bed. Pearl earrings? The ones she'd 'lost'? I have those too. And plenty more besides. I was nearly inside her the other night. Me. You might think you have control but I can tell you, I am the one for all I look strange, different and odd. I have control because you don't have the first idea. He took some pleasure from the fact that PC Anderton was in ignorance. He wasn't so very clever.

He swaggered off, trying to imitate Johnny Depp's swaying walk in *Pirates of the Caribbean*. Vanda struggled to keep up with him. 'Hey,' she said, 'wait for me.'

He barely acknowledged her.

Brian continued to cruise up the High Street, scanning the crowds for Daniel Gregory. Plenty of people were walking to the bonfire, he noticed, passing Claudine and Bethan walking purposefully up the hill towards the gate. He pipped his horn at them and they both turned and waved.

He couldn't be sure if it was his imagination but it seemed to him that Claudine still looked wary. Even when he eyed her in his nearside wing mirror. Wary or guilty?

He spotted Gregory and his mother, also walking in the same direction no more than a few yards behind his wife. Gregory's mother, he noticed, was holding Holly very tightly by the hand. He nodded approvingly. One should always watch children carefully in such a noisy, dangerous, confused and dark environment. Everyone from the entire town seemed to be walking in the same direction, towards the same place, the huge stack in the centre of the field, roped off by the local farmer. Brian smiled at himself. He would wait until the bonfire was lit, the flames dancing and the fireworks screaming and cracking. He could easily lure Gregory to the far corner of the field. Only a murderer can appreciate what pleasure it gives to commit the crime over and over again in your mind. You watch your intended victim suffer a thousand times, see him die a hundred times. Premeditated murder is to kill over and over again.

He had already planned how he would lure Daniel away from the rest of the crowd. This is the nice thing about your target being a doctor. It was so easy. He could make something up. Anything.

An old lady, having struggled up the hill, seized with a crushing pain in her chest. A child who had been burnt by a sparkler, a vain young woman, ill-advisedly wearing high heels into a farmer's field, twisting her ankle from a careless step into a rabbit hole. Brian could think up dozens of these simple stories. The simpler the better – the more credible. In fact, he would not decide which one he would use until he actually started speaking.

And then, Doctor Gregory, he thought, I will pay you back for your duplicity, in pretending to be a good, loyal, trustworthy family doctor when all the time you were a monstrous perversion. A sad stalker who stole my wife's personal belongings so you could drool over them like a sex-starved bloodhound. A sexual predator on an underage woman, a doctor who profits by his mistaken diagnoses, a doctor who watches a tiny child die without lifting a finger to help it. This is who you are.

Yes, Daniel. Even if you had not stolen my wife's belongings you would still deserve to die because you have failed the people of this town. You and I both have an important role to protect the citizens of Eccleston. I have carried out my duty faithfully. But you…!

A doctor who commits so many cardinal sins is surely capable of anything.

His first smile of the evening came as he watched the nurse from the surgery strolling nonchalantly a few paces behind Gregory. The doctor, he noticed, was unaware that he was about to be 'bumped into'. WPC Shirley Evans noted the smile and misinterpreted it. She thought that her colleague's mood had lifted. And then Brian Anderton saw someone else – or he *thought* he saw someone, a ghostly vision from his past. He watched the woman walk slowly towards the bonfire. Surely. It could not be her?

Yet he watched, mesmerised.

She was thinner than he remembered her, but just as insignificant. Almost a shadow, a wraith walking with the crowd but somehow not quite part of it. She had always been like that. There – yet not there. Never quite real.

Daniel was unaware of the policeman's presence. He saw Claudine and Bethan from a distance but made no attempt to approach them. The girls smiled and waved shyly at each other but neither asked if she could join her friend.

The bonfire was finally lit and the air filled with crackling sparks and the whoosh of the flames as they soared heavenwards. It was a clear sky now with a sprinkling of stars but as the fire grew brighter and hotter the stars appeared to fade.

Everyone's attention was now on the display of fireworks. The *oohs* and *aahs* as starry cobwebs filled the sky, the shock of bangs as staccato and deafening as gunfire, the explosions of stars, gold and red, silver and the brightest magnesium white.

Holly was at once in awe, entranced and frightened. Daniel's mother grasped her hand tightly and he suddenly realised how important this role was to her.

He had made mistakes and one of these had been to think of his mother in that one role when she had another one, much more important to her now. That of grandmother.

He watched them with a warmth of affection. This, now, was his family.

And from the back of the field Brian Anderton watched too. He searched for the woman he had noticed earlier but she had vanished. Perhaps she had never been there except in his mind.

Something, he never knew what, made Daniel turn around. There was activity in the far corner of the field. A large big-bosomed woman was towering over a shrinking girl. He frowned. It was hard to make out exactly what was happening because they were on the very edge of the light from the fire. But it seemed as though the larger woman was holding a sparkler too near the girl's hand. He started forward. It was so close it must be burning her. So why didn't the girl pull away? Why did the two women simply stare at each other?

Perhaps he had always known the reason why.

Bobby Millin was hurting Vanda. Torturing her own daughter.

And that was when it all started to fall into place.

Not Vanda was his first confused, instinctive thought. Of course not Vanda. She had cared for the child in the best way she could. It was Bobby. Life-saving, angel of mercy, Bobby. *She* had been the one. Oh, that he could have been so blind.

Daniel's eyes narrowed. The number of times Bobby had 'resuscitated' her tiny, silent granddaughter. And who had been with Anna-Louise the night the little girl had died?

So who had *really* pressed the pillow to the toddler's face until she had finally stopped breathing?

He knew now.

Proving it was going to be the problem.

Brian hadn't made precise plans. He simply knew that tonight was the night. After all, he had been the one who had planned it so. He knew that tonight would change everything as surely as if he had been blessed with prescience.

And in a way he was. He could picture Daniel's startled amazement as he doused him with petrol, watch his surprise turn to terror as the lighter clicked. Only as he was burning and screaming would Brian finally tell him why.

The fireworks were still exploding, the fire sending sparks high into the night as he started away from the crowd. It was time he fetched the petrol can. 'Best check on the car,' he said, adding in response to the WPC's enquiring look. 'No need for you to come, Shirley,' he said kindly. She instantly turned her attention back to a group of youths who were too engrossed in rolling a spliff to notice her. She breathed in deeply, caught the sweet scent of the one they had already lit and sighed. It brought back happy memories of when she had been a student, footloose and fancy-free. No wretched job then. No home to run to, no husband and no baby. She sucked in another deep breath and sighed. She hadn't appreciated her freedom then.

Daniel was engrossed in his latest problem when the hand tapped his shoulder. 'Excuse me, Doctor.'

Brian Anderton was looking concerned. Strange, anxious and concerned. There was no trace of his previous hostility, which deceived Daniel into believing that this was a professional plea.

'Yeah?'

'There's an elderly lady over in the corner of the field. She's been taken ill. I just wondered if you'd have a look at her.'

Daniel was not suspicious. His doctor's training came to the fore. All he was thinking about was concern for this unknown woman who had come to the bonfire only to fall ill.

'Yes. Yes. Of course, Brian.'

He followed the policeman across the field towards the darkest corner without even wondering why an 'old lady' who was feeling ill would have chosen the remotest corner of the field to fall in.

Unseen by either of them, Cora Moseby was standing near

enough to hear the policeman's words. Like an automaton she followed at a distance.

Guy Malkin was inching around the edge of the field, moving closer to Claudine Anderton, circling her like a hyena moving in for the kill. If he could only get close enough to whisper in her ear, tug at her sleeve, she would know how he felt and she would come to him. There were plenty of dark, quiet corners in this English field.

Marie Westbrook had planned to 'bump' into Daniel at the bonfire so had sidled close to him. When she saw him following the policeman away from the bonfire, she too walked behind at a safe distance.

Chapter Twenty

Then everything happened fast, like one of the fireworks exploding into the arena.

First Vanda started screaming terrible things to her mother.

'You killed her. You killed my baby. My little Anna-Louise. You hurt her more and more. Every day of her life you hurt her like you hurt me. And when you thought you had hurt her enough you killed her. I know you did it.' She was facing her mother, her anger and grief making her appear bigger, taller, stronger. Frighteningly powerful.

Bobby Millin stood perfectly still, her mouth slack, her eyes unfocused, shocked. She opened her mouth to speak but no words came out, only a strangled croak.

Vanda took a step towards her but her brother restrained her with a hand on her arm. 'Hey,' he said. 'Steady on there, Vand. Mum wouldn't—'

Vanda withered him with a look. From somewhere – who knows where – she had found a huge source of strength. 'You always were the stupid one,' she said, half turning towards him. 'You couldn't see what was under your ruddy nose.'

Arnie gaped at her. 'What's brought this on?' he began. 'What is this?' He looked from his mother to his sister then gave up. He had no words in his entire vocabulary to encompass the situation.

Bobby Millin's shoulders crumpled. As her daughter had appeared, physically, to expand, so she had appeared to shrink. She was staring straight out, into the distance, as though desperate to abstract herself from the scene. No one watching could tell whether she was listening to her daughter's rantings or whether the allegations were so dreadful that she had been struck stone deaf and dumb. She said nothing in her defence and apart from the dropping of her shoulders she did not appear to react. Around the family group was a ring of shocked faces. No one dared speak. It was as though they were all holding their breath, waiting for something more to happen, for someone to make a sound and break the spell of ice that had dropped over the scene.

It was like a horrid, pagan festival, the roaring fire, the dancing fireworks, the bright explosions – and in the foreground, a furious young woman, held back by her minder, accusing her mother of the murder of her child.

What made it infinitely worse was that they had all known the child. As they knew Bobby, the helpful nursing assistant, Vanda, the downtrodden teenager, Arnie, the local psycho.

These were not strangers to the Ecclestonians. They were people they passed in the street day by day. Neighbours, if not friends. Familiars.

Like everyone else Daniel had been mesmerised by the drama that was playing out in front of his eyes. Feeling he should play an active role he started towards the group but Brian Anderton couldn't afford to waste the time on this. While resenting the tableaux he realised, *this* was playing right into his hands. A distraction. While everybody was looking the other way it was the perfect opportunity to carry out his plan.

He touched Daniel's shoulder. 'Umm, Doctor.'

Daniel turned.

Somewhere, far back in his mind, he had registered that Anderton was carrying a petrol can but he didn't question it. He followed him towards the edge of the field, where the rim of light met absolute darkness and stumbled behind the policeman.

All the time he walked across the field he was aware that something was wrong. He hesitated, stringing events together. Surely Anderton should be speaking into a two-way radio; where was the ambulance, the back up? The flashlight?

He struggled to find normality. 'Brian,' he said lightly, 'I'm not going to be able to do much in the dark.'

'My colleague is with her. We have a light. I *think* she's OK but if you would just check?'

Daniel peered into the darkness and could see nothing.

Still his mind struggled.

Anderton had been working with a WPC. Of course. *She* would have stayed by the old lady's side, comforting her, while Anderton had crossed the field to fetch the doctor. Then Anderton had been sidetracked by the family drama which had played out in front of their eyes.

Panic only set in when Daniel recalled seeing the WPC standing behind Roberta Millin as her daughter had pointed the accusing finger at her.

Daniel hesitated, undecided whether to turn back.

But our instincts tell us to trust and obey a policeman.

He suddenly wished Anderton would say something. 'Hey, Brian,' he tried.

But the policeman kept walking.

* * *

He knew when he had reached the right spot.

But what Brian Anderton had *not* realised was that Claudine had noticed him leading Daniel towards the edge of the field and had felt the apprehension that had been building up inside her over the past few weeks. She knew that something besides the fireworks would explode tonight on this field.

'Here,' she said quickly to Bethan, 'stay with Holly and her grandmother. Don't stray. I need to have a word with Daddy.' She placed the little girl's hand in Daniel's mother's, ignoring the inevitable startled look and the, 'Well, she might at least have asked,' from Holly's grandmother, and hurried after Brian.

Guy Malkin had not taken his eyes off Claudine since he had arrived at the field. He knew that he was in love with her and would be for ever and she had given him signs that she felt exactly the same about him. Why wouldn't she? He was a man now. It was time they told Anderton that his day was over anyway.

Daniel turned. 'So where is she?' He didn't know what the policeman's game was but there was something very odd going on. He wasn't sure when he had realised that there *was* no old woman in a state of collapse. That he'd been lured here.

He faced Anderton, expecting a confrontation.

That was when he felt the splash. Followed by another splash. Then he was drenched in the stuff and his nostrils were full of the stink of petrol and he could not speak for terror because now he could see right into the policeman's mind. And it was bonfire night. Sparks were everywhere, filling the night sky like fireflies. Children were brandishing sparklers. He tried to pull at his clothes but his fingers were stiff with panic. Rockets were exploding in the sky, showering golden, brilliant tendrils of fire – any one of which could ignite him. Each one threatening to explode him into pain and death. Then he heard the click of a cigarette lighter. He remembered it now. Clearly and too late. The way Anderton had toyed with the yellow, plastic Bic lighter in his hand, clicking it over and over again.

'No,' he said. 'No. Please.'

We all make this appeal, for mercy, for pity. But we are wrong to do this. Our killers have no pity. So it is useless to appeal to it.

Yet we do it.

Daniel watched the flame, saw the hand bring it nearer and nearer.

That was when Cora Moseby began to scream. But the scream mingled in with the other shouts and screams of Bonfire Night. It melted into the night air.

Claudine drew in her breath. One word. The wrong word. 'Brian,' she breathed. 'No. No. It's just Daniel. He doesn't mean any harm.'

Brian Anderton gave an almost animal groan. 'How do you know?' The cigarette lighter was no more than a foot away from Daniel. Daniel backed away and felt the prickle of a hawthorn hedge against his hand.

He could sense the heat already and he had nowhere to escape to.

Anderton clicked the lighter. It didn't even spark.

Anderton clicked the lighter again.

Still it was stubborn.

No flame.

He clicked it a third time.

Chapter Twenty-One

Malkin had misunderstood so much in his short life. He had watched the scene around the bonfire, confused at what was happening. He hadn't understood what Vanda was talking about, her anger directed at her mother. He'd looked from one to the other and given up.

Now he watched another scene with the same bafflement.

He'd seen Anderton move towards Daniel with the cigarette lighter. He smelt the petrol but made no connection.

He saw Claudine launch herself at her husband and that was enough. It was time for him, Guy Malkin, to act the cartoon hero.

In his mind's eye he saw himself knock Brian Anderton to the ground and so, yelling and screaming like a Zulu, he did just that.

Anderton did not have a clue what was happening. His focus was all on Daniel, his quarry. *He* was in control here. It was dark. Malkin was dressed in black jeans and a hooded top. All Anderton felt was himself being felled. Shocked, he dropped the can. The petrol splashed over him just as the lighter, contrary and fickle to the last, spluttered its flame to ignite him.

His last conscious thought was a terrible, searing understanding.

So this had been the meaning of it all.

He heard screams and more screams and then he tried to run away from the flames.

But they were faster than him. With him and around him. He was inside them. The flames were him.

Marie Westbrook was a nurse, well versed in first aid and quick to react.

Rule one is to prevent further harm and that included to her. She knew the petrol can could blow up at any moment. A bomb waiting to ignite. She kicked it away from Anderton, spilling more of the volatile fluid as it jerked along the grass. She set it upright, ignoring, for the moment, the screams of the human torch, the scene straight up from Hell, Dante's *Inferno*, the rim of watching faces demonic and reddened by the fire and the terrible, visible agony of the man, his lips peeled back in agony like an early Christian painting.

Her next priority was to protect Daniel. 'Take your clothes off,' she screamed. 'All of them.'

Oblivious to embarrassment he stripped naked and she tossed him her coat to cover up. Her challenge now was to stop Anderton running around, whipping the flames into activity, the watchers shrinking away whenever he neared one. Anderton, driven into insanity, was screaming, while Claudine stood nearby, absolutely still, watching her husband, her hands covering her mouth, her eyes wide open with horror. Parents covered their children's faces. They did not want this picture seared into their tender brains. Finally Daniel caught Anderton's ankles in a flying rugby tackle of the sort he had been renowned for at school. Marie called to the watchers for coats, blankets – anything to damp down the terrible flames.

She worked beside Daniel in shocked silence, the only sound Anderton's low moans and the mutterings of the crowd. Privately Marie revelled in the fact that they were working together. She and him, how it was always meant to be. Even in the horror, the panic and the darkness she smiled. Happy.

She recalled the second rule from the lecture on burns: *You do not remove the clothes of a burns victim because they form a sterile dressing over the area of damage. Besides, the skin will come away with the clothes, peeling away the flesh down to the sinews and the bones.*

Firemen were running helter-skelter across the field with fire extinguishers and arc lights and the scene was transformed to a sea of slippery foam around which stood a ring of shivering, frightened, pale people, shocked at what they had witnessed. The festival was abandoned; the bonfire left to burn out and fireworks suddenly seemed a threat too terrifying to ignite. Blue lights flashed, sirens wailed. Two ambulances, a ring of police cars, officers slowly taking charge, trying to restore order before taking statements and finding what had happened on this dreadful night.

Now the initial shock was over, Daniel felt shaky. His thoughts were all on what might have been. He could not rid himself of the image of the evening, which had exploded so suddenly into terrifying chaos, or the picture of a man turning to charcoal in front of his eyes. He looked around at the pale, frightened faces of the familiar families who had gathered to celebrate and enjoy themselves and knew that none of them would ever forget this night. He saw his mother shielding Holly from the scene, the way his daughter clung to her, and was glad she was there. An ambulance man ushered him into the back of his van and he sat for a while as they found a spare pair of trousers and a sweater. He peered around the back door. They were stretchering Anderton into a second ambulance but he knew they were too late. He could not live.

Brian Anderton died four days later of shock, infection and fluid loss. He had sixty-five per cent burns.

Had he lived he would have faced a lifetime of surgery and prison.

Daniel Gregory refused the offer of a 'check-up' in hospital and returned home with his mother and his daughter. Marie slipped away, unseen, into the darkness. Claudine and Bethan were 'cared for by a neighbour'.

Once home, Daniel bathed and showered and shampooed his hair to get rid of the smell of smoke. Then he sat in his dressing gown, staring in front of him. He could still smell petrol in his nostrils; still see the man in flames, dancing his macabre dance every time he closed his eyes. He turned his head sharply to the side, convinced he could still hear hysterical screams.

It would take him a long time to forget.

For months he would see the man flailing. Even to fill up his car with petrol and breathe in its pungent perfume would become a terrifying ordeal. Presented with any naked flame for more than a year, he would shrink away.

WPC Shirley White had comforted a hysterical Cora Moseby and it was from her that she learnt a fuller story, that she had been stalked, that PC Brian Anderton had promised to protect her and what form that protection had ultimately taken. 'When David Sankey doused himself in petrol,' Cora said, her face white and shaken, 'in front of my bedroom window, it was Brian who set him alight. *He* set him alight,' she'd said – again and again. 'It was *he* who burnt him. Not Sankey. I think Sankey was just doing it to frighten me but Brian Anderton put the flame to him. He clicked his lighter and Sankey exploded into fire.' She hid her face. 'Just like Brian did tonight. He did it', she turned her face to WPC White, 'to protect me. I thought he always would. He was,' she paused, 'chivalrous.'

It was an epitaph of sorts.

'When I found out where he'd moved to I followed him to Eccleston because I knew I would be safe here. He would always protect me.'

WPC White had found the woman pathetic, sad and damaged. She'd put her arm around her and tried to quiet the terrified sobs.

Chapter Twenty-Two

Five months later

It was the warmest day so far this year, the middle of April, a perfect day in a perfect spring that seemed to be full of golden daffodils, scarlet tulips and bright, clean sunshine. Daniel had been waiting for this moment. In his hand he held the key to Applegate Cottage. The building work was finished, his belongings packed in a van, waiting for them to move in. As he opened the wicket gate he could see the field beyond, the chestnut pony grazing, pale-pink apple blossom making the orchard dazzlingly bright and filling the air with heavy scent. The first of the bees were starting to buzz around the temptation. The key was old-fashioned, heavy iron and huge in his hand.

He inserted it into the arched door and stepped inside.

It was perfect. The builders had cleaned up and moved out a month ago and his cleaner and the gardener had spent most of their time up here, preparing the house. The Yellow House was sold subject to contract and Holly had been living with him since Christmas. Elaine was expecting her first child of the new marriage so was less possessive over Holly than she might otherwise have been. He was aware that all their lives had moved in a different direction, taken a different course than he had anticipated a year ago. He stepped inside. In spite of his cleaner's efforts, the cottage still smelt of damp plaster and brick dust, but as he moved from room to room he seemed to see his life unfolding before him. He and Holly, his mother nearby, in this happy cottage, away from his patients. It would be a private life, a privileged life and a happy life, he had no doubt. His heart gave a little skip as he recalled the bright, intelligent eyes, the wisdom that had shone from Maud Allen's face. Her influence would live on, a woman who was not afraid to make brave choices.

Claudine and Bethan had moved back to France. She had spent an evening with him just before Christmas to explain while the two girls had behaved shyly and awkwardly towards each other. Too much had happened for them to resume an innocent, childish friendship.

'England has bad memories for me, Daniel,' Claudine had said, 'and this pretty town has the worst memories of all. I shall live in the countryside in my own land, speaking my own language. I am not sure I understand English.'

He knew she meant *the* English.

Her smile had been sad and tinged with regret but he knew she was right. She had to leave. 'I can't stay here, Daniel, you must understand. I can't *possibly* stay here. I am seen as that foreign woman who sent her husband mad, who incited such terrible events that led to his death, who teased a young man, who flirted with the doctor. It will all come out in the court case. Everything will be blamed on the fact that I am a foreigner who led my husband a merry dance until he lost his reason. Yes. That is the plea his solicitor would have entered had he lived: that Brian was sent mad by me.'

She looked at him then and he caught the sadness in her face. 'He was not really a bad man,' she said, 'but something happened to him, Daniel, long ago, that planted a small, bad seed in his brain. When those things happened again and somebody stole my personal clothes…' She coloured slightly. It amused him to think that underneath Claudine was a bit of a prude.

'When that happened, because by then we were making friends, he believed it was you and that I was enticing you, inviting you by dangling things on the washing line. Leaving secret messages, waving, like semaphore. Hah.' She gave a mirthless laugh. 'For goodness' sake. How sick was he?'

It was the best way to think of it.

'Keep in touch, Claudine,' he urged, but she shook her head sadly.

'It's best not to. Too much damage has been inflicted. Apart from Bethan, I must close the door on this country and on this part of my life.' She cast her eyes up the High Street. 'For all that this little town is so pretty it does not have happy memories for me. I shall not return. I go next week, Daniel, back to France. I shall not return to England. Ever.'

She gave a tiny shudder. 'I close the door,' she said. And then she was gone.

His mother, with typical alacrity and efficiency, had sold her house and bought one of the flats in Tanner's Row. She was moving down next week, full of plans and excitement. He knew that she was excited at the thought of living nearer to them.

Correction. What she was excited about was being *invited* to live near them. And Holly was equally excited at the thought of having her grandmother so close by. She also loved the small, exclusive complex, the swimming pool that belonged to the flat-owners, the access to the river and the gymnasium.

In a small town it is impossible not to bump into people. Guy Malkin pushing the pushchair along the pavement, Vanda clinging onto his arm, Arnie walking purposefully two steps behind them, as though he was a minder for the entire family.

Bobby Millin had been charged with the murder of Anna-Louise, but WPC Shirley White had confided in him. 'Our case is weak,' she'd said, 'even with Vanda's evidence we can't prove that Anna-Louise was smothered. She can testify that her mother abused her, but she wasn't actually in the room when Anna-Louise died. And of course,' she said as an afterthought, 'the child can't speak for herself.'

So Daniel returned to the original picture, of the doll-like child, the tiny pink tongue flicking in and out of her mouth, saying nothing.

And now she never would.

Holly was walking up the path, school over. And then the furniture van turned into the drive. It was time to begin his new life.

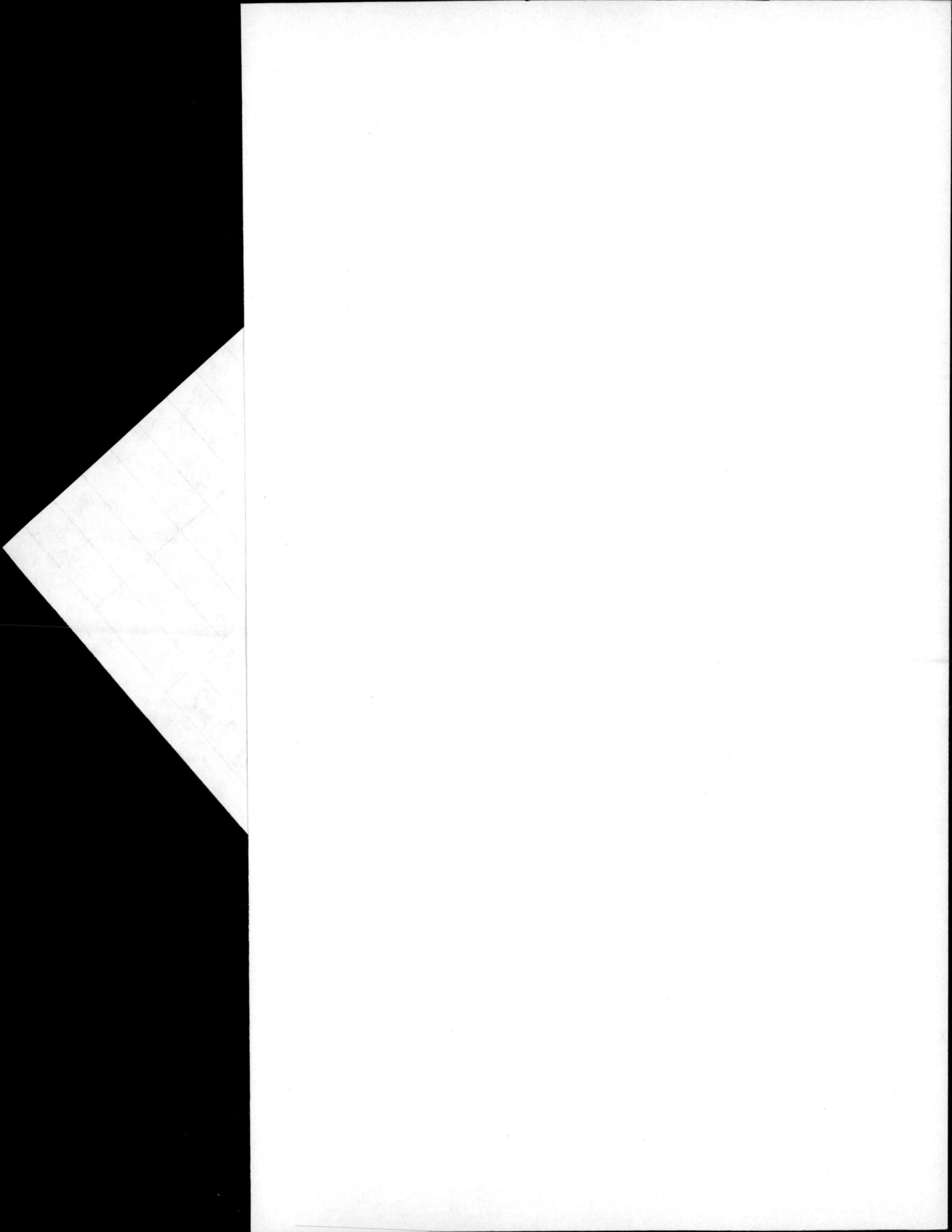

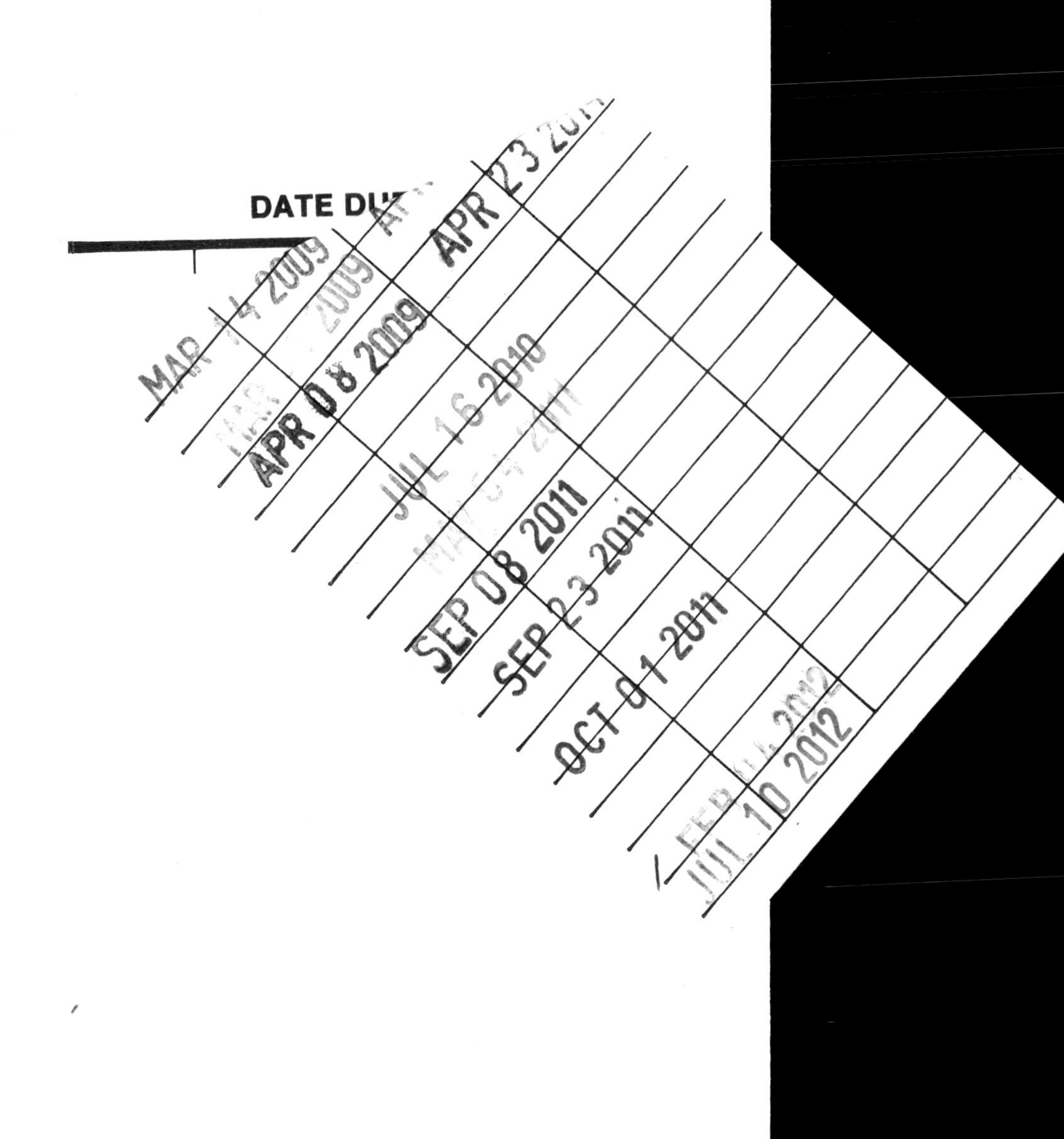
DATE DU
MAR 14 2009
APR 08 2009
APR 23 2011
JUL 16 2010
SEP 08 2011
SEP 23 2011
OCT 01 2011
JUL 10 2012